A Wedding
HOMERUN
IN LOVELAND, OHIO

A Wedding
HOMERUN
IN LOVELAND, OHIO

CATHY LIGGETT

BARBOUR
PUBLISHING

Cover design: Faceout Studio, www.faceoutstudio.com

Published by Barbour Publishing, Inc., P.O. Box 719, Uhrichsville, Ohio 44683, www.barbourbooks.com

Our mission is to publish and distribute inspirational products offering exceptional value and biblical encouragement to the masses.

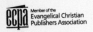 Member of the
Evangelical Christian
Publishers Association

Printed in the United States of America.

Dedication

To all those in my community who have
inspired this book and blessed my life. . .
I know who you are—and God does too!

Chapter 1

If this lightning and thunder doesn't stop soon—Megan O'Donnell's entire body stiffened with tension as she tried to see through the quarter-sized raindrops pummeling the windshield of her SUV. She'd had just about enough of the teeming rain and the nerve-shattering booms that shook her mid-sized car.

More than once it crossed her mind to jump right out into the downpour, shake her fists at the dim, menacing evening sky, and make it stop. Make the skies calm again. As if she could. As if she could really control the weather and the heavens.

But. . .she would if she could. She'd do that for Sammy, knowing how frightened the claps of thunder and slashes of lightning made him. She'd do anything for her six-year-old guy. Because that's what moms did, right? Anything and everything they could.

"How are you doing, honey?"

Loosening her death grip on the steering wheel, she reached into the back passenger seat with her right hand, patting his knee where it hung out from under his army-green cargo shorts. "You okay?"

" 'Kay."

Sammy barely had the syllable out of his mouth when another jolting round of thunder surprised them. Megan jumped, her hand flying back to the steering wheel, working to steady the car against the beating rain. But, of course, Sammy didn't jump, didn't react much—not in an overtly physical way. Not in a way that most people would notice.

But then, he didn't have control over his body like most people did. Still. . .that didn't mean he wasn't scared. And she didn't have to turn around and touch him to know his already uncooperative limbs had grown even more rigid with fright. She knew it. She could sense his tension from where she sat in the driver's seat. Could hear the fear in his quivering voice.

"Lau."

"Yes, it was loud, wasn't it, honey?" Gripping the steering wheel tightly, with all her might, she worked to hide her own unease with words that sounded loose and light. "Even louder than Grandpa's snoring." She forced a soft chuckle she wasn't really feeling at the moment.

Flicking on her turn signal, she started to make a right turn off Route 22 onto Columbia, but didn't make it around the corner before a semi flew by in the lane next to her, deluging the left side of her car with sprays of rainwater. She flinched involuntarily as if the water had splashed straight through the window.

"You're being brave, Sammy."

"Bray?"

"Yes, brave. You're my brave guy."

Wishing her car had a rudder or at least four-wheel drive, she cautiously made the turn, making her way through a half-foot-deep puddle. The rain-soaked road grew darker and narrower the farther she drove from the intersection. Water gushed like miniature rapids in the gullies at the sides of the road. Broken-off twigs lay scattered on the lawns of the ranch-style homes and all over the street, too, resembling a gargantuan game of pick-up sticks. Luckily, the debris couldn't camouflage the winding road she knew so well and had been driving on since she'd first gotten her license as a teenager.

Still, what a night to be out, backtracking all over Loveland.

But promises were promises—and she'd told Sammy days ago that, yes, they could get a bite to eat at Paxton's Grill before her meeting that night. Even though, logistically, it wasn't a sound idea at all. Not when she'd had to leave work in downtown Loveland, go past their house to pick him up at after-school care on Route 22 and 3 then drive back by their house again to go to Paxton's right in the heart of town. After dinner, of course, she'd have to repeat her steps pretty much the same way, driving north from town to drop off Sammy at home so Mrs. Biddle could watch him for the evening, before turning south again to go to the high school where she'd be holding her meeting.

No, none of it made sense. Except for the fact that Paxton's french fries were Sammy's favorite, and she was quite fond of them herself. And honestly, munching on the best fries in town seemed oddly comforting at the moment—no matter how much driving it entailed.

It had been a day and a half at the clinic, with one physical therapy session after another. Record high temperatures the past few days hinted that summer was in the wings, creating as much havoc in the way of twisted ankles, bad knees, and pained shoulders as the first weeks of spring had. And if the day hadn't been challenging enough, she was anxious the evening might be even more so. Never having facilitated a meeting before, she'd been nervous all day long. No, that wasn't true. All week long was more like it.

"Music, Maw-mee?" Sammy's voice, barely audible over the racket from the rain, quavered some as he made his request.

"No problem, honey." She clicked on the radio, already tuned in to his favorite station. Nothing soothed him like country music, and she felt bad she'd been too preoccupied with her own anxieties not to think of it sooner. But there were so many questions—"what-ifs"— plaguing her mind about her All-Stars Sports Day meeting.

As in, what if no one responded to the flyers she'd put up around town? What if the only people at the meeting were the girls she knew from downtown Loveland—like her longtime friend Janey from Sweet Sensations Bakery or Maria from Miss Annabella's Tea Parlor? Or what if, considering the weather, the two of them didn't even show up and it was just—her?

On the other hand, what if the high school cafeteria was buzzing with volunteers? And there were more people there than she'd imagined? Would she really know how to organize more than a dozen volunteers or so?

She'd been so worried about it all she'd barely slept the night before. And she'd brought a change of clothes to work, hoping a more professional look would help ease her jitters. Slipping out of her work uniform—khakis and a black polo—she'd donned a pair of neatly pressed navy capris, a crisp white three-quarter-sleeve blouse with a sash that tied at the side, and a pair of navy heels. The heels were painfully pointy; she'd bought them on sale the season before. But still, standing before the mirror in the clinic's restroom, she felt the look said "take charge." And she would try her best to do just that—for Sammy's sake and for the other kids like him. She'd gut her way through the experience like she did everything else. And no one would be the wiser.

Hopefully.

Good evening, ladies and gentlemen. No. *Good evening, friends.* Or. *It's so good to see everyone here this evening.* Better. *You know. . .* Pause. *For a long time it's been a dream of mine to organize an All-Stars Sports Day event especially for our special-needs kids and—*

"There ye'?" Between the ending of a Blake Shelton song and the first sweet notes of a Carrie Underwood tune, Sammy spoke up from the backseat again.

"Are you hungry?"

"Hun-gey."

"Well, we're almost there. Here we go—down the hill and over the bridge that crosses the water."

Gazing out the window, she looked to see if the river was as high as she imagined it might be. It seemed the closer they got to their destination, the more the rain was actually starting to let up some, now just a slow, steady rhythm. Even so, the river water surged and swirled still turbulent and dangerous looking. "Hey Sammy, you remember the river that cuts through town, don't you? The Little Miami River?"

"Li'l?"

"Yes, little. Not big. Little." She'd gotten used to describing things to Sammy outside the car window. Things that he could've seen for himself if only he could reposition his body to sit up high, or stretch, or lift himself to press his nose against the glass like other kids might.

"Now we're passing the bike rental shop," she added, doing her best to keep her voice upbeat. "No riders on the bike trail tonight though, huh?"

"No bike riders."

"And there's Scoops. We love that place, don't we?"

The mention of the ice cream parlor must've made Sammy's mouth water even more.

"Paxton?"

"Oh yes. There it is. Paxton's Grill. Just a few blocks away. I can see the round yellow-and-red neon sign." Her foot hovered over the brake pedal. "Maybe Allie will be working."

"Like Allie."

"I know. She loves you, too."

"Justin an' Carrie love me?"

"Yes, and Justin and Carrie."

Justin and Carrie, Allie's kids, were like a brother and sister to Sammy—just like Allie had always been to her. She and Allie had practically shared infant seats together. At least, that's the way their moms liked to tell it, and their moms knew all about sister-like friendships. Laura O'Donnell and Pamela Matthews had shared one since they were young girls. And these days, the empty-nest moms were more than friends—they were the owners of one of Loveland's most successful businesses, the We Do! Wedding Planners. The pair had also garnered a well-deserved reputation for doing a bit of matchmaking on the side.

Turning on her blinker, Megan tapped the brake, creeping the car to a halt, wistfully wishing Allie would be hosting tonight. Allie helped her husband as much as she could since they'd taken over Paxton's Grill from Greg's parents the year before, leaving little time for socializing these days. It would be such a treat to see her even if they only had a moment to catch up.

"Okay, Samster. Here we are. All I have to do is make a left turn so we can park in the community lot and—"

Before she could finish the sentence, an old-model pickup truck swerved toward their SUV, barreling down West Loveland Avenue from the opposite direction. Wasn't it going to stop? Slow down? Wasn't the driver going to notice? Do something?

She froze, trying to think. Turn left? Right?

Her fingers gripped the vinyl-covered steering wheel, and she yanked it hard. Not even sure what she was doing—except for following some unfathomable gut instinct—she veered the car to the right, putting herself at risk while protecting Sammy's side of the car, in case of impact.

Closing her eyes tight, she prayed with all her might, listening to the moaning, groaning, screeching truck brakes. Coming closer. And closer still. Until finally there was silence. The frightening noise stopped.

But her hands were still shaking. Her heart still racing. Anger fueled by fear, she hopped out of the car and began ranting.

MacNeill Hattaway jumped out of the rust-fringed pickup truck, slamming the creaking door behind him.

That was close. Way too close!

He'd decided to drive his uncle's rattletrap thinking it'd be less showy and conspicuous than his red Corvette, but water-slick roads or not, the thing really just wasn't safe. He couldn't—wouldn't—do it again. Not when he couldn't trust the brakes, and not when the questionable steering locked up without a moment's notice.

Of course, it hadn't helped that a deer had lunged across the road in front of him at the same time he'd turned the truck off Route 48 and onto West Loveland. Still, he'd almost gotten himself killed and all because he'd had a craving for a burger from Paxton's before meeting up with a friend later that evening.

Even worse, he'd almost maimed another driver—a woman—who had every right to be standing in the street screaming uncontrollably at him.

Not that he wasn't accustomed to people screaming at him.

Actually he was fairly used to it, being that it was pretty much a part of his job. As a pro pitcher, he'd heard way more than his share of fevered remarks from the Tristate Hawks' fans over the years—both good and bad—all depending on how precisely he could get an orange-sized ball to cross over a seventeen-inch plate from a little over sixty feet away, preferably at a speed of ninety miles an hour or so.

Sometimes he managed to do that handily. Other times, he

couldn't do it to save his life, his ego, or his ears from the deafening cries of disgust from the stands.

So, yeah, he was used to people yelling all right.

But he could tell the woman wasn't used to it—or at least she wasn't used to being the one doing the yelling. Instead of flailing arms, hers were crossed over her chest, hugging her petite body. And her voice sort of trembled as it got louder, as if it was usually softer, more controlled, and not used to such extremes.

"What were you thinking? You could have killed us. All of us!"

At least she was kind enough to include him in the mix, he noticed.

"Hey, I'm sorry, miss. I really am. I'm sure I scared you to—"

"To death. Yes! You certainly did scare me to death." She shoved a tendril of dark, wet hair back from her forehead, attempting to tuck it into her ponytail. Letting more of her face show. . .a really nice, pretty face, he could tell that much even through the drizzle. "Do you always drive like that?"

"Do I what? Well, no. I mean, actually there was a deer. A deer that came out of nowhere, leaping across the road. I tried to swerve away, but then"—he pointed to his uncle's truck, ready to explain about the apparently lousy brakes and major lack of steering, but she cut him off.

"Do you know I have a child in my car?"

"A kid? You do? Is he—is she—all right?"

"He. Yes, he's all right. But you frightened him. That's for sure. As if he wasn't already scared enough from the storm."

Oh, great! A new infraction to add to his list. Frightening children without even meaning to.

"You scared my Sammy." She suddenly pounced closer, right in his face, as if mentioning her son's name had given her a surge of adrenaline, a boost of courage.

Mac couldn't help but think she reminded him of the geese that had taken up residence around the pond out at his uncle's farm. The mother geese—squawking, hissing, protecting their young at all costs. Ready to chase off an intruder—or go beak-to-toe, if they had to, with anything—or anyone—that got too near.

Of course, unlike the geese, Mac didn't mind the woman getting close. So close he'd caught a whiff of her sweet-smelling perfume. The fragrance wrapped around his head, overriding the competing scents of the rain-cresting river and his running truck engine. And even if her words were harsh, and deservedly so, there was an underlying sweetness about her he detected right away.

"You could've really hurt him." She jabbed a pointed finger in the air, nearly into his shoulder. "You could've killed him, and—and, are you a parent, Mr.—"

"The name's MacNeill."

"Mr. Neil, are you—"

"No, it's MacNeill," he corrected, enunciating slowly. Of course, as soon as he did, he wondered why he even cared.

"That's what I said. Mr. Neil."

"No, my first name is—"

"Whatever!" She planted her hands on her hips. "Are you a parent?"

"A parent?" What was the woman getting at? He scratched his forehead, protected from the drizzling rain by the bill of his baseball cap.

Unbelievably, her voice got shriller. "Yes. Are you?"

"No, but I—I mean. . ." Was not being a parent supposed to make him a total monster? Insensitive to children and their safety? Is that what she was implying?

"Well, Mr. Neil, you should learn to drive like you're one."

"MacNeill." He repeated his name again, this time grinding it out, his jaw tightening. So that *had been* what she was getting at. Which pretty much irritated him to no end. Who was she to make such a jibe? Mother Teresa?

Sure, maybe in the past he'd been reckless in a lot of ways. He'd used his celebrity status inappropriately—for his own good and for illicit pleasures. And yeah, he'd driven many cars many times too fast and too often under the influence. No doubt the tabloids had had plenty to write about him over the years because he'd given them plenty of material. But he could tell she didn't even recognize him as the baseball player most everyone else knew him as. She had no clue as to who he was. . .where he'd been and where he was now in his life.

He hadn't left his custom-built home and taken up residence at his deceased Uncle Jake's farm in Loveland on a whim. He'd done it for a reason. It was because he wasn't the same person he used to be. The injury to his elbow had changed him. No, that wasn't altogether accurate. God had changed him. His Creator had given him a second chance. An opportunity to redeem himself and all his bad boy ways.

Couldn't she give him a moment to redeem himself with her, too?

He drew in a deep breath, attempting to maintain full control of himself as he tried again with the pretty but exasperating woman.

"Hey, look—" he started, keeping his voice soft, non-adversarial.

But it was no use. She turned, huffing back to her car without giving him so much as another second to explain himself. Standing there with his mouth half open, he blinked out into the rain. Obviously, protective moms were a lot tougher audience—and a lot less forgiving—than the Almighty Himself.

Chapter 2

"We almost gaw hit," Sammy told Allie as she set down a brimming mound of french fries and a kid-sized burger in front of him.

Megan noted they were definitely getting the royal treatment just as they always did when visiting their friends at Paxton's. Allie even put them at a table at the rear of the restaurant, a cozy nook, where there was more room for Sammy's wheelchair.

"But we didn't get hit, Sammy," Megan countered, disregarding the grilled chicken Caesar salad that Allie had just served her. Instead, she first grabbed for the container of catsup sitting in the center of the wooden table. Shaking it in the air, she reached across the table, squirting a few blobs onto Sammy's plate.

"We're fine," she told him. "Really," she added, bobbing her head in confirmation at her lifelong friend.

Allie slunk down into a black vinyl chair next to Sammy, her eyes narrowing in concern. "But it was a close call, huh?" Biting her lip, she shook her head of loose blond curls. "How scary!" she said, looking both incredulous and pretty at the same time.

Ever since Megan could remember, people always thought she and Allie looked alike when in reality, they didn't one bit. But it must have been some kind of osmosis or best friend thing that kept onlookers saying so. Not that Megan ever minded really. All throughout their growing up years, she'd always thought Allie was the prettiest girl in their class, inside and out.

"Are you okay, honey?" Allie ruffled Sammy's tufts of toffee-colored hair, shades lighter than Megan's own deep brown. "A little shaken up? Need some more fries?"

"We're fine, Allie," Megan repeated, picking up her fork, stabbing at layers of romaine lettuce. "You know how people get when it rains around here. A little bit of precipitation and everyone turns crazy."

"Cray-hee," Sammy mimicked. Pausing from his munching, he slowly turned his head, looking straight at Allie. "Maw-mee yell at man."

Wasn't it funny how she could never get Sammy to talk when she wanted him to? But now, when it wasn't something she necessarily wanted the whole world to know, or at least something she'd prefer to have the option of sharing with her best friend when and if she felt like it, her child couldn't keep quiet. Of course, she was glad he felt so at home with Allie that he could talk freely with her—but still, it never failed, did it?

"Your mommy yelled at the man? The other driver?" Instantly, Allie's head flew around to face her. *"You? Yelled?"* She could tell from Allie's shocked expression her friend didn't know whether to be worried or amused. "So, it *was* really, really close."

"Well, it was. . ." Megan's gaze dropped from her friend's inquisitive eyes down to her plate without really seeing it, playing out the scene in her mind once more. Yes, it had been close. Too close really. Not just Mr. Neil's truck and her car, but at one point she'd actually almost leaped on the man. Had entirely invaded his space, and gotten in his face, and almost poked her finger into his shoulder, and. . . Oh, how her face burned at the memory of her outburst.

And it wasn't just her outburst that was causing her some discomfit, it was the realization that she hadn't been that close to a man since—well, there'd been the time with Aaron Jensen—but that was several months ago. She and Aaron had taken Sammy to a pumpkin patch and they'd been all scrunched into a hay wagon together with a group of strangers. But that was her last sort of contact with the male species that she could remember.

Really, how had she let herself get so out of control with Mr. Neil? She usually wasn't like that. Sure, she'd defend her child to her death, but in a calmer, more dignified manner.

But then was it really her fault? The man was a maniac on wheels! Even if he didn't look like one. . .even if his eyes appeared sympathetic when she mentioned having a child in the car.

But he could've just been faking that, trying to placate her. Trying to smooth over the fact that he was, after all, the one who had been out of control behind the wheel and had gotten her acting so nutty. To the point where she'd jumped out of the car, into the drizzling rain, calling him names that she wouldn't even call her dog—if she owned one.

Feeling suddenly self-conscious and overheated, she laid her fork aside, taking a long sip of her water, not even finishing her reply to Allie. But it didn't matter. Apparently Sammy had a lot more to say, and Allie leaned closer to him, eager to listen.

Smacking his lips, his hand wrapped around several fries, he gave Allie a hint of description regarding "the man." "Man was tall," he told her.

"Oh?" Allie's eyes widened at Sammy's disclosure and Megan's did likewise, astonished by the little tell-all.

It was more information than Megan even realized he knew. Somehow from the way her car had been angled, and the way she and Mr. Neil had been standing in the street, Sammy must've seen far more than she'd imagined from between the front seats and through the windshield. Because, yes, Sammy was right. The man had been at least six feet tall. He'd crossed his arms over his chest, and he'd had to sort of lean down a bit to her, as if listening hard to hear what she had to say.

Or—no, that wasn't it at all, was it? He leaned down as if to taunt her. Yes, that's why she lost her temper and behaved so wildly. Because he was taunting her with those sympathetic eyes of his. Which was confusing and frustrating and—

"Anything else?" Allie wanted to know, quirking a brow at Sammy.

Sammy nodded. "Dark hat."

"Hmm. . .is that right, Meg? Tall, dark hat, and—dangerous?" Allie's eyes twinkled at Megan. "Those are the very best kind." She giggled.

"Please, Allie."

"Did you exchange information?"

"No, of course not. He didn't hit us—he almost hit us. Came really, really close to hitting us." Her mind tried not to linger on the word close again. Reaching across her salad, she scooped up a handful of fries from Sammy's plate, downing them before her taste buds barely had time to register what had hit them.

"So you didn't get his name or number?"

"No I did not get his phone number, silly."

"But you did get his name."

Of course, Allie had noticed her exclusion. "His name was. . . Neil. Mac Neil." Fork in hand again, she pierced the lettuce maybe a tad aggressively, remembering how he'd even been irritable telling her his name. That hadn't been very nice of him, had it? Not nice at all.

"Wait a minute—Mac Neil? Or MacNeill? Are you sure he didn't say—"

But before Allie could finish her question, a blast of Orphan Annie's voice singing "Tomorrow" erupted from Megan's purse, interrupting her friend. Hastily wiping her hands on her napkin, she fished out her cell phone and eyed the incoming number. "Sorry, Al. It's Mrs. Biddle. She might need a ride."

Flipping open her phone, Megan tried to half listen to Allie and Sammy's conversation while Mrs. Biddle prattled on, as she normally did, always taking her time to get to the crux of her call.

But she couldn't make out what Allie and Sammy were talking about. Although she could just imagine as she watched her best friend reach into the pocket of her bib apron and pull out a few after-dinner mints for Sammy. It was Allie's way, her bribe, Megan knew, to get more information about the stranger out of Sammy.

Megan had to smile. Leave it to her happily married friend to continually try to make romantic connections on her behalf. Just because their moms supposedly had a talent for matchmaking, Allie had always thought she'd inherited the trait as well.

"I'm sorry, Mrs. Biddle," Megan apologized into the phone. "I lost you on that last part. You asked if I'd been out in the rain? Yes, I have. And I can come pick you up if that's what you're asking."

Sometimes Mrs. Biddle's husband ran her over to Megan's house and the couple watched Sammy together. Other times Megan provided transportation—which was more than fine with her. A little extra driving was well worth it for her to have the retired schoolteacher to depend on. When Megan counted her blessings, for sure, Mrs. Biddle was someone she always counted twice.

"What?" Megan sat up straight, trying to wrap her head around what Mrs. Biddle was saying. "You're in the emergency room?"

Megan realized she must've said the words a bit loudly because Allie and Sammy ceased their conversation and were both looking straight at her. Meanwhile she listened intently as her usually dependable babysitter told her how she'd slipped in the rain and may have possibly fractured her hip.

Taking in a deep breath, she tried to focus on the other woman, rather than her own concerns about finding another sitter. A replacement sitter she'd need for how many months if Mrs. Biddle needed surgery? Six maybe? At the very least?

Oh, but she shouldn't even be thinking about that right now. How awful of her to even think about her own needs first. Mrs.

Biddle was the one who'd been hurt. She could hear the discomfort in her voice.

"Mrs. Biddle, don't worry. We'll be fine. You need to take good care of you. And please have your husband call and let me know how you're doing. Okay?"

"Miss Biddle hurt?" Sammy wanted to know before Megan could even hang up the phone and toss it back into her purse.

"She's at the hospital?" Allie frowned.

Luckily, Allie had served Sammy a mountain's worth of fries because Megan had been eating more than she'd intended to. Anxious about the turn of events, she grabbed another fistful before answering. "She was coming out of the grocery and slipped on the curb in the rain. They're running tests now to see how bad her hip is. She said her husband will call with her prognosis." She bit off the top of several fries all at once. "I don't know. . .maybe I should reschedule the meeting. The problem is, I wouldn't know how to get a hold of anyone. That is, if anyone is coming."

"No way, Meg. You've wanted to do this for so long. Sammy can stay here with Greg and me." Allie pulled his wheelchair closer to the table. "He can help us close up. Right, Sammy?"

"Thanks, Allie, but you guys have work to do and dinners to serve." Megan shook her head. "And I'm sure you'd like to cut out early to get home to Justin and Carrie if the opportunity arises. Besides, I really don't know how long the meeting will last. It could be two minutes or two hours, who knows?" She felt her shoulders slump forward, knowing full well the next call she had to make.

But still, she hesitated. She never did like calling her mom and dad for help. Not that they didn't love seeing their grandson any and every chance they got. But they worked all day long, her mom planning weddings and plotting romances, and her father as a counselor at the high school. Although for Megan, it wasn't just their work schedules that made her hate to call so much. She didn't like to lean on them. It had always made her feel "less than" somehow.

But since she didn't have any other choice. . .

"I'll call Mom and Dad. They'll be happy to see their Sammy."

Retrieving her cell phone once more, after a quick call and a thrilled "yes" from her mother, Megan glanced at her watch. "Sorry, Al." She frowned. "I guess we'll need to-go boxes for our dinners since we'll have to spend extra time running over to their house now."

Her best friend nodded and offered to watch Sammy one more time, before popping up and heading back to the kitchen for boxes.

Sitting at the table waiting for Allie's return, Megan sighed, slogging another several fries through the dabs of catsup left on Sammy's plate. How she hoped the All-Stars Sports Day meeting went well—at least better than the rest of the evening had gone so far anyway. What, with a near car crash and a sitter with a possible broken hip. . .

Could the rainy evening get any worse? she wondered, and then wished she hadn't put that negative thought out into the cosmos.

By the time MacNeill walked back to his uncle's truck, the brunette with some of the more annoying accusations he'd ever heard—and the most interesting eyes he'd ever seen—had already pulled away and was gone from sight.

For a minute, he considered turning around and heading back to his uncle's farm, maybe making some scrambled eggs for supper. It would be a fitting penance since he'd probably shaken up the woman and her child and possibly ruined their dinners. It would also give him a chance to switch out vehicles before meeting up with his old buddy Ted Slater in a couple of hours.

But even through the haze of light rain, Paxton's neon sign beckoned him like it always did. And so did fond memories.

Righting the truck back into the line of traffic, he promised himself he'd retrace his route up the winding country road back to the farm to grab his Corvette after a visit to the local grill.

Driving a short ways up the street, he found an empty parking space and waited for a few cars to go around him before parallel parking there. The truck door creaked again as he shut it behind him, and with a light step, he hopped up onto the paved sidewalk that outlined downtown Loveland. The same sidewalk he used to ride his Stingray bike on.

Back when he was ten, he'd known every crack and bump in the surface. Back and forth, he'd ride his bike to baseball practice, balancing so well that half the time he didn't even bother clasping the handlebars.

When he was a bit older, he and his friends had hung out on the sidewalk for hours at a time, popping wheelies and getting in the way of passersby. All in the hopes of catching some cute girl's attention.

More than once, Mr. Keller had come running out of his hardware store to shoo their group away from the front of his business. And the pharmacist at the drugstore ran them off a few times as well, except when they had enough spare change in their pockets to come into his place to buy pops and candy.

But both of those businesses were long gone now. And as Mac clomped along in the cowboy boots he'd found in the back of his uncle's closet—more comfortable and broken in than the expensive leather loafers he usually wore—he felt as if a part of his past had gone missing, too.

Not that there weren't plenty of new businesses framing Loveland's downtown strip these days. Because there were. Unique, cutesy establishments like the Loveland Music Academy, a tea parlor, a yarn store, and a gift shop—all of which seemed to be more the trend now. In fact, downtown Loveland had become a colorful place since the last time he'd visited, and he figured it had to have been a committee of women who had made it that way.

Who but a woman would think of the window boxes and urns full of plants and flowers spilling out from everywhere? And the American flags and fun-looking flags that poked out of doorways or hung next to awnings? Plus, there were park benches and antique lampposts strewn along the sidewalks in a picturesque style.

No doubt about it, Mac shook his head, the look of West Loveland Avenue had changed considerably since his family had moved away to Florida at the end of his sixth-grade year. Even his beloved Paxton's had undergone a minor makeover, he noted, as he closed in on his destination.

Named after Colonel Thomas Paxton, the first settler to the area, the grill had a foothold on the main corner of downtown and was still the hub of the strip. But it looked slightly more sophisticated than he remembered, with a black wrought iron fence surrounding it, sandwich board signs announcing specials, and outside—in front of the restaurant—were café tables, vacated at the moment due to the inclement weather.

One thing hadn't changed though. Mac smiled thankfully as he whiffed the air: the mouth-watering aroma of Paxton's charbroiled burgers. Even after all the places he'd traveled to and all the restaurants and hamburger joints he'd eaten in, nothing compared to the delectable scent of a Paxton burger. It seeped out of the place, drifting toward him temptingly, making his mouth water. The sensation hit him full force as a handful of patrons poured out the door. Mac sidestepped them, letting them pass by before he entered, conditioned to protecting his mending elbow, keeping it out of the way of being bumped.

Stepping inside, he immediately tugged on his cap, pulling it a little lower, hoping no one recognized him. But then he caught himself.

All that was in his past. In the other circles he used to run in. Used to be men would approach him, wanting to buy him a drink. Women used to smile flirtatiously, their eyes full of promises. All had wanted something or had some proposition in mind, but that had been okay with him then. He'd been more than happy to give everything he had to take all they had to offer in return.

It wasn't until after the accident he stopped to realize how empty most of those exchanges had made him feel.

But since he'd been living in Loveland throughout his entire recovery, to date no one had made a big deal about his residing in their midst. For the most part anyway. Sure, every now and then a person here or there would ask for an autograph or come up to chat with him. But mostly everyone acted respectful of him and his privacy.

The hostess station was empty. Still, Mac stood there politely waiting—for a minute or two anyway. Then when a hostess never showed up, he helped himself to a seat, slipping into a red vinyl booth by the front window.

Being in the half-filled establishment always brought back flashes from the past. Like the times he'd come there as a kid after a win at the baseball diamonds just across the bridge. Coaches and teammates along with proud moms and dads would nearly take over the eatery on those summer evenings, all charged up and ready to chow down after a victory.

He even recalled double dates that started out at Paxton's, in particular one on a Fourth of July when he kissed childhood sweetheart Becca Cannon at a table—the third table along the right wall—creating his own kind of fireworks.

Caught up in old memories, he hardly noticed when a middle-aged waitress showed up at his side out of nowhere.

"Need a menu?" she asked, puffing upward at her bangs, sending them flying off her forehead.

"Not unless you've changed things since I was here two weeks ago," he teased. "You still have the best burgers in town?" He smiled up at her.

"Still do. Haven't changed a thing." The woman reached in her pocket for an order pad, a bemused glint in her eye.

"Good. Then I'll have one with everything on it."

"Everything, huh?" She scribbled the order. "You're a brave one."

He chuckled at her comment, adding, "And some fries."

"You got it."

Mac watched as the waitress made her way to another table, thinking she looked like someone he might've known as a kid. But then a lot of people looked familiar to him. As she started back to the kitchen, he was still trying to figure it out—until his eyes got diverted to another woman. At the back table—a woman he *did* recognize. With a little boy, presumably her son, sitting across from her in a wheelchair. The lady he'd almost run into.

He had to admit, the lady—the mom—biting her lip with a cell phone at her ear, still appeared somewhat flustered, which made him cringe some. Hopefully, he hadn't been the main cause of the stressed look on her face. It didn't make him feel great either to see that her son was obviously handicapped. No wonder she'd been so upset.

Not that he'd nearly hit her on purpose, of course. But still. . .

He let out a deep breath, berating himself once again for driving his uncle's truck in the first place. But something about living out at the farm. . .something about not being in the limelight lately. . .made him notice how frivolously he'd been living and how materialistic he'd become, making him yearn for simpler things. But he still had to be responsible about it. If he wanted to continue driving the truck, then he needed to pour some money into it and get it fixed. Or start looking around for a safer model.

Well, one thing he could be thankful for, he thought, gazing at the lady and her son, at least he'd been given another opportunity to try to apologize to her. And that's just what he intended to do.

Scooting to the edge of the booth, he was just about to go make amends, when a portly guy in a John Deere cap and a forest green Stihl chainsaw T-shirt blocked his path. "Hey, aren't you Troy Clinger?"

Mac looked up at the stranger towering over the booth. "Nope, sorry. Not me."

"I don't mean Clinger." The man shook a finger close to Mac's face. "I mean, I mean. . .oh, you know. . ." The man bent over, placing his fingertips on the table, as if drawing the answer from the Formica tabletop. "Danzer!" He straightened. "Carl Danzer, that's it."

"That's not me either."

"Well, you're someone." The man's eyes narrowed. "I know you are."

"We're all someone." Mac had a ready-made answer, having gone through the same scenario often enough.

"Oh!" The man clicked his fingers in revelation. "Hattaway. MacNeill Hattaway. I knew it all along. My brother went to school with you."

"Oh yeah? Who's your brother?" he asked, then wanted to kick himself for doing so as the man took a trip down memory lane, reciting names, places, and past events which were mainly on the hazy side for Mac.

By the time the guy finally produced a napkin and a pen, and got what he'd initially come over to the booth for—an autograph—Mac looked up and saw that the woman and her son were gone.

It was a shame. Not only would he have liked to apologize, but he could've invited her to the meeting Ted had asked him to attend. It might've been something she'd be interested in.

Oh well. He pushed his cap back from his forehead, remaining positive. It was a small town. More than likely he'd run into her again sometime—though hopefully not literally.

Chapter 3

Megan stood staring at the group of volunteers staring back at her as a drop of rain slid down the back of her neck, paused at the rise of flesh between her shoulders, then tumbled downward like a rollercoaster car, gathering momentum till it hit the gulley at the base of her spine and then disappeared into the waistband of her pressed, polished cotton capris.

Or, at least the capris had been pressed. And dry. And, yes, she'd even thought she looked good and somewhat professional in the navy pants and her once crisp three-quarter-sleeve white blouse. But that had been earlier in the evening before the torrential downpour hit.

Before she'd stood under the lightning-crackling sky getting Sammy into the car and his wheelchair into the trunk.

Before she'd stood out in the drizzling rain, yelling at a maniac driver.

Before she'd dropped Sammy off at his nana and pappy's and

had gotten spat on by the gray skies again.

And before some insensitive, careless driver had zoomed by her in the high school parking lot in his Corvette, splashing her, soaking her to the bone.

Oh, this is so not how she'd pictured things going, she thought, as she braced her shoulders, feeling another drop of rainwater begin its course. Or was it perspiration? Now that she was standing in front of nearly two dozen people—All-Stars Sports Day volunteers—looking at her, waiting for her to say something.

But, no. It definitely couldn't be sweat. The room was freezing. She hadn't remembered the Loveland High School cafeteria being air-conditioned when she'd been in school. But it certainly was now. Her jaw tightened and she could barely feel her hands. Only because she was freezing? Or also because she was anxious from the twenty-plus sets of eyes all directed on her?

"Well, everyone. . .thank you for coming. This is so. . . I just want to say. . ."

What was it she'd planned to say? She'd thought it all out the night before. And she'd practiced every free minute she'd had since. But now—crunch time—nothing would come to her.

She squeezed at her shoulder-length ponytail the way she always did when she was nervous. Big mistake. She'd forgotten it was drenched, sending more water running down her back, along with a chill that followed. She'd been wrong not to have the meeting in Miss Annabella's Tea Parlor when Maria had offered. Spring or not, it was a chilly evening, and it would've been the perfect place to meet on this rainy night.

"I'm sorry there's not something hot to drink." She worked to brace her jaw in an effort to keep her teeth from chattering. "That would sure warm us all up, I know. What a dreary night, huh, for this time of year?"

Only when she looked at the rows of men and women, none of them appeared to be waterlogged like her. Because they hadn't dragged their handicapped child out in the storm? Because they had spouses who could stay at home and watch their kids? Or because they had sitters who had come to their houses, who weren't in the emergency room at the moment?

Suddenly Maria's hand popped up, much to Megan's relief. Maria—her acquaintance from town—who didn't have any off-spring but had been kind enough to brave the nasty night along with Janey, a dear friend from grade school whose only "baby" was her bakery. "I could check if there's a coffeemaker in the back kitchen," she offered.

"Would you all like some coffee?" Megan asked the group, but most all of them simply stared at her, mute. How could they all be here for the same cause—a sports day for their special-needs kids—and not be a bit more effusive and friendly?

"I guess we're okay, Maria. But thank you." She nodded before turning her full attention back to the not-so-responsive group. "And thank you, everyone, for coming. And for caring enough to help organize a special day of sporting events for our great kids."

Hugging herself to keep warm in front of the blank eyes that stared at her, she continued, "You know, as a physical therapist, I work with a lot of athletes of all ages. We are continually helping the athletes to heal, and teaching them how to use their bodies properly so they can go out and play a sport, compete safely, and have fun.

"I guess after watching so many kids know the joy of performing at a sport, I've longed to have the same opportunity for my son, Sammy, who was born with cerebral palsy. And I'm sure that's why most of you are here, because you also desire the same sort of fun event for your children."

Seeing a few nods in the audience, she loosened the grip on her arms, feeling encouraged to continue. "Sammy is really excited about the prospect of having this All-Stars Sports Day come together, and I have to tell you, he said the cutest thing the other day when we were talking about it. He said that parents are special and they need a special sports day. Of course, I told him we'd look into that next year after we see how this year's event goes." She smiled at the volunteers, who finally seemed to be responding to her. Talking about kids always was an icebreaker; she felt thankful she'd thought of it.

She spoke for a few more minutes, taking care to touch on several important points, one of them being fundraising for the event. No one noticeably flinched at the word. Quite the opposite, in fact.

Yes, suddenly the men and women appeared to be tuning in to her. All grinning and sitting up straighter in their metal folding chairs.

"Wow, if you could only see what I'm seeing now. You all look so enthusiastic and eager, ready to forge on with this project. It's exciting."

Only. . .well. . .they did look enthused and animated. But they weren't really looking in her direction, were they? They were looking to the left of her actually. She paused her talk, craning her neck to see—

"This is Cammie Larking, reporting from the cafeteria of Loveland High School. Tonight we're here to let viewers know about a meeting taking place for a very special cause. . ."

Megan heard the reporter's voice before she could really take in and grasp the sudden commotion taking place around her. A cameraman with a Channel 4 News emblem plastered on the side of his video camera was walking backward on bent knees, obviously taping the reporter with her mic in hand. While right behind her, Ted Slater, Cincinnati's top homebuilder, waved at the cameraman.

It had crossed her mind earlier that she hadn't noticed Ted in the group of volunteers. She and Sammy had bumped into Ted and his wife and their daughter Hannah, who suffered from cystic fibrosis, at Scoop's ice cream shop a few days earlier. Ted had been adamant he'd be at the meeting to support Megan and the cause.

Of course, she'd never dreamed he meant he'd be bringing a news crew along with him, for goodness' sakes. But she should have guessed. Around town, Ted was known to be as much a promotion man as he was a homebuilder, always landing on the news or in an infomercial for some reason or another. With his ties to the media, having Ted on the committee could really be a help. Except for. . . the cameraman wasn't really angled in on Ted, was he?

No, he zoomed in on the man walking in behind Ted, causing the volunteers to lean forward in their seats to see. Megan leaned closer, too, until finally a man emerged out from behind Ted's shadow. A man taller than Ted and younger. Certainly more fit than the homebuilder, and wearing a baseball cap just like—

Mr. Neil? The maniac who had almost run her down? What on earth was he doing here? And why did all the volunteers and parents suddenly look so pleased about his presence? And why was Cammie glowing and smiling, standing closer to him than need be with her mic?

"So you've finally come out of hiding?" For some reason, the reporter's voice sounded more coy than professional.

"I've been recouping, not hiding, Cammie," Mr. Neil answered.

"Well, whatever you want to call it, we've missed seeing you out on the field."

"Thanks, Cammie, I appreciate that."

"Ted Slater, Cincinnati's most prominent homebuilder, says your help is what's going to make this first-annual All-Stars Sports Day project a grand slam." Cammie poised the mic at him, waiting for a response.

"A grand slam? Well, I—"

"Come on now. You've never been shy before," Cammie half-cooed, as if she knew that from personal experience. "No reason to be shy now, MacNeill Hattaway."

Megan couldn't believe it. Mr. Neil. Mac Neil. Was really MacNeill Hattaway? Oh, how stupid of her! She'd been so upset at the near-crash, she hadn't put it together.

"I'm planning to do everything I can to help the folks here make it a great event, Cammie," MacNeill was saying.

"I'm sure you will, Mac." Cammie beamed. "I'm sure you will," she added before suddenly swinging the mic around, thrusting it in Megan's face. "And I've been told you're Megan O'Donnell. Megan, all of us women are envious that you'll be working side-by-side with Mac, your new co-chair of the All-Stars Sports Day event—"

Her new co-chair? Of her own brainchild? When had that happened?

Plus, MacNeill Hattaway? She was actually being paired up to work with him? A person who didn't have any children, only plenty of childlike, bad-boy behavior if the tabloids in recent years had been even slightly accurate.

The man had nearly sideswiped her earlier in the evening, and now he'd officially blindsided her, too.

"Do you have anything to add to that?" Cammie moved closer, pressing for an answer.

"Anything to add?" Megan blinked at the news reporter. "Well, I—um. . ." Her cheeks burned and she certainly wasn't chilled any longer. No, she was on fire, beyond steaming. Nothing about this evening had gone as planned from the very beginning. Not one thing.

But then. . .averting her eyes from the ultra-white light of the camera, Megan glanced at the group of parents and volunteers. Their faces had certainly lit up when MacNeill walked in. And their glistening eyes were on her now, at full attention, eager to actually hear what she thought.

And what she thought was—well, what she thought was she had to put her feelings aside, didn't she? Or at least pretend to. Because it really wasn't about her, was it? It was about the kids and the special day that could bring fun, and closeness, and a sense of accomplishment for them. Oh, how she needed to remember that.

She swallowed hard, straining to regain her composure.

"Why, Cammie, I say we're all working together to make this a great event." She forced a bright smile. "Let's play ball!" She raised her fist in the air in a cheer.

"Mac, you're really going to be helping us?"

"Can you sign the back of my T-shirt?"

"Hey, how do you think the Hawks will do this year without you?"

The volunteers swarmed Mac the moment Cammie and her crew departed, everyone apparently delighted he was there.

Well, not everyone. Peering over the group circling him, he searched out Megan O'Donnell across the cafeteria and saw her talking to an older man who was in a wheelchair himself.

If only he could make eye contact with her, mouth out a "sorry," or give her an apologetic smile.

Staring long and hard in her direction, halfway ignoring the hubbub going on around him, in his mind he willed her to look at him. Oh, and she did. For about a split second anyway. She glared at him, and then glanced away, obviously wanting to avoid him.

All he could think was "strike two!"

Yep, he'd done it to the pretty woman again. Caught her totally off guard with the news crew and all. This time, he'd hit her full force without even meaning to—without even having a hand in it.

True, when Ted had asked him to come to the meeting, he'd been thrilled. More than willing to come, excited even to help. He felt like he had so much time to make up for in the "thinking of others" department.

Ted told him he'd be pitching in—no pun intended—like everyone else. Oh, and maybe using his celebrity status to garner a few local sponsors for the event.

But Ted had never mentioned this. Who knew Channel 4 was going to be there? Mac certainly didn't. Although he should've guessed as much, being that Ted was involved. His friend was no stranger to promotion for his homebuilding business, and surely Mac should've realized that where Ted's daughter Hannah was concerned, his friend would undoubtedly use whatever tactics he could to gain support and recognition for the special-needs kids' day.

But the news reporter, the grand entrance—it was all a surprise to him. And so was seeing the mom he'd almost crashed into running the meeting.

And, man. . . She wasn't happy about him being there, news crew or no news crew—he could tell. He'd trained himself to read body language throughout his career, mostly the body language of batters up at the plate and runners on base. It was all part of the game for him and an area where he definitely excelled.

Megan O'Donnell might've fooled the volunteers and the media with her quick cheerleader smile and team-inspired words, but she couldn't fool him. He could tell she hadn't known a thing about Ted's invitation to him, about Cammie's visit, and contrary to the rest of the group, she wasn't happy about it. Her pursed lips and narrowed eyes told him so. Her deadly glare shouted so.

"Hey folks, I appreciate you all giving me such a warm greeting," he said to the volunteers huddled around him. "But, uh, I'll be around for the next few months, and I'll be happy to sign anything. I promise. Right now though, I think I should properly introduce myself to the woman who started all of this. Can you all excuse me for a minute? I need to shake hands with Mrs. O'Donnell."

"Miss," the lady closest to him said. "*Miss* O'Donnell."

"Miss?" Something inside his chest did a skip.

"I should know. I'm an old friend of hers. My name's Janey. I own Sweet Sensations Bakery."

He dipped his head toward the cute blond. He'd seen her often enough in the bakery, but had never guessed she was the owner. "Greatest bear claws ever. Blueberry muffins are topnotch, too." He nodded the compliment.

"Thanks." She grinned, obviously pleased. "Can I quote you on that?"

"Well, sure. It's true." He grinned. "So. . .*Miss* O'Donnell, huh?"

"Miss. Just like me." She preened.

Mac excused himself then snaked his way through the throng of volunteers toward Megan. Apparently having finished her conversation with the handicapped gentleman, she looked like she was pouring more energy—or was it frustration?—than was necessary into gathering up her papers and purse from the lunch table behind her.

Having already experienced the brunt of her wrath earlier in the evening, he suddenly felt a little apprehensive. Hard to imagine that a pretty, petite thing like her could stop all two hundred pounds of him with one direct glower, but she certainly could and did.

Halting momentarily, he took a deep breath and steeled himself, feeling as young and intimidated as a high school boy asking a girl to the movies. He inched closer. "I, uh, wanted to see if we could try to patch things up."

"Since now we're going to be working together?"

"Exactly." When she continued to glare, he held out a hand.

"Look. I really am sorry about earlier. I was completely at fault. I'm glad my stupidity in driving that old truck didn't hurt you or your son."

She looked at his hand like it might bite. "Apology accepted, Mr. *Hattaway*."

Feeling like a fool, he let his hand drop to his side. "I tried to tell you my name. . ."

"Yes, you did. You definitely tried to tell me that you were MacNeill Hattaway, world-famous pitcher."

Now he was getting irritated. "Look, I'm trying to be friends here. And it's Mac. . .just plain old Mac."

"And my new co-chair, to boot."

He could detect the agitation in her tone, and hated hearing it. Still, it wasn't easy keeping the aggravation from his own voice as he answered her.

"Hey, I don't know where Cammie came up with that. I really didn't know about any of the press hoopla. Or some of the things she was saying. Honest. I didn't."

She finally looked at him. Really looked, and he could tell her mind was busy scrutinizing him, weighing what she'd heard in the past and what she'd seen tonight against what he had to say.

Doubt flickered in those big blue eyes of hers. She wasn't buying it.

"You don't believe me, do you? You think I'm here—you think this is all a media stunt for me."

She stared more intently.

"Seriously? That's what you really think?" he prodded.

"Well, you have to admit. . ." She looked away from him, glancing toward the cafeteria door instead. "That was quite an entrance."

"You can be sure that's not what I'm looking for with this experience, Megan O'Donnell. I want this to be all about the kids." That word seemed to bring her focus back on him. "The other thing—the media dwelling on me—I don't need it. I don't want it."

"And that's what I want. This needs to be all about the kids, Mr. Nei—" She caught herself. "Mr. Hattaway."

"Mac," he countered again. "So then. . .that's good, isn't it? We both want the same thing," he said. But even as he was staring into her eyes and saying that, he felt a strange tug. As if maybe—just maybe—with this new co-chairperson there might be something more.

But Megan still wasn't ready to concede. "I guess time will tell." She looped her purse strap over her shoulder and was just about to turn away from him when the Janey girl appeared.

"Hey, can I get a picture of our co-chairs together?" A small digital camera surfaced in Janey's hands. "I'm helping with some of the PR for the event," she informed him as she waved Megan closer to his side. "You need to get a little closer, Meg. Here, let me take your purse for a minute."

Janey grabbed Megan's purse, setting it down by her own feet, and then with a free hand pushed Megan toward him.

He could feel the rigidity in her shoulder next to his. Could literally feel her reluctance instead of just sensing it. But apparently her friend didn't notice.

"Okay, that's way better." Janey glanced into the camera. "Now, both of you, smile."

Megan's stiffness and aloofness was a bit of an ego bruising to be sure. Certainly, he wasn't used to females not wanting to be around him—reacting to him that way.

But what bothered him even more was the idea that she didn't believe him. Something inside him wanted Megan O'Donnell to take him at his word. The thought that she didn't troubled him, made him start to frown.

Yet. . .he'd had plenty of years experience putting on a show for the camera. And as Janey snapped a handful of photos of them, Megan wasn't the only one forcing a smile.

Chapter 4

The rain had let up by the time Megan made her way back to her parents' house. Not that it mattered really. Rain or shine, the place she'd called home until she'd moved out on her ill-fated wedding day had always been a warm, cozy haven. That was especially true of the kitchen where her mom's curio cabinets lined the walls, plants and knick knacks adorned the bay window, and where she found her parents and Sammy sitting at the round oak table for four—which could always fit six in a pinch.

"Back so soon, honey?"

Megan honestly thought her mother sounded somewhat disappointed.

In fact, she realized neither of her parents gave her barely so much as a glance when she walked into the room. But then, how could she fault them for that? Both Laura and Kurt O'Donnell had their eyes pinned on Sammy, watching him eat freshly-baked cookies—oatmeal cranberry walnut—Megan easily detected from the familiar scent lingering in the air. The grandparents gazed at their grandson adoringly, completely captivated as if they'd never seen such a charming creature eat before.

As much as she didn't want to depend on them for anything, and as much as their love could be stifling at times, she had to admit she was lucky they were doting and devoted. They hadn't been all that thrilled when she announced her engagement to Bryan; they thought it was too quick and their trip to town hall to be married by a justice of the peace even hastier. The doubt was always there in her mom's eyes and forced smiles when Bryan was around. Megan knew he certainly wasn't the match her matchmaking mother would've made for her. And certainly not the kind of stark, non-traditional ceremony her wedding planning mother would have helped her design either.

But after her parents once expressed their concerns about her decision to marry him, the two of them never said anything again. Not even a "we told you so" when Bryan walked out on her and Sammy just a few short months after it was determined Sammy had cerebral palsy.

In a way, it might've been easier if they had said something. If they had clucked their tongues or self-righteously reminded her they'd never thought Bryan was good husband and father material to begin with. It would've given her a chance to say it out loud, how wrong she'd been about him, instead of carrying around feelings of self-loathing about the bad choice she'd made in him—in men— years ago. But conversely, her parents acted like Bryan had never existed. Like marriage vows had never been exchanged.

Instead, through the entire Bryan ordeal, her parents' focus remained steadfast on Sammy. Their eyes always twinkling at the sight of their newborn grandson. And glistening when Megan went to legal lengths to make sure Sammy carried the O'Donnell family name. Her parents thought Sammy was just perfect and poured their love into his heart and life from day one.

Or at least whenever Megan gave them the opportunity.

"It's almost nine," she countered. "The meeting actually lasted longer than I expected." Although it hadn't been all that much of a meeting, had it? With MacNeill Hattaway involved, it'd been more of a media event.

"Have a seat." Her mom nodded to the empty chair at the table. "And some cookies."

Her dad chuckled delightedly. "We were just sitting here watching Sammy chow down."

"So I see." Megan half-smiled at her parents' usual fascination with her son. "This is a big night for you, Sammy O'Donnell. Paxton's fries. And Nana's homemade cookies. What a lot of treats!"

Cookie crumbs dotting his lips, Sammy bounced his head wildly, an over-the-top grin lighting his face. Megan walked around the table, kissing his crown of tousled hair before taking a seat herself.

"We can only stay another minute or so."

"Oh Meggie, you have time for a cookie, don't you?" Her mom scooted the platter toward her. "And a cup of hot tea? You probably need it after running around in the rain and lightning all evening."

Before she could begin to protest, her mother was already on her feet, at the sink, filling the teapot. As if it were a given. As if Megan had all the time in the world to sit and sip a cup of tea. As if she didn't need to drive home, get Sammy bathed and ready for bed, get a sandwich packed for the next day, and get herself ready for bed as well.

That's why it was so much easier to have a sitter. That's why she was going to miss Mrs. Biddle so, so much. The woman was loving, but efficient. She knew how to stick to a schedule. Just thinking about all the chaos and disruptions she might be in for the next few months made Megan want to groan out loud.

"Rain an' lightning?" Sammy interrupted her thoughts, looking up from actively splashing his cookie in his cup of milk. "Bray maw-mee. You my bray maw-mee." He repeated the compliment she'd paid him earlier in the evening.

His good-heartedness quelled her irritation immediately the way it always did. Well, maybe one cookie. . . Maybe they had time for one cookie and one cup of tea.

She picked a cookie from the pile, the largest one she could find, thinking that might prevent her from eating a second or even third one.

"So." Her father leaned forward. "How did the meeting go?"

Something about his posture made him look overly anxious to know. Megan could feel her radar naturally turn onto alert, her words coming out hesitantly when she answered him.

"Good. Good, I think. I mean. . . We have at least twenty volunteers or so."

"Oh honey, that's wonderful." Laura O'Donnell beat her husband to a reply, her voice a little louder than usual as she competed with the simmering teapot. "Did Janey and Maria come? They're such nice girls. I love working down the street from their shops. I stop in to visit every chance I get."

"They were both there." Megan nodded. "And of course, lots of parents." She broke her warm cookie in half, taking small savory bites.

"Great, great," her dad replied, though he eagerly brushed off the information. "Was there anything else? Anything else happen?"

"Happen?"

A feeling of déjà vu crept into her bones. Oh, how many times had she sat at this same table in her younger days, lured by a plateful of cookies and lulled into such a complacent confidence that she'd said more than she'd meant to about a certain boy she liked or had given away secrets about the things she and her friends were up to.

Well, that wasn't about to happen now. She was older and in control. Her parents weren't about to get her going on and on about what was on her mind. Like Mac and his grand entrance. And his self-appointed co-chair position. And about his—her heart stopped for a moment thinking of his eyes, of all things. The way he stared at her so intently when he'd come over to give her his made-up story about how he didn't know anything about the news reporter or cameraman.

An involuntary shiver coursed its way up her back, shimmying her shoulders.

"See, you're shivering." Her mother set a steaming mug down in front of her. "A cup of tea is exactly what you need."

Before she could mumble a thank you, her dad kept prodding. "Yeah, happen. Did anyone else show up? You know, besides those girls you and your mom know. And the parent volunteers. Anyone else?"

Her light bulb might've been dim, but it didn't take too long for it to go off.

"Oh, this town." She shook her head. "This small, small town. Did you run into Ted or something, Dad?"

Her father nodded. "Sure did." His grin was slightly comparable to Sammy's ecstatic one moments earlier.

"And you didn't warn me?"

"Warn you?" His head jerked back.

"What's there to warn about, honey?" Her mother chirped in, a bit too quickly. "Hattaway—he's—well, he's very nice looking. And he's—"

"You knew, too?" She'd been set up to be run over and no one had bothered to tell her? Stomach churning, Megan set the cookie aside.

"Oh yes!" Her mom settled back down in the chair next to her. "Can you believe it? Your wonderful idea—it's going to be bigger than ever now! With celebrity backing. It's so, so exciting."

"What exciting, Na-naw?"

"MacNeill Hattaway, Sammy." The look on her dad's face as he answered his grandson shone with pride as if just being in on Ted's secret meant he'd had a hand in things where Hattaway was concerned. "That all-star pitcher is going to help your mom with your special sports day event."

"MaaNil?" Sammy's eyes grew as round as the cookies he chomped on.

"That's right, MacNeill." Her dad turned to Sammy with his hand in the air. It took a struggled few moments before Sammy managed to lift his right hand and high-five her father.

Oh, great. MacNeill Hattaway was a name Sammy was familiar with. She should've known.

Even when Sammy didn't have the chance to watch sports with his pappy, he wanted the television tuned in to the sports channels at home. And even though he couldn't participate in the community's organized sports, sports were his all-time favorite thing—even ahead of country music, Paxton's fries, and his nana's cookies. Hadn't that been the reason she'd thought of the All-Stars Sports Day event in the first place?

"But Hattaway doesn't even have kids." Megan grimaced at the beaming faces surrounding her. "Why should he care?"

"Why wouldn't he care?" her dad retorted. "You don't need to father a child to care about one."

"Besides, Meggie," her mom added, "perhaps Mr. Hattaway wants to redeem himself." She didn't have to say why the pro ballplayer might be in need of redemption. Everyone at the table—well, excepting Sammy—had read or heard plenty about the questionable life and times of MacNeill Hattaway.

"Redeem himself?" Megan rolled her eyes. "You mean get good publicity is probably more like it."

"Don't you think you're being a little harsh, honey?" Her mom put a hand over hers. "People do deserve second chances, don't you think?"

For a moment Megan wondered if her mom would think Bryan deserved a second chance, too. Not that Megan would've given him one anyway. But then she realized her mom hadn't thought Bryan worthy of a first chance. Once again, Megan wished she'd listened to her mother's warnings back then.

"I just don't want the focus to be all on MacNeill Hattaway and not on the kids." She frowned at her parents.

But even as Megan said the words out loud, she knew there was something more she wasn't saying. Thoughts she was keeping all to herself.

No, she didn't want the spotlight off the special-needs kids. But she also didn't want a man coming along to "save the day" like some Disney prince. Because not only was that such a non-reality in her non-fairytale world, but really and truly, she didn't need some male doing that.

She could manage just fine, like she always had. All by herself.

As Mac made a slow turn onto his uncle's property, the low, wide tires on the Corvette clawed at the nuggets of gravel lining the driveway, tossing them aside in every direction, threatening to nick the red glossy paint.

He let up on the gas pedal a little more. Even though the car wasn't his, even though he was only driving it to be helpful since a friend of a friend had a father-in-law with a waning car dealership who wanted his endorsement, he still felt compelled to take good care of the vehicle.

Luckily he hadn't been driving the sporty classic last November though. November sixth to be exact. The night of his near-fatal crash.

Inching up the drive, the fullness of the opal moon shed a forgiving light on the weather-worn boards of his uncle's oak barn, making it appear almost unblemished under the redemptive glow. For more years than he cared to remember, he'd forgotten how awesome moonlight could be.

Instead, living in his high-rise condo in the city, he'd always been charmed by the sight of urban lights—the flickers of neon, the lit-up billboards. They always lured him. Jazzed him up. Made him want to prowl the streets, many, many times when he would've been better off home alone.

As he pulled the Corvette up close to the side of the barn, Bitty, the stray cat making its home there, froze and stared into the headlights before jumping off a bale of hay and skittering away into the night. Mac got out, and leaning against the car, felt like he wouldn't mind disappearing into the night, too. The rain had stopped hours before, leaving the acres of grass and wildflowers smelling cleansed and fresh. The moon included him in its light, giving off a feeling of comfort that the city's tempting glitter never held for him. Everything around him had a feel and smell of healing. He felt grateful for that.

Yeah. . .if he'd been driving the Corvette the night of the accident—the night he'd been under the influence, totally inebriated, he wouldn't be standing in the moonlight now. He would've been a dead man for sure. But the Corvette had been in the repair shop that week, ironically. The loner car he'd been given was an SUV that protected him a bit more than the sports car ever would've when he lost control and ran into a brick building at top speed. Not that the SUV spared him injuries. Not by a long shot. From what he learned later, he was thrown from the crumpled vehicle and lay on the side of the road, unconscious, bleeding, and broken. He woke up in the hospital days later clueless as to when or how he got there.

But if I had to go there to get here. . .Lord, it's a good thing, I guess.

Turning toward the house, boots scraping the skillet-sized earth-sunken stones that formed the sidewalk, Mac wished the same thing he always did as he made his way up the wooden steps and across the width of the wraparound porch to the front screen door.

He wished that his uncle would be waiting for him inside.

A few inches shorter than Mac, but with a heart at least twice the size, Jake Lochen, his mother's brother, was a man he enjoyed immensely. Truly a man to be admired, though not for his worldly status necessarily.

Years ago, in fact, when his parents confided that his uncle was ill and having trouble keeping up with payments on the farm, Mac had stepped in and paid off the mortgage. He couldn't stand the idea of his uncle losing the property and not living out his final days there, finding whatever joy he could in his "piece of heaven on earth" as he fondly called it.

Of course, Mac couldn't handle the thought of losing the farm either. Jake had taught him an awful lot on those ten acres when he was a young boy. He had many good memories of his visits there, and of his uncle, who never ceased giving him lessons on pitching. Lessons about life. And teaching him about God.

Mac had gone on to perfect his pitching just as his uncle had trained him, and was lucky enough to play in the major leagues, in his former hometown, no less. Problem was, as his pitching led him to more and more success and fame, he'd pretty much turned his back on everything else.

Making his way into the old farmhouse, he turned on the floor lamp sidled up against his uncle's favorite worn leather chair. Mac hadn't yet sat in that chair. He still had too clear a vision of his uncle sitting there, reading his Bible on summer mornings before they went out to toss. Or visions of Jake bent forward over a newspaper on the floor, whittling some knickknack or another on evenings when it was too brisk to be outside on the porch doing the same thing.

Instead Mac walked past it, shucking his spring jacket and removing his baseball cap, tossing them onto an antique church pew on the opposite wall. The pew had always been a catch-all for everything. Jackets, hats, baseball mitts. It was also the spot where his uncle parked his walking stick.

Uncle Jake had used a walking stick daily—long, long before he'd ever become ill. As a young boy, Mac had never understood since he couldn't detect any problem with his uncle's legs or gait.

"It's a reminder," his uncle told him when Mac, at about eight years of age, finally got up the nerve to ask.

"Reminder?" Mac had been totally confused. "Like of how to walk?"

"In a way." His uncle chuckled. "It's a reminder for me to depend on God. Not to try to make the walk alone."

Mac picked up the walking stick, rubbing the smoothness of the carved pine, marveling not for the first time at his uncle's talent. Jake had made many a walking stick and handed them out to friends and visitors alike. Some had intricately carved knobs and handles; others were awesome combinations of wood, braided and glazed like some fancy bakery bread. Just holding the walking stick in his hand also forced Mac to recall the essence of his uncle's faith.

And to reflect on his own.

If only Uncle Jake were still around the see the changes in him since the accident! Not that the man had ever criticized him for his scandalous behavior—he never had. Jake Lochen never judged and rarely lectured. Instead, the very few occasions they'd spent any time together in the past years, Uncle Jake had only promised to pray for Mac.

"I'm trying, Uncle Jake," Mac whispered into the silence. "God knows I'm trying."

As he used his uncle's walking stick to make his way upstairs to the bedroom, he thought about all the handicapped kids who were in need of assistance just to eat, walk, and barely play. Hopefully, his volunteering for the All-Stars Sports Day really could make a difference.

Hopefully, too, someday the Megan O'Donnell lady would look at him with a smile in those pretty blue eyes of hers. Instead of gazing at him in a distant way. . .unable to connect or trust.

Chapter 5

"Oh Megan, I'm so glad you stopped in."

Megan watched Janey slide a tray of Morning Glory muffins into the bakery case, making her decision even more difficult. Without fail, Sammy always asked for jelly doughnuts from her friend's Sweet Sensations Bakery. But Megan couldn't help eyeing all of the yummy choices and considering them. What should she get this time? A freshly-baked muffin? Or her usual cinnamon twist?

"It's Saturday. Why wouldn't I stop in?"

A visit to Janey's bakery was part of her and Sammy's Saturday morning routine. If the weather conditions were even so much as passable, she'd come in, chat with Janey, and gather up their order. Meanwhile Sammy waited outside right where he wanted to be, with his wheelchair parked on the edge of the community basketball court on the opposite side of the bike path. That put him in prime position to watch the groups of kids who gathered there to shoot hoops and play pickup games on their day off school. Generally kids who were used to him and the other way around.

Sammy enjoyed that time immensely and the bit of freedom that came with it. But so many times as Megan glanced out the bakery window and saw him sitting across the bike path in his wheelchair, on the sideline, unable to be a part of the action, an all-too familiar pang tugged at her heart. This morning was no exception.

"I just e-mailed you." Janey pulled her from her thoughts. "I have pictures to show you."

"Pictures?" Megan's eyes darted between the muffins and doughnuts. "Pictures of what?"

"From the other night. At the meeting." Her friend's voice turned slightly accusing. "Megan, why didn't you tell me MacNeill Hattaway was going to be there?"

Megan looked up to see Janey pull her hands to her hips. "I would've at least redone my makeup. Or brought cupcakes or something," she prattled on. "Did I tell you he complimented my bear claws?" A proud smile erupted on her face.

Megan stared at her friend, blankly, mostly not understanding one wee bit why everyone seemed to care so much about what MacNeill Hattaway thought. Did everyone really need to hang on to his every last word?

"Janey, I don't have time to look at pictures. Sammy's over there at the basketball court, and—"

"It'll only take a minute, I promise. Cindy Duncan wants a photo to accompany the press release she's written for the *Loveland Herald* and the *Cincinnati Enquirer.* I thought you'd want to decide which photo it should be."

"I'm sure you can choose, Janey. I trust your artistic eye."

Truly, Megan wasn't trying to heap undue flattery on her friend. Janey had always had a creative streak in everything she did. It was even obvious in the way she'd decorated her bakery. The shop was surprisingly unique, with an art deco style that was both striking and homey at the same time.

Plus, Megan flat out didn't need to see pictures of MacNeill Hattaway. His face was already imprinted on her mind, thank you very much. And she would be seeing him at their next All-Stars meeting on Wednesday night. Wasn't that soon enough?

But before she could protest any further, Janey dusted off her hands, pulling a digital camera out of her apron pocket.

"Seriously, Janey. Sammy's out there. I really don't have time. If I could just get my latte and our doughnuts?"

Glancing into the sunshine that poured in the bakery window, Janey waved toward the basketball court. "You worry about him too much, Meg. Sammy is less than ten yards away. He looks perfectly content. Perfectly comfortable."

She followed Janey's line of vision and knew it was true. Sammy did look fine. But the fact of the matter was, she wasn't.

Even after nights and days of stewing, she still wasn't comfortable at all with the entire Hattaway hubbub. And she really, truly didn't care to see photos of her and him, standing side-by-side.

"I'm not making this decision on my own," Janey said firmly, coming from behind the bakery cases. "Besides," she said with a giggle, "you should look at these pictures, for real. Hattaway's so gorgeous and hunky. Maybe you'll want to blow one up. Poster-sized."

Right. Megan could barely refrain from rolling her eyes.

"Did I tell you Mac also likes my blueberry muffins?" Janey preened.

Megan wanted to groan. A few fast-flung compliments here and there, a couple of appearances at fundraisers, and soon MacNeill Hattaway would be up for sainthood, all of his past forgiven.

"He should. Your sweets are incredible, Janey. I've told you that a zillion times." But somehow her compliments didn't carry much weight. Not like Hattaway's anyway.

In fact, Janey dismissed what she'd said with a wave of her hand and started up about the photos all over again. "Here. You have to look." She thrust the camera's screen in Megan's face. "Don't you two look great together? I'd thought of nabbing him for myself, but after I saw that picture of you two. . .well, guess I'll have to find my own baseball star."

Forced to look at the photos of Mac and her, Megan could readily see what Janey was talking about. They did look good together. Aesthetically speaking of course. And why wouldn't they? Her dark hair contrasted perfectly with his sun-streaked blond. And his athletic look and build complemented the girl-next-door persona everyone always told her she exuded. Yes, they went together "picture perfectly" like two people in a car advertisement or something. Only, unfortunately, she wasn't a model getting paid to smile. She'd forced that on her own.

"So which one?" Janey clicked through the series of pictures she'd taken.

"How about the first shot you showed me?" *Did it matter?*

"Oh, great. I like that one best." Janey nodded with approval, sliding the camera back into her pocket. "I like the way Mac's kind of looking at you in that picture. I'll copy you on it when we send it to the newspaper so you can have a record."

"Really, Janey, don't worry about it. It's not a big deal."

"Are you kidding? MacNeill Hattaway not a big deal?"

Megan couldn't stand to hear it any longer. "Hey Janey, I hate to be a nudge, but I should be getting back to Sammy. Do you mind getting my latte and his doughnuts together? And I'll take a cinnamon twist. I really hate leaving him alone for so long, you know?"

It was the perfect excuse, one she didn't mind dredging up. Anything to remove herself from anymore talk of the local baseball hero. But as soon as the words left her mouth and she glanced out the window again at her son, the excuse had turned to reality.

"Oh my—" Words froze in her mouth. Her heart lurched in her chest.

In the short time she and Janey had been looking at photos, the younger kids had disappeared from the basketball court. Apparently, they'd been shooed off by a gang of teenaged boys who had taken over the area. That might have been more normal than frightening, except for the fact that the boys weren't shooting hoops. In fact, she noticed the ball had rolled off past the edge of the court. And Sammy's eyes were wide as the boys turned their focus on him and his wheelchair. In fact one of them stood behind the chair, rocking it back and forth, hoisting it up and down.

She wasn't sure what was going on. But that was all she had to see. Heart pounding, her maternal instincts at full throttle, she bolted out the door.

Hands at his waist, Mac gazed up into the sunlight flickering through the branches of the birch trees lining the running path, trying to catch his breath.

Jogging three miles had never been so hard in his life! How he'd ever been as stupid as to get behind the wheel drunk all those months ago was certainly beyond him.

For at least the thousandth time he inwardly chided himself for ever being so irresponsible. For ever being so negligent as to cause the accident that left him with pins everywhere in his body—his ankles, his knee. . .and though his pitching elbow was healing, there was still the question if it would ever be completely right again.

These days it was hard to believe he'd ever been that dumb. But obviously he had been. *Really dumb.*

Shaking his head at himself, he glanced around at the serene setting, squinting at the glistening strip of river that ran along the jogging path.

Many a time, he'd heard his uncle talk about having a heart of gratitude. How a man needed to humble himself and realize where all good things came from. He finally knew what Uncle Jake had meant. Feelings of thankfulness came easy nowadays. Such as, he was thankful that he hadn't hurt anyone else the night of the accident. Of course, he was also thankful that his life had been spared despite his recklessness. He'd really needed the chance he'd been given to reacquaint himself with the things that mattered in life. God being at the top of the list.

Claiming one of the iron benches off to the side of the path, he closed his eyes. Raising his face to the sun, he soaked in the warm, healing rays. But all too quickly the peacefulness of the moment was interrupted by jeering voices. Most likely coming from teenaged boys, he guessed.

Slowly opening one eye, he glanced in the direction of the disruptive sound. Yeah, there was a tribe of them, all right, all huddled together on the basketball court that flanked the jogging path.

Only. . .whatever they were up to didn't look like anything good. His other eye shot open.

Not a one of them was dribbling the ball. Actually not a one of them had a basketball in their hands. In fact, the only ball in sight had rolled over onto the grass. And there was a wheelchair he could see, right in the middle of the noisy bunch.

Could it be—? He peered more closely.

It was! Megan's son sat in the wheelchair, in the center of the group. And it looked like the boys were moving in on him, on— what did Megan say his name was again?

Sammy. She had called her son Sammy the night the two of them had stood out in the pouring rain together, her finger nearly jabbing his chest.

Instinctively, Mac's jaws tightened. So did his fists. Whether it was Sammy or not, the idea of a bunch of boys ganging up on a defenseless kid made him crazy. Hustling toward the court in long, quick strides, he struggled to keep his temper in check. But it wasn't easy—especially when the kid behind the wheelchair kept jostling the thing, acting like he was going to dump Sammy out of it.

The name MacNeill Hattaway might've been synonymous with

a lot of rotten things in the past—but "bully" wasn't one of them. It was also something he had never tolerated very well. Not since he'd been friends with a neighbor kid Robbie, who had Coke-bottle glasses and had always been picked last in gym.

"Hey guys." He stepped onto the court and crossed his arms over his chest, tucking his closed fists under his armpits. "What's going on here?"

"Who wants to know?" The tall, lanky kid standing behind Sammy's wheelchair didn't even bother looking up from under the oversized cap, sunk down over his eyes and face.

Even so, Mac leveled his eyes at the kid, felt his teeth clench. "I do," he ground out.

But the kid didn't flinch. Kept his eyes downward. "Don't worry, dude. He likes it. He's my kid brother." He nodded toward Sammy.

"Brother, huh?"

"Yeah." The kid shrugged. "Brother."

Mac eyed the other boys, who for the most part, couldn't keep from smirking. He shot the kid another stone-cold expression, but again the kid wasn't looking anyway. "So what's your last name, *dude*?" he repeated the boy's own word emphatically.

"Smith." The kid didn't skip a beat.

"Yeah? Smith, huh? That's interesting."

"Yeah, why?"

"Because that's not his name."

"Oh, right. Like you know his name? Who are you, the bike path police or something?" The teenager snorted at his own not-so-clever joke, and then glanced around in search of his friends' knowing grins. Mac figured him to be the ringleader of the group since most of the boys chuckled along with him.

"His name is Sammy O'Donnell."

"Wha?" Sammy, who had been sitting stiffly, not moving an inch, slowly turned his head toward Mac's voice, coming face-to-face with him. "You know my name?"

"Yes, I do, Sammy."

"Hey." Sammy's face lit up suddenly. "I know you name, too."

"He talks weird," Mac heard one of the boys in the group say.

"Probably because he is weird." Another smart-aleck boy answered back.

But Sammy didn't appear to hear the jibes from the boys. "You MaaNil. MaaNil Haa-away." His tense face broke into a smile.

"What?" Unable to contain his surprise, the boy behind the chair finally looked straight up at Mac. "It's you."

Mac recognized the teen right away and snatched the concealing hat off his head. "Reese? Reese Calvin. Are you serious? What do you think you're doing?"

What's going on now?

Megan stopped and froze just yards from the basketball court, her heart still pounding. It was all she could do to stand back for a moment and not run the rest of the way to Sammy's defense. But it looked like MacNeill Hattaway, of all people, had already done that.

When she'd sprinted down the bakery steps and across the bike path, she'd seen a man jogging up to her son. Fit looking, in running shorts and a sweatshirt. Tall, and towering over the teenagers and Sammy's wheelchair. The man had looked familiar from a distance. But she'd never dreamed it would be Hattaway.

Yet there he was, surprising her again. He seemed to be everywhere these days.

Unbelievably, he also apparently knew the teen who had a grip on Sammy's wheelchair.

"I thought you liked sports, Reese," she overheard him saying. "That's what you told me at the baseball clinic."

"Who says I don't?" The boy shrugged.

"Well, hmm. . ." She noticed Mac uncross his arms and rub at his chin as if pondering the question. "You have a basketball court here. And a basketball. Yet instead of playing a game, what you choose to do is taunt Sammy here in his wheelchair. That's not cool, Reese. And it makes me think you like bullying a whole lot more than sports."

"What do you mean *taunt*?"

She thought Mac might lose his temper a bit when the kid asked that. But Mac remained patient, unfettered.

"I think you know what it means. If you don't, somebody can look it up on their iPhone."

She didn't know if it was the derisive tone in Mac's voice that caused the Reese boy to drop his hands from the wheelchair grips or not. But he did and was quiet about it.

"Now, what do you think your next move is?" Mac asked him, to which Reese gave a dull, "Huh?"

Mac repeated the question, nodding his head toward Sammy. "What do you think your next move should be?"

Reese shifted from foot to foot.

"He wants you to apologize," one of the boys at the helm of the group, about the same size as Reese, shouted out.

"I know that, doofus," Reese sputtered back at him.

"Actually"—Mac looked around—"I think a group apology would be real nice," he said with a sardonic smile.

Murmurs of "sorry" filled the air. Some of the boys, Megan noticed, even went so far as to pat Sammy on his shoulder or hand. All the while, Sammy smiled, not a begrudging bone in his body, just looking happy to be sitting in the midst of the action.

That taken care of, Mac addressed the group again. "Now it looks like to me, there's a basketball over in the grass. Somebody needs to go get it."

"I will!" The least virile-looking boy in the bunch suddenly appeared empowered by Mac's command. He ran as fast as he could to retrieve the ball.

"So what do I do with it?" the boy asked as he dribbled the ball awkwardly back onto the court.

Megan was just as curious, wondering what Mac could possibly be up to. He may have been wondering himself because he paused, taking a moment to scratch at his head.

"Uh, okay. Here's the deal," Mac told the boys. "How about we do something constructive? How about you ten guys divide yourselves into teams? An 'A' team and a 'B' team. Make it fair. Because if the teams aren't even, Sammy and I are going to make them that way. Aren't we, Sammy?"

She watched Sammy's grin grow to cover his face.

"Then you're going to play a quick game of b-ball—let's say

twenty minutes. I'll time it. Whichever team has the most points when time's up wins doughnuts from Sweet Sensations."

A mingling of cheers erupted then dissipated quickly. The boys got down to business, forming their two ragtag teams.

Chapter 6

Being a mom had its rights. Walking onto the basketball court where there was a group of ten males or so who had been teasing her son was one of them.

But. . .

Even though Megan still had emotions coursing through her, wanting to knock some heads together for the way the boys had been treating Sammy—and scaring the wits out of her—and wanting to let MacNeill Hattaway know that she could handle matters with her son on her own, thank you very much, she bit her tongue. She kept her cool. At least this time anyway.

Mostly because Janey was right, at least to a certain small degree. Though Sammy might be six years old and handicapped, he really wasn't exactly a baby anymore or oblivious to the world around him. He was becoming more impressionable, beginning to notice things she wasn't even aware he was noticing. Just like how he'd sat at Paxton's the other night and told Allie all about the near crash with Mac and how she had "yell at man."

Six-year-old perspective or not, she had to realize how her reactions and emotions affected him. Though she'd protect him to her last dying breath—which she hoped wasn't any time soon since she was his only guardian—better to do it in a more controlled way, for sure.

So as the teen boys sized up their teams and began to play, she settled herself on the opposite side of Sammy's wheelchair, where she could easily witness Mac's zeal for the game. Like the true competitor he was, he was taking the rivalry between the boys very seriously. She completely startled when he apparently sensed her presence, immediately turning his attention from the action on the court to greet her.

"Hey," he said quietly, with warmth in his voice.

Or was she imagining it? The intense expression on his face smoothed for an instant at the sight of her. He even smiled. And for a reason she couldn't fathom, it didn't look to be a strained smile, like the ones they both wore in the picture Janey had shown her minutes earlier.

Nonetheless, it was a quick, confusing greeting, and before she knew it he was back to business again, shouting out coaching tips to the boys and calling fouls on them.

In contrast, Sammy sang out her name. "Maw-mee!" he shrilled, unable to contain himself with all the excitement going on around him.

Truly, her son's face couldn't have been any brighter or his smile any wider, making her realize even more that she'd been right not to run over and fuss at the boys or Mac and ruin things. Though he looked happy to see her, she could tell he was nowhere near ready to be ripped from Mac's presence.

And certainly, she had no trouble understanding that.

He probably felt more like a part of the game than he ever had before. It wasn't every day a kid got to hang side-by-side with a baseball superstar or any superstar for that matter. And for Sammy, a true fan, it had to be even more special.

"Who's winning?" she asked, since she hadn't been paying all that much attention to the game.

"The Tees," Mac told her. "But the Skins are going to clinch it."

So MacNeill Hattaway was psychic, too? *Of course!* She should've known.

"Why do you say that?"

He offered a knowing, sideways grin. "They want it more."

"They're big doughnut fans? I overheard what you told them. They're vying for doughnuts, right?"

"It's about the doughnuts to the Tees. It's about winning to the Skins. They want to win more."

"Ahh."

She squinted, trying to see the game through Mac's eyes. As the minutes ticked off Mac's game watch, she really did begin to discern what he meant. The players on the Skins kept looking to him for approval when they made a basket or defended well. It was obvious they shared something with him—the love of the game? The sport of it all? Who knew? His watching them, his approving nods, apparently meant a lot though.

Whether she wanted to admit it or not, there was a sort of magnetism about the legendary MacNeill Hattaway. She could see it, even more, she could feel it—now that she experienced him in his element. His love for the game, apparently any game, unmistakably overflowed and seeped into most everyone around him. And he was right. The Skins caught up with the Tees and surpassed them in the last minutes.

"Cover your ears," he warned her as he bent down slightly to cover Sammy's ears with his hands.

"What?" She barely had time to comprehend what he was up to. Before she knew it, he pursed his lips and with some freaky skill he possessed, let loose with the loudest whistle she'd ever heard come from anyone's lips. A definite and nearly deafening signal that the basketball game was over.

"Time's up!" he shouted. "Way to go, Skins! Nice work, Tees."

Sweating and cheering, the Skins picked up their T-shirts from the side of the court, twirling them in the air, before high-fiving Mac and making a run for it across the jogging path over to Sweet Sensations.

"Can udder boys come?" Megan heard Sammy ask Mac, his voice nearly being drowned out by the hoopla.

Mac's forehead wrinkled as he studied her son's face. "You really want the Tees to come, Sammy?"

Sammy nodded. "He, too." Her son made a wobbly attempt to point at Reese, the boy who'd teased him most.

"Okay." At Sammy's request, Mac invited the rest of the boys, and more cheering resulted.

Meanwhile Reese rushed over to offer his services. "I'll push Sammy over to the bakery." He grabbed the wheelchair handles.

Mac raised a brow. "Gently?"

"Of course, gently."

Ironically, Megan noticed, Reese almost appeared offended by Mac's question. She had to smile at that, but didn't mind Reese's change of heart, especially since she was close by and could keep an eye on how he treated, or mistreated, her Sammy.

"So how should we do this?" Mac asked her after the boys took off ahead of them.

"Well, we can't let all these kids go into Janey's shop." She glanced at the group whose all-out exuberance could be mistaken for plain old rowdiness. "How about we go in and grab a few dozen doughnuts and some drinks and let them wait outside at the café tables? Or better yet. . ." Her thoughts suddenly turned to Janey who she knew would make a fuss of her and Mac being together. "You stay with the boys. Let me go in alone."

"Alone? Don't be silly." Mac splayed out his hand, inviting her to go up the wooden bakery steps ahead of him. "My treat, remember?"

Only, after Megan had tolerated Janey's uncontrollable gushing over Mac, and after dozens of doughnuts were boxed up and ready to be paid for, Mac patted his hips for his wallet.

"Oh, no way." He groaned. "Forgot I had on running shorts. I don't have a dime on me."

"No problem!" Janey exclaimed. "They're on the house, you two."

"You are not giving us the doughnuts for free, Janey." *Or turning this into a "we two" situation.* Megan reached into her purse for her wallet.

"But this is exciting! Having you both here, you know, at the same time," her friend chattered, over-splashing coffee into their to-go cups.

"Exciting or not, I'm paying. So you may as well tell me how much. Unless you want me to overpay."

After squaring up with Janey and getting back outside, Megan noticed Reese had already pulled Sammy's chair up to a table and was sitting next to him. All the other boys filled the remaining seats. Distributing doughnuts all around, Megan pointed to the only place left for her and Mac to sit—a waist-high rock ledge that also served as a flower bed in spots. They hoisted themselves up on it.

"That was pretty lame," Mac confided. "I invite the guys for doughnuts. And you end up buying."

He bit into his bear claw, and Megan was suddenly aware—almost mesmerized—by the size of his hands. No wonder he could handle a baseball so deftly. Although. . .at the moment he didn't look like the poster boy for a tall, handsome pro athlete the way he typically did. Unshaven, his hair disheveled, with a slight tear in an old college T-shirt. In a way, he actually looked more interesting to her than he usually had. More human. More. . .likeable really. Well, maybe that was going a bit far too fast.

Working to take her eyes from him, she tried to focus on what he was saying instead. He was still embarrassed about not having his wallet.

At first, she had to admit, she had been put-off back in the bakery, wondering if he was trying to pull the Hattaway charm thing. Get something for nothing. But even if he was, did it matter? In a way, she'd been glad to pay.

This was probably the best Saturday morning Sammy had ever had at the basketball court, what with the "high stakes" game and the camaraderie of the other boys. Even now she knew he was soaking in as much as he could. Maybe he couldn't entirely follow all of the boys' banter about sports and whatever else they were saying. But he was glowing, sitting in the middle of it all, with a few of the guys asking if he needed any help with his milk and doughnuts from time to time.

And it had all started with MacNeill Hattaway coming to Sammy's defense.

Maybe she needed to let down her defense as well. At least just a bit.

"These kids will probably never forget this," she told him. "The Saturday morning MacNeill Hattaway bought them doughnuts."

"*Almost* bought them doughnuts." He corrected her with the same easy smile he'd given her earlier.

"Ha! True."

"And, trust me, they went crazier at the mention of free doughnuts than they did at the mention of my name."

"Maybe that saying is true? You know, the one about 'the way to a man's heart is through his stomach.' "

"Could be." He grinned and she sensed he was enjoying himself, or at least enjoying their repartee. Which maybe was a good thing after all, she supposed. They would be working together. A lot. For the next several months.

"I really will get the money back to you, Megan."

"Do I look like I'm worried?"

It was rhetorical of course, so she didn't expect an answer. She also didn't expect the way Mac looked at her. Really took a minute to look at her as if appraising her expression. As if seeing something more than she wanted to share.

Yes, they'd been talking easily, making some of the strain from a few nights prior begin to fade away. Even so, it was only talk. And his looking at her felt like more than that.

Turning away from his gaze, totally aware of her burning cheeks, she busied herself, dusting off the sugar from her hands. Wiping them with a napkin. Placing the napkin in her empty white doughnut bag. Crumpling the bag into a small ball.

"Finished with that?" Mac hopped down from the ledge, reaching out for the bag. As he walked over toward the trash can, she tried to not watch him, tried not to notice the way he moved with such agility.

Instead, she glanced over at Sammy and once again saw him beaming. She felt her heart relax and warm, and if it could speak it would've surely cooed "aahhh" at that moment. It was a feeling, a deep contentment she didn't experience often. No, not often enough.

Once again, whether she liked it or not, a small voice niggled inside her, reminding how they'd gotten to this place, this moment.

MacNeill Hattaway.

He was rubbing his right elbow as he walked back to their spot along the wall. Second nature to her, she couldn't help but ask, "Is it bothering you? Your elbow?"

"Not so much anymore, honestly. Just acts up once in a while."

"Have you been seeing a physical therapist?"

"Not really. I'm past that phase. It's been a lot of months since the accident. I still do some exercises on my own to continue to strengthen it though."

"Did you do something to make it act up?"

"Yeah." He laughed. "You might say that. I fell the other night."

"Dare I ask?"

"Probably not." He half-chuckled, shaking his head. "Not one of my brightest moves. Why? Are you a doctor or something?"

"I'm an 'or something,'" she told him. "A physical therapist."

"Really? That's great. Everyone needs a physical therapist from time to time. Actually," he harrumphed, "I seem to need one almost all the time. Where do you work?"

"See that? Right over there?" She pointed to the building where she spent at least forty hours of each week.

"With the green roof?"

"That's the place. I could. . . I can give you a quick ultrasound treatment if you want. It may help ease the discomfort."

As soon as the words were out of her mouth, she wished she could retract them. Is this what MacNeill Hattaway did to people? How he got them to react to him? By being charming? Humble? And smiling a lot?

Make a person forget about his past. . .

Maybe even make me forget mine, too?

Well, she wasn't going to get caught up in him like everyone else always seemed to do. She couldn't afford to. If he took her up on her offer, that was fine. In the clinic she'd be on her own turf. In a place where she was in command. Where she felt comfortable. Even if she was alone with MacNeill Hattaway, it would be absolutely no problem. She could handle the situation without a doubt.

"The clinic's not open on Saturdays?" Mac asked as Megan pulled out her keys, unlocking the wooden door to LPTC, the Loveland Physical Therapy Clinic.

"Every other," she told him. "But I'm lucky enough that I don't have to work on Saturdays so I can spend the time with Sammy. Plus, going to Janey's on Saturday mornings is a family tradition of ours. We'd both go through withdrawal if we had to stop."

She laughed, and to Mac, the sound filled the place, causing the rows of metal exam tables and exercise equipment to instantly feel less sterile, homier. He watched as she moved around the room in her jeans and flip-flops, set down her purse, washed her hands. She started to flick on some lights, but then changed her mind, which was fine. There was so much sunshine pouring in the arched windows, making her dark, shiny hair even shinier, that lights were unnecessary. Plus they were only going to be there fifteen minutes or so. Her friend Janey had said she'd be more than happy to keep an eye on Sammy, who was still content to be sitting with the other kids, listening to them talk sports.

"So this is your home away from home?" Mac asked her.

"Monday through Friday." She nodded to the exam table closest to him. "Want to hop up there?"

Pushing a small portable cart in front of her, she made her way over to him. As she pulled the cart up close to the table, he was familiar enough with the ultrasound equipment it housed not to have any questions.

Except for one or two about her.

"How long have you been doing this?"

"Why?" Her eyes smiled into his, taunting. "Are you nervous?"

"Uh-uh. Not at all. I'm sure I'm in capable hands."

At least her hands felt good anyway as she squirted cold gel on his bare arm then proceeded to warm the substance and his skin with her soothing, expert touch.

"I've been here eight years now." She lifted the handpiece and began rubbing it in a circular motion around his elbow area. "Now I have a question for you. . ." she hedged.

"Okay."

"How did you hurt your elbow?"

"You mean the first time? Or the other night?"

"Let's start with the most recent incident," she suggested.

"Fair enough. . ." Plus, he imagined she'd already heard about his prior car accident. Hadn't everyone? A person had to be living in a cave not to.

"You said you fell?"

He nodded. "I couldn't sleep the other night. So I got up, grabbed a flashlight, and went outside looking for something and fell into a ditch. Pretty much hit elbow-first."

Megan stopped rubbing. "Excuse me, say that again. You were doing what?"

He sighed. Apparently, vague wasn't going to cut it with her. "I've been living out at my uncle's farm for the past few months. He passed away last year, but I'd already bought—well, that doesn't matter. The fact is, my uncle used to whittle. He whittled canes mostly, dozens of them. Like I said, I couldn't sleep. I started thinking about my uncle Jake and his whittling. So I got up." He shrugged. "And I went searching for a good piece of wood I could use."

"To whittle?" She sounded shocked, still holding the handpiece upright. "You whittle?"

"I, uh, I'm just getting started," he admitted.

Her forehead crinkled slightly. "Was your uncle crippled?" She cued in on the fact about the canes.

"No, he wasn't. Not physically. He just thought most everyone was spiritually."

He thought for sure she'd press him for clarification about that statement, but instead as she went back to work on his arm, her questions turned back to whittling, as if she just couldn't get over the fact he was attempting to try it.

"I like to do stuff with my hands," he explained. "Especially now that I'm not pitching."

"You're probably used to working out a lot, I imagine."

"Yeah. It's been quite a change all around. My body misses the practices, the workouts. I can't do everything to the degree I did prior to the accident, but it's getting better. I'm getting there." He paused. "It's all good. Good it happened. I guess that sounds a little crazy to you?"

"Honestly, I've heard it before."

He chuckled, feeling a little chagrined he'd exposed himself like that only to hear such a nonchalant response. "So I'm kind of like 'same old, same old'?"

"I'm sorry." She paused, looking up at him in a way that made her eyes collaborate with the words coming from her lips. "I apologize if I made it sound like that. I'm just saying I've had a lot of mangled people come in the door saying they think their accidents were good things. That they were out of control, and the accident saved their lives."

"It not only saved my life. It saved my soul."

He didn't know why he was telling her all this. Except for the fact he'd asked God for a chance to see her again, to makes amends with her, and here was that chance. It wasn't like he was trying to win her over—Megan O'Donnell wasn't a game to him. Not like so many other women had been in the past. It wasn't the way he wanted to operate anymore. But she didn't know that. And somehow he wanted her to. Which was crazy. They were only going to be working together on a sports day event, and then beyond that. . .

Why did his mind keep going there?

"So what are you doing tonight?" The question slipped out of his mouth just as she placed the handpiece back in its spot and grabbed for a cloth to wipe the goo from his arm. It surprised him almost as much as he could see it surprised her.

"What?" Her hands stilled. Her eyes grew wide. "Tonight?"

"What I meant to say is, I need to repay you for the doughnuts. Do you and Sammy have dinner plans?"

"No. . ." She swiped his arm quickly, deftly, tossing the cloth in a receptacle on the cart. "No," she repeated.

"Do you want some? Plans, I mean?"

He watched her body almost twitch in response to the question. Standing there, biting her lip, he wondered what all was going through her mind.

Or did he really want to know?

All he knew for sure is that hesitation was rarely a good sign. At least on the field it never had been. He doubted it was in this case either.

"I should say no," she said finally.

"Should?" He stuck his neck forward. "Or are you saying no?" He wasn't sure how much to push. This was definitely unfamiliar territory to him. When had a woman ever said anything but yes to him?

"I guess. . .yes."

Yes? Dear Lord in heaven, she was killing him with her ambiguity. "Yes, dinner? You and Sammy?"

She shook her head. "I mean yes—I'm saying no."

"Oh." His head lolled back on his shoulders as if he'd deflected an imaginary blow. "Yeah, okay. That's okay." He gathered his bearings and nodded.

He thought he'd been tired after his run! But asking a simple question and getting a not-so-simple answer had taken another kind of toll on him. One he wasn't accustomed to.

"But thank you anyway," she added politely.

"Sure." He shrugged, trying hard to sound indifferent. "No problem." He slid down from the table. "Thank you for the treatment. I'm sure my elbow will be feeling a whole lot better." He started to make his way toward the door. "Really appreciate it. Hey, and tell that son of yours—tell Sammy, I said good-bye, okay?"

"Sure." She nodded. "Unless, if you're going past the bakery, you could tell him yourself."

"Naw, I'm sure he's doing fine. Plus, it's about time I get home and shower." He glanced down at his sweatshirt. "You know, get the day started."

"Yeah, me, too." To his ears, she sounded almost relieved. "Thank you for helping out Sammy today. That was nice of you."

"Not a problem." He grabbed the doorknob to let himself out before they could politely thank each other for one more thing one more time. "I guess I'll be seeing you around. . ."

"At the meeting on Wednesday."

"Right. Wednesday. Meeting. Wouldn't want to miss it," he said easily, tipping his hand good-bye.

Closing the door behind him, he walked down the sidewalk through Loveland, making his way toward his car. Until a thought stopped him in his tracks. A startling realization. One he couldn't totally grasp.

He really had meant it, hadn't he? What he'd said back there?

He really didn't want to miss the meeting on Wednesday. More than that, he didn't want to miss the chance to see Megan O'Donnell again.

Chapter 7

"Na-naw! You pretty!"

Sammy spotted his nana's reflection across the shop the moment Megan pushed his wheelchair through the handicap entrance of We Do! Wedding Planners.

As Laura O'Donnell turned from an oval antique wall mirror, the pearl-trimmed, shoulder-length wedding veil donning her head turned with her, its rustle as hushed as a whisper.

Megan had to agree with Sammy. Her mom did look pretty, almost glowing in fact.

But then everything in the We Do! Wedding Planners shop always seemed to have an ethereal quality about it. Almost as elusive and otherworldly as love itself, Megan had always thought—and still did, as she glanced around the establishment.

The evening sun shone through the storefront windows, its shimmering beams bringing out the lively amber luster in the giant oak armoire that stood behind the petite Louis XIV reception desk.

Nearly tall enough for castle decor, the armoire's doors were flung wide open like welcoming arms, white satin and lace spilling out from the formidable piece of furniture from sample wedding dresses stuffed inside.

Two overstuffed upholstered love seats the same color as pink candy hearts sat in a room to the right of the entry, cozily arced around a diminutive coffee table. On top of the table sat a delicately-painted floral china tea setting that looked fit for a princess, no less, with photo albums of exquisite We Do! brides who had already taken their walk down the aisle. And on this late spring day, instead of burning logs, the fireplace was filled with a huge pot of late-blooming tulips in a variety of corals, pinks, and yellows.

To the left of that sitting area, a staircase with a banister wrapped in eucalyptus garland accented with baby-cheek pink bows led to the upstairs workroom and computers. But as a young girl, Megan imagined more than once it looked like winding steps that just might lead to heaven.

In the middle of all that fluffiness, Sammy had a practical question. "You getting married, Na-naw?" He frowned.

Megan unzipped his light windbreaker and removed the baseball cap from his head. Ruffling his smooshed-down hair, she noted the confused look on his face. She would've been baffled as well if she hadn't caught her mom on numerous occasions doing the very same thing—trying on wedding veils.

The "veil thing" was, after all, how her mom and best friend Pam had gotten their start as wedding planners. Once upon a time, many summers ago as little girls, the two of them had organized pretend weddings in their backyards, attended by all their favorite stuffed animals of course. The bride's main prop for those special occasions had been a lacy half-slip—size 6x—that they'd used as a wedding veil. Tattered from many summers of use, and yellowed from time, that same half-slip hung in a shadowbox frame on the wall at We Do! Wedding Planners, displayed like a well-earned diploma.

"Getting married?" Her mom giggled at Sammy's inquiry. "I'm already married, Sammy, you know that. To the most wonderful man in the world."

"Pap-ee?"

"Yes, your pappy. But"—she slid the veil from her head—"I think there's someone else I know who may be getting married soon." She smiled broadly in Megan's direction.

"Why—why are you looking at me like that?" Megan suddenly felt her shoulders stiffen. But then maybe it was the surroundings. For the past several years, she hadn't been all that comfortable in her mom's shop. The place was so different from Megan's work environment. And her mom so different than her, she realized.

Every hour of her mother's work day appeared to be wrapped in love and romance and frills. While Megan, well, she just didn't have time or energy or even the interest to fuss with those sorts of things.

"I'm not looking at you like anything, honey. I'm thinking about Sylvia Pruitt."

"Sylvia Pruitt? The old maid who lived in the Victorian on the riverbanks?"

"She still lives there, and she isn't an old maid, Meg. She's been unlucky in love, that's all. But that's behind her now. Thanks to Pam."

"A little Pamela Matthews matchmaking, huh?"

Her mom nodded. "Both of us were involved to some degree, but I suppose most of the credit goes to Pam." She reached for a hanger. "I was just trying on veils thinking about which one might suit Sylvia best if she—"

"Decides to marry?" Megan stuffed Sammy's baseball hat in his backpack.

"Oh no. If she decides to buy her veil and gown through us. No doubt, she'll be getting married. And soon."

"To whom?" Megan knew her voice sounded incredulous, and she didn't mean to be mean, but she couldn't fathom it. *Sylvia Pruitt? Getting married?* As kids they used to dare each other to run across Old Maid Pruitt's yard, hoping not to get caught in case she really had gone crazy without love and might cast some sort of weird spell on them.

"Martin Chandler." Her mom's eyes flashed bright. "Sylvia and Martin, together at last. Isn't it perfect?"

Megan would've never thought of pairing up the spinster and funeral home director together. But now that her mom mentioned it, in an odd way the two did conjure up a likely match. "I guess it could work." She shrugged.

Watching as her mom tucked the veils she'd been trying on back into the armoire, Megan noted how gently she nudged the satiny puffs of pristine white dresses into their places before shutting the cabinet doors for the day. Once again she couldn't help thinking how farfetched it was that her mom, along with her We Do! business partner, spent their days—their lives actually—in such a way. Treating love like it was something palpable.

"So!" Her mom turned to Sammy. "Are you ready to have some

fun with me and your pappy tonight while your mommy's at her meeting?" She bent over and gave Sammy a kiss on the top of his head.

He nodded excitedly. "You an' Pap-ee wach me?"

"We sure are."

"Miss Biddle can't. She hurt. She like her flowers though."

"You took flowers to Mrs. Biddle? That's sweet."

Sammy nodded again while Megan filled in the blanks. "We went to see her last night after work. She's still at the assisted living facility recovering from the surgery and doing rehab."

"Miss Biddle give me a kiss, too," Sammy spoke up.

"Well, how could she resist?" Her mom chuckled softly. "You're such a handsome guy, you," she said, giving Sammy reason to beam. "So it sounds like poor Mrs. Biddle has a ways to go yet in her recovery."

"I'm looking for another sitter though. I have a few leads," Megan stressed. Of course, she didn't know how successful any of them would be. It wasn't easy finding someone reliable and trustworthy who was also comfortable with a special-needs child. "I'll find someone soon. You don't have to worry."

"Worry?" Her mom looked more crushed by Megan's words than fretful.

"I mean if you have other things you have to—"

"Nothing is more important than our Sammy." She shot Megan a stern look.

Oh, they'd covered this ground before. Round and round so many times. And it didn't matter what her mother said, or what her father said either, Megan simply hated to ask them for help. Point blank.

"You try to do too much yourself." They'd pleaded. *"We're not meant to do life alone."* They'd lecture. Which just wasn't true in the first place. She wasn't doing life alone. She was doing it with Sammy. And there were plenty of single moms out there doing even more than she was. All by themselves.

"I hear what you're saying, Mom," she appeased, not having time to rehash it all again. "I just meant—well, you and Dad work all day and—"

"Speaking of which," her mom interrupted, turning her attention to Sammy, "your pappy is so excited that you'll be there tonight to watch the baseball game with him."

"Baseball game?" Sammy's eyes grew wide. Her mom was definitely speaking his language. "To-nigh?"

"Oh yes." Megan's mom nodded. "The Hawks are playing the Cubs."

"MaaNil buy me doughnuts."

"What did you say?" Her mom gave a little chuckle. "Doughnuts? MacNeill? MacNeill Hattaway bought you doughnuts? Did I just hear that right?" She glanced back and forth between Sammy and Megan, the smile on her face growing so wide Megan thought her face might crack in two.

"Well, Hattaway didn't really—" Megan started to explain the entire story, but she couldn't burst Sammy's bubble that way. "Well, he didn't really have to," she repeated, switching gears. "But yes, it was his idea to buy doughnuts for some of the boys."

Her mom shook her head. "I don't get it. Where? When?"

"Saturday morning, down on the bike path." Megan checked her watch. "But really, Mom, I don't have time to go into it."

Yet that didn't stop Laura O'Donnell, matchmaker extraordinaire—and curious mom.

"You mean you're *seeing* MacNeill? Besides when you're at the meetings?"

And that's when her mom got that funny look on her face. The one with the slightly raised eyebrows, the faint smile, and dreamy eyes. The one that spoke of romantic possibilities and happily-ever-afters.

Oh, thank goodness she hadn't accepted Mac's dinner invitation. Neither her son nor her mother would've ever gotten their heads out of the clouds again!

As it was, Sammy hadn't stopped talking about Mac and the doughnuts for a second over the past five days, telling everyone they ran into all about his special morning at the bike path. Not only did he repeat the tale to whoever would listen, but he woke up talking about it and went to sleep with MacNeill Hattaway's name on his lips, too.

No wonder it had been so hard for her to get her mind off Mac since Saturday. The scene on the basketball court. . .eating doughnuts outside Janey's shop. . .the time they'd spent alone at the clinic together. If Sammy hadn't kept mentioning his name, surely she wouldn't still be thinking about Mac. Stewing over all he had confided to her. Wondering who he really was—what he was all about. Remembering how he'd looked at her while they were sharing time on the rock ledge together. A look that had definitely unnerved her. And surprised her. Although she shouldn't have been surprised at all since. . .hadn't he had as much practice with women as he had with pitching a baseball?

Suddenly her cheeks warmed again as they'd been doing the past several days. Spring allergies possibly? Hopefully her mom wouldn't notice. Knowing her, she'd read more into it than was true.

"No, Mom, I'm not seeing MacNeill," Megan answered flatly. "Not besides the meetings," she added, emphatically.

"But Sammy just said—"

"Well, yeah. I mean, we bumped into him on Saturday but—"

"Maw-mee and MaaNil go 'way together," Sammy piped up. Unfortunately.

"Ya'll went away together?" her mom asked breathily.

Now her mom's eyes didn't just look dreamy, they were wide with amazement. Approval and amazement. No doubt her mother could twist her and Mac's trip to the clinic into a romantic rendezvous. Which it wasn't. At all.

She let go of a sigh. She was so tired of all the MacNeill Hattaway jibber-jabber. And it sure didn't help quell the uneasiness she felt thinking about seeing him again in just a matter of minutes.

"Mom, really, please."

"Please, what?"

"Please don't look at me like that."

"But Sammy just said—"

"Mom, Sammy is the best son in the world, but he's an impressionable six-year-old. An impressionable six-year-old with a very big mouth." She arched her brows at Sammy, hoping to reprimand him with her best evil-eye look. But his grin grew all the wider.

Exasperated, she shook her head. "Look, really Mom, I need to run. I'm going to be late for my own meeting."

"You mean the meeting with you and MacNeill?"

"I mean the meeting that I'm facilitating with Hattaway where there will be dozens of other volunteers in attendance." She handed over Sammy's backpack. "Sammy has a little bit of homework in his folder. A paper on shapes, right, Sammy?"

"Yes," he answered, before retelling his encounter with Mac for the hundredth or so time. "Doughnuts good. MaaNil nice!" he told his nana, who of course, looked delighted, savoring every tidbit of information.

"I bet they were very good, Sammy," she cooed at her grandson. "And I bet MacNeill is very, very nice."

Oh. My. Goodness!

Megan felt as if her blood pressure was rising sky high. If she didn't make a quick exit, she was afraid she'd let out a scream. Or a very loud groan. Or who knew? "Okay, I've really got to run, Mom. Really." She pecked her mom on the cheek. "Thanks."

"You're welcome, sweetie. And don't worry. Stay out as late as you want. We'll get Sammy's work finished. Your dad can help him while I make dinner. But first"—she squatted down alongside the wheelchair—"I think we should visit the garden, Sammy, don't you? We'll cut some flowers to take home to Pappy."

Sammy nodded eagerly, and as Megan watched her mom push the wheelchair to the back door of the shop, her heart conflicted in a million ways.

She felt inadequate, needing to lean on her mother, but glad Sammy had a grandmother who loved him so.

She wished she could linger more often with Sammy just like her mom was getting the chance to, but it seemed she always had to rush to the next thing and the next, or their world would surely fall apart.

And while she felt happy that her mom was teaching her son about flowers, she wondered why she wasn't a flower person.

Unlike her mom, she didn't know the first practical thing about growing and nurturing a garden. Why she hadn't absorbed some of that knowledge long ago, she didn't know. All she remembered as a young girl was marveling at her mom's springtime peonies that grew to be nearly as tall as she was. And in the summer, there would be daisies lining the white fence, armloads of them, plentiful enough to pick. Back then, while she'd wait for her mom to finish up work for the day, she'd sit on the back porch of We Do! Wedding Planners pulling at the daisy petals.

He loves me, he loves me not, she'd repeat over and over in her head, with little regard for the plucked petals falling to the ground. She said it just the way her mom had taught her. She said it all the while dreaming of love and marriage and never-ending bliss.

But that was only because that's what little girls do. . .

Chapter 8

Mac caught a whiff of something sweet—the same scent he recognized from his night out in the rain a week earlier—and knew Megan had arrived early for the meeting.

Looking up from an article he'd been reading in the *Loveland Herald*, he watched as she set her purse and meeting notebook on the cafeteria table and then switched her cell phone from the cream-colored jacket into the front pocket of her jeans, keeping it handy for emergency purposes he supposed. He'd never seen her hair down before. It waved around her face before falling to her shoulders, its ebony darkness making her clear blue eyes shine even bluer.

He thought he'd just sit tight and let her come to him for a change, not wanting to appear overly eager, especially after his awkward exit from her clinic the other day. But somehow that thought didn't hang in his head very long. The metal folding chair squeaked as he set down the paper and got up to greet her. "Hey."

"Hey." She glanced up at him, and then over his shoulders at the clock above the exit. "You're early, aren't you?"

He gave a slight smile. "It's another Uncle Jake-ism. He always said, 'If you're not early, you're late.' "

"I had a grandmother who shared the same maxim." She returned a polite smile before grabbing up her notebook. "Well, since we're both here ahead of time, I guess we could sit and organize our thoughts some."

"How about over there?" He pointed to the same row of chairs he'd just been sitting in, chairs which faced the lone cafeteria table and were already lined up with other rows for the volunteers who were due to arrive in the next few minutes. All the other tables had been folded upright and were pushed against a side wall.

"So, let me guess," he said as they settled in their seats. "You were a cheerleader, right? When you went to high school here?"

She tilted her head and stared at him. A reaction he realized he deserved. After all, the question did sound odd—even to him. But truth was, when he'd been sitting earlier, his mind had wandered from the newspaper he'd been reading. Looking around the cafeteria, he'd imagined Megan O'Donnell there years ago, eating lunch with her high school friends. Talking. Laughing.

"Uh, no," she answered. "Actually, I was a bandie. Played the french horn."

"A bandie, huh?" Somehow that didn't jibe with his image of her. With her petite figure, pretty face, and go-get-'em personality, he pictured her more with a pair of pompoms in her hands. "Really? Well, I always thought the french horn would be a great instrument to play."

"You're kidding, right?"

"More like faking it." He relaxed, letting go of a grin. "I'm not sure I even know what a french horn is."

"It's kind of like an italian horn, but different."

"An italian horn? I don't think I. . ." He caught the glimmer in her bright eyes and laughed. "Okay. Guess I had that coming," he conceded. "So where did you bandies sit for lunch? Over there?" He pointed to the south side of the cafeteria where some residual glow from the setting sun illuminated the red maples outside an oblong picture window.

"Nope. The more popular kids sat there. Bandies sat over there." She raised her arm in the opposite direction, to a darker corner of the cafeteria.

"Oh." He frowned.

"Don't worry." She laughed—he sensed more at his expression than anything else. "It didn't scar me for life or anything, not being one of the more popular kids."

"No, it's not that. It's just, I thought—" Chagrined, he scratched at his clean-shaven cheek. "Hmm. . .guess I'm not so smart after all."

She raised a brow as if astonished by his admission, but kindly kept any smart retorts she might've had to herself. "You were in Florida for high school, weren't you?"

As she spoke, he tried to keep his mind off those glossy pink lips of hers. But it wasn't easy. Blinking, he nodded. "Uh, yeah. But being back here. . .well, you know, sometimes I wonder what things would've been like if my family had stayed." No, that wasn't true. He'd only started musing over thoughts like that since he'd met her. Wasn't that right? Not letting that realization sink in any deeper, he switched gears. "So, what's on the agenda for this evening?"

She flipped open her notebook, clearly more than ready to get down to business as she scribbled some notes. "Well, I thought we'd talk about how we're going to divide the volunteers into groups to—"

"You know. . ." he drawled, interrupting her—not because he wanted to, but because he couldn't hold off any longer. "I, uh, there's something I need to talk to you about before we get started."

"Uh-huh." She kept writing.

"The head of the school board called me."

The pen stopped, her hand hovering over the page. The heavy lashes that shadowed her cheeks suddenly flew up. "Phil Ellis? Really? I didn't realize you knew Phil."

"I don't. But he called the other night. Said he graduated a couple of years ahead of you, right? In the class of—"

"He called to tell you we went to high school together?" Her eyes narrowed warily and those pretty, full lips of hers went thin. So much for the smiles he'd won from her just minutes earlier.

"Ahh, not exactly. He wanted to get some autographed photos from me."

"Autographed photos? And you're telling me this because. . ." She squinted, obviously puzzled and rightfully so. He was even confusing himself with his cryptic account of the conversation. He needed to man up and tell her the main reason for Phil's call. Even though he dreaded doing it. He had to give it to her straight.

Taking a deep breath, he spat out the bad news. "Aw, it wasn't just about autographs. Phil called to let us know the school's going to have to renege on their promise. We're not going to be able to use the stadium for our All-Stars Sports Day."

Her mouth fell open at first, but then she apparently recovered quickly, jotting notes in her book. Her reaction surprised him until she shook her head and replied, "That's not funny, Mac."

"Funny?" Putting his hand on the back of her chair, he leaned in close, able to keep his voice soft but unable to hide the irritation he suddenly felt. "You really think I'd joke about something like that?"

Her face was only inches from his when she looked up, searching his eyes. Obviously she found the truth there. "Oh no. You *are* serious." He watched her face crumple. "But, I don't get it—why?"

"There're some problems with the field. They're going to have to tear it up and redo it and the track this summer. So the stadium's out of the picture."

Volunteers started to trickle in, and she put up a good front, feigning smiles and friendly waves in between his explanation, but he knew inside she had to be in turmoil.

"And they didn't know that before they gave us the go-ahead?"

"Initially they'd planned to wait and put in the new field next summer. But now they're afraid if they don't take the money from the state this summer to make the improvements, they might risk losing the funds altogether."

He hated to hear the heavy sigh that came out of her. Hated to see the way her face and body went slack. It was a look of defeat so unlike her that it about did him in. Making him want to comfort her. To take her in his arms and let her know it'd all be okay as he knew it would be.

But before he could do more than blink, her body language changed.

"Well. . ." She shifted, tilting her chin upward, raising herself in the chair. "We just have to think of someplace else, that's all. I'm not putting this event off until next year. I'm just not," she added, a defiant tone in her voice. "The kids are so excited. And people are here, wanting to help." She glanced over her shoulder at the chairs filling up behind them. "We just have to figure out—wait a minute, I know—Ted! He'll have some ideas. We can talk to him about it tonight." A sparkle regenerated in her eyes.

"I don't think he's going to make it tonight."

"He's not? How do you know?"

"He called me the other day. After he heard the news."

"Ted called you, too? You both knew and I—I didn't?"

"Well, I—"

One of the dads stopped him mid-thought with a clasp on the back of his shoulder. "Hey Mac. Sorry to interrupt, Megan." Shane Dugan leaned down between the two of them. "Mind if I get that autographed baseball hat from you tonight? Hate to push, but Chase's birthday is this Friday and—"

"It's in my car, Shane. How about I grab it after the meeting?"

"Great." Shane clapped him on the shoulder again. "Really appreciate it, man."

Megan gave a warm smile in Shane's direction, but the moment he walked away, her mouth tightened again. "I don't get it. I wish— You should've called me, Mac."

"Yes, I should've. But there's only one problem. You've never given me your number."

Her cheeks reddened at that, making him believe it was intentional and not just an oversight that she hadn't shared her number with him. A low blow to his pride for sure. But his pride was what had been getting him into trouble over the years, and he was trying—hard as it was—to put it aside most of the time now. Haggling about should'ves and could'ves wasn't going to make things any better for either of them at this point.

"Look. That's the bad news, but there's some good news," he told her.

She looked up at him tentatively, biting her lip.

"I ran into some of the guys—some of the volunteers—at the gym, and they all agreed. We can have the All-Stars Sports Day at my place. Out at the farm. It's perfect. Plenty of fields in those ten acres where we can set up the activities. Plenty of space for parking."

He had hoped by offering the farm for the event, and getting some preliminary okays from several of the dads, that it would be a help to her. Make it one less thing on her list to stress over. Something to make her life easier. After all, she did have a job. And a child. A handicapped child at that. The woman definitely had her hands full and seemed happy to be doing it all, something he truly admired about her.

Still, he wasn't sure his suggestion met with her approval. Not until she scribbled something else in her notebook and then ripped out the page, handing it to him.

"No need for a thank you note," he teased. "Not necessary."

"It's my cell number."

"Ah."

Folding the paper into squares, he started to tell her not to fret, that he'd only call for their event planning purposes not for pleasure. But then he wasn't sure he wanted to make a statement that he might want to retract someday. All he knew as he tucked the paper into his shirt pocket was that he'd never, ever, had such a hard time getting a girl's phone number before. In fact, in the past, he'd rarely had to ask. Numbers just appeared everywhere—in his pockets, in his gym bag, on his windshield. Wherever. But not so with Megan.

He'd learned a long, long time ago, however, that nothing worth having ever came easy. And crazily, there was something about Megan that made him think and feel she might be worth the irritation and degradation she put him through.

As they both rose from the chairs to greet the volunteers, she paused and laid a hand on his arm. "Thank you, Mac," she said softly, a fervent sheen of appreciation glimmering in her eyes.

Oh yeah, he thought, as his heart did an involuntary flip. Megan O'Donnell definitely had his number, too.

Chapter 9

"Notice anything different?"

Megan gave Janey the once-over as her friend handed her the to-go cup of coffee she'd ordered. Taking the lid off the cup, she blew into the steaming brew, appraising Janey's appearance at the same time.

"You just got your hair highlighted, right? It looks good. I like the caramel color running through it."

"No, silly. Not me." Janey waved a hand in the air. "The bakery. Notice anything different about the bakery?"

Megan had noticed a lot of "different" things about the bakery—mainly the signs. Everywhere. Signs that looked tacky and out of place. Signs that she wanted to ask Janey about, but didn't for fear she'd say something that might hurt her friend's feelings. But since Janey brought it up. . .

"You mean, that maybe?" Megan pointed to just one sign, the closest one on the glass bakery case right in front of her. A neon green rectangular thing which looked shoddy and out of context in light of Janey's usual good taste. "That's, um, different."

"Exactly! Since MacNeill Hattaway said my bear claws are his all-time favorites, I thought a little sign saying so would entice my customers."

A *little* sign? Megan didn't reply, but instead continued to blow, blow, and blow some more, pretending to fixate on her too-hot coffee.

"So what do you think?" Janey asked.

"Well, I. . ." Megan stalled, replacing the lid on her cup, searching her mind frantically for something constructive to say. But she didn't have to come up with anything. Unknowing to him, Sammy came to her rescue.

"Where my jelly doughnuts go?" He pointed at the same bakery case from his wheelchair right beside her.

"Right where they always are, little guy," Janey answered him. "They're right next to"—she scuttled around to the front of the case to have a look for herself—"the bear claws." Her shoulders slumped. "Oh, I guess the sign is kind of big, isn't it? You can't see the jelly doughnuts at all and only a part of the glazed tray. Hmm. . ." She bit her lip, frustration clouding her face. "Well, what do you think of those signs?" She pointed to a trio of white shelves lining the wall, all stacked with a variety of breads. "Do you think they're oversized?"

"I certainly don't have a problem seeing them," Megan replied as diplomatically as she could. She read the two closest to her. " 'Mayor Goodwin's Favorite Sensation: Pumpernickel Rye.' 'Librarian Martha's Favorite Sensation: Cinnamon Raisin Bread.' "

"Sammy's favorite is—"

"Jelly doughnuts. I know, honey, that's why I have a couple right here." Megan waved the doughnut-filled bag in her hand at him before turning back to Janey. "I guess I don't understand why you're doing this, Janey. Sweet Sensations is so cute and warm and inviting—and you do a great business. With the signs, well, do you think they might detract just a bit from the homey atmosphere you've got going here?"

Janey shook her head, bringing a defensive hand to her hip. "You don't understand, Megan."

Isn't that what she'd just said?

"Remember Sean Shaffer?" her friend continued.

"Your almost-prom-date-senior-year-of-high-school Sean Shaffer?"

"Exactly. Hard to forget, isn't he? The way he dumped me and went to prom with Amanda Richter?"

It certainly had been easy for Megan to forget Sean. She'd never thought of him again after graduation when everyone had gone their separate ways to college. Apparently, Janey had never gotten over him or past their senior prom fiasco. However, Janey's side of the story had never quite jibed with Sean's. He'd always claimed it was her who dumped him first and that's why he'd asked Amanda.

"What does Sean have to do with Sweet Sensations?"

"Everything!" Janey blurted out. "Everything!" she repeated.

Megan shifted on her feet, and even Sammy sensed Janey's explanation was going to take more than just a minute.

"Maw-mee, doughnut please?" he asked.

She'd just heard his little stomach growl and didn't want to put him off any longer. Her plan had been to take their time and eat their doughnuts outside. But they'd already gotten to Janey's later than she'd hoped to, and she sure hadn't planned on a lengthy conversation with her friend, voyaging into past loves, dumpers and dumpees. "Sure, honey." She set her coffee cup on the counter, plucked some napkins from the dispenser there and laid them across Sammy's lap. "Go ahead and eat your jelly doughnut here." She pulled one from the bag. "Then we have to get going. We don't want to be late."

"Late?" Janey's ears perked up as she moved back behind the counter and started making a fresh pot of coffee. "Late to where?" She poured out what little residual coffee was still in the pot and began to refill it with fresh water.

"Oh, you know, we're, uh, taking a ride."

"See Mac farm," Sammy sputtered between chomps of doughnut and spurts of jelly.

Janey immediately set the carafe down. "You're going out to MacNeill's?" Her eyes widenend.

"Just to check out the place for the event." Megan nodded. "Allie and her kids were going to come along, but Carrie has a bad cold and Allie didn't want Sammy to catch it."

She'd asked Mac if it'd be okay for Allie and her kids to come out to the farm along with her, making it sound like his place would be something fun for all of them to experience. But that was only half the truth.

In reality, she was just plain nervous to be alone with him. He confused her. He didn't make sense. No, MacNeill Hattaway didn't make sense at all. Not in the way he looked at her. Not the way he was so nice to her. Not the way he acted interested in her. Not when he could have his pick of almost any woman on the planet.

Was it because they were using his farm for the event? Was he thinking that meant there was something more going on between them? Something he expected? Although honestly, he had even been acting nice and interested long before the farm situation came up.

And the worst of it was, when she was around him lately, she confused herself, too. Why did she have such a hard time looking into his eyes? Was she afraid of who she might see there? Maybe a man so different than the one she first believed him to be? Not that it mattered. It really, really didn't. She'd vowed long ago not to let a man—especially not a man like MacNeill Hattaway—into her and Sammy's life again. But then, oh—she had to be crazy to even be thinking thoughts along those lines.

"Take a lot of notes." Janey's voice interrupted her thoughts.

"Notes?" She shook her head, trying to clear it of one MacNeill Hattaway. "Oh, I will. For sure. We have to figure out where to set up the parking area. Then we need to know where all the booths and events will be situated around the property."

"No. I mean, take lots of notes so you can tell me everything about the place."

"Janey, it's the old Lochen farm out on Route 48. You know the place well."

"I know, but it can't be the same old farm anymore. Not with MacNeill living there now. That's different. . .oh, hold on. Can I help you, sir?"

Saved by one of Janey's customers, Megan swiped at Sammy's gooey mouth then gathered up the used napkins and threw them away along with her half-empty coffee cup. Tugging her purse onto her shoulder, she was ready to push his wheelchair toward the door where she could call out a good-bye to Janey, when her friend returned, stopping her short with another guy matter.

"So, I never finished my story about Sean Shaffer."

"Oh, right. What's going on with him?"

In a millisecond, Janey's pretty hazel eyes narrowed, making her look atypically malicious. "He's back in town; that's what's going on with him," she practically hissed. "He's back in town, and he's doing it to me all over again."

Megan tried to make the connection. Was there a community dance coming up she didn't know about? Had Sean tried to invite Janey or something? "Sorry, Janey, I'm not getting it."

"The Donut Emporium? The one in the gas station right across the bridge?" Megan noted that Janey refrained from saying "duh," even though her tone implied she wanted to. "That's his, Megan. That's Sean's place."

"The Donut Emporium?" She knew of the small doughnut shop of course, but had never considered stopping there. After all, her allegiance was to Janey, and besides that, she and Sammy had enjoyed their routine at Sweet Sensations for forever.

"But Janey, your place is totally different. It's not a little shop; it's more like a haven. A really comfortable one. And you have breads and coffeecakes and birthday cakes, all in addition to your doughnuts. Plus a variety of great coffee drinks, did I mention that? And—"

But Janey wasn't listening. "I just can't believe him. It's like the guy has it out for me or something, always ruining my life."

"Oh Janey. People change, don't you think? I doubt if he's the same old Sean you remember him to be." Not that Megan remembered him as the sneaky, conniving guy Janey thought him to be anyway. "Besides, hasn't the Donut Emporium always been there?" she asked her friend. "Like ever since we can remember?"

"Well, yeah, but now Sean's running specials. And he's sponsoring a girl's softball team. And he's sending out those coupon mailers. I got one in my mailbox yesterday. My heart about sank to my knees."

"Oh." Megan could just imagine what that must've felt like. She was almost afraid to ask her friend the next question. "Have you—have you noticed a decrease in your store traffic?"

"Yes. Not a lot," Janey said somberly. "But some."

"And that's why you made all the signs?"

Janey nodded.

Her friend had always had the ability to create quality bakery products and had a great sense about what it took to create a charming atmosphere for Sweet Sensations. But Janey's strong suit had never included marketing. Of course, in the past that had never been an issue. Sweet Sensations never required much advertising and pretty much sold itself on its own merits.

But if Sean was going to keep chipping away, trying to attain a bigger piece of the pie, so to speak, Janey probably did need to take some action.

"Well, what if you did this? What if you made the signs a tad smaller for starters?" Megan suggested. "You know, get some of those starburst things you can buy at a craft store. You want them to be visible of course—just not in the way, you know? And then, maybe you could turn it into a promotion so it all makes sense."

"Meaning?"

"Meaning, uh, a contest." She tried to think fast. "A contest where all your customers have to do to enter is to write down their favorite Sweet Sensation. They can enter each time they visit your bakery. Whoever's name you draw wins a Sweet Sensations gift card or free baked goods for a week. Or whatever you decide."

"That's a great idea." Janey's eyes lit up as she brainstormed. "I can run it in conjunction with the upcoming Amazing Race. Maybe I'll even get some new customers that way."

"Who knows if it'll work?" Megan shrugged. "But you can try it."

"I just don't know why Sean Shaffer is doing this to me, Megan." Janey finally picked up the carafe again and poured water into the coffeemaker. "First the prom, and then this." She pushed the brew button.

"Janey. . ." Once again Megan started to tell her she suspected that wasn't Sean's primary intention. He was probably just trying to make a life for himself back in Loveland. But doubting her friend would care to hear that, she gave Janey a reassuring smile instead. "It'll all be okay. Don't worry."

Janey nodded and gave Megan a smile, too, though a wan one at best. Her friend taken care of for the time being, Megan bent down to Sammy who had been patient beyond belief. Removing his ball cap, she kissed him on the forehead. "Ready, Samster?"

"Reh-hee," he replied, taking his cap from her hand and clumsily fitting it back on his head.

"Oh! I packed up some bear claws for MacNeill." Janey came from behind the counter with a bakery box. "And there're extras for you guys." She settled the box into Sammy's lap. "Don't eat them all up on the way to the farm."

"Not to worry," Megan promised.

Just hearing Mac's name—or even thinking about him—created an instant quiver in her stomach. She hadn't been able to eat anything all morning and didn't plan to anytime soon.

Mac was just pulling a navy T-shirt over his head when he heard the crunch of Megan's SUV on the gravel drive. He'd cut the time close, but everything had taken him longer to get ready than he thought it would.

Though he'd been getting better at cooking for himself the past few months, and even forced himself to settle in and watch a cooking show every now and then, it wasn't like he was a whiz in the kitchen by any means.

Pizzas might look easy with a little sauce and cheese and whatnot on top, but when you were trying to make one from scratch—crust and all—there was more preparation involved than he would've thought. And the worst part was definitely the clean-up. Somehow he'd managed to have more sauce on the counters, floor, and wall than on the pizzas themselves.

He wasn't sure how the end result would taste, but he thought the house sure smelled good when he took the pizzas from the oven. Wrapping them in foil, he packed them with three drinks, a salad, and some plates and plastic utensils in a broken-down but still usable picnic basket he'd found in his uncle's hall closet.

Setting the lunch on the island, he noticed his phone vibrating alongside it on the counter. Picking it up, he checked the display. Hal Halvorsen, his agent. Well, Hal's weekly check-in call would have to wait, Mac decided. Because he had something—actually a pair of someones—more important to attend to.

Sliding into a pair of Reefs by the front door, he sent a word of thanks heavenward for the sunshine as he sauntered outside to the driveway. Of course, the prettiness of the day wasn't even a contender where Megan was concerned. Already out of the car and opening up the trunk door, her hair was piled on top of her head and she had on some kind of yellowish dress that hit just above her knees, showing off the curve of her calves. She peeked at him over her sunglasses as he shuffled down the stone walkway toward her.

"Hey! Glad you made it. Let me help you with Sammy's wheelchair." He sidled up next to her.

"Hi." She seemed unusually shy to see him, and he had to admit as much as he was looking forward to her coming, he also felt a sudden twinge of awkwardness.

"Oh no—it's okay. I can get it. I'm used to it."

"I'm sure you are," he said, as he stepped closer and grabbed at the metal frame, his hands just inches from hers. "Got it." He lifted the chair out of the car, over her head, and onto the ground, suddenly aware of how many times a day—a week—a year—that Megan went through the same motions. Unfolding the chair, he took it upon himself to push it over to the rear passenger door where Sammy was buckled in.

"Mac. It you," Sammy chirped as Mac opened the car door.

"Yes, it's me, Sammy. How you doing, bud?" He unclipped the seat belt and lifted Sammy out of the car and into the wheelchair.

"Do good," Sammy answered him.

"He's always doing good, isn't he?" Mac smiled at Megan.

"Most of the time he is." She smiled back.

Mac pushed the chair out of the gravel and into a grassy area to the side of the driveway, feeling somewhat silly about how happy he was about the news he had to share. "So, Sammy. . .do you like surprises?"

Sammy gave a vigorous nod.

"Great, because I have a surprise for you."

"Suprise? For me?" Sammy grinned up at him before turning to his mom. "Buh it not my birt-day, is it, Maw-mee?"

"No." She laughed. "You've got a ways to go yet. Your birthday isn't until the week after All-Stars Sports Day."

"This is an everyday sort of surprise," Mac told them. "Actually it's just something I've been fiddling with."

"More whittling?" She lifted her sunglasses from her eyes, settling them on top of her head, exposing every pretty feature of her face to him.

So she'd remembered, had she? The thought made him smile.

"No, I've been doing some of that off and on. But this is something I made that's a lot different and a whole lot bigger. Something for Sammy and the other kids for the All-Stars Sports Day. I figured he could be the first one to test it out today before we get started on our work. If that's okay with you, that is."

He could see the curiosity in Megan's eyes—how she squinted at him even though the sun wasn't shining in her eyes in the least. Looking at him as if she was trying to figure it all out. Figure out why he was going to such ends. Couldn't she just believe he was doing things simply because he wanted to? Wasn't that reason enough?

She glanced at her son whose face glowed with excitement then back at Mac. Mac figured his excitement probably showed on his face as well. She shook her head, smiling as if she'd been outnumbered. "It's fine with me, Mac."

"Where surprise?" Sammy asked.

Mac motioned toward the clearing to the left of the house and barn. "It's right over there. Ready to see?"

Again, Sammy nodded with earnest, and having Megan's permission, Mac pushed on through the grass.

"Did you have a hard time finding the farm?" he asked as Megan walked by his side.

"Oh no. I'm somewhat familiar with these back roads. The only hard thing was getting away from Janey's bakery."

"Bring you bear claws," Sammy spurted out.

"Bear claws?" Mac chuckled. "My favorite."

"Oh, believe me, we know. Janey has signs all over Sweet Sensations."

"Signs?" He couldn't imagine what she was talking about.

"It's a long story, trust me, and. . ."

He'd been enjoying the first easy flow of conversation they'd had since she got there. It had taken Megan some time to even look his way when she spoke to him. But her chatter came to a halt when she spotted the wooden structure he'd created. She paused in her tracks. "What's that?"

"That's the surprise."

"Surprise for me," Sammy stated, growing more excited at the sight of the mass of wood.

"Yes, for you."

"I like it," Sammy said brightly, his enthusiasm never lacking.

"I like it, Mac."

Mac laughed from his belly. "Like it? You don't even know what it is, do you?"

"No. Buh, I like it," Sammy answered him. "It from you."

Sammy's words caught Mac off guard, jarring his heart in an unexpected, touching way. Megan had raised one sweet kid. No wonder she wanted to protect him fiercely from all there was out there that could harm him or his spirit in any way. Mac could certainly understand and appreciate that. Why, just the way Sammy looked at him—with no judgment, no expectation—just pure joy and trust, like the world rose and set in him, made Mac want to make that happen.

"I hope you like bowling," he told Sammy.

"Like it on TV."

"Now you can do it yourself," he informed Sammy, pushing the wheelchair up against the wooden ramp. "At least I think it'll work," he told Megan. "I sort of did a test-drive myself. But we'll see how Sammy does. The ramp might need a little tweaking."

He grabbed a light bowling ball from a plastic container sitting next to the ramp and pulled out ten bowling pins from the bin.

"You're serious." Megan's lips crinkled into a mystified smile. "Aren't you?"

"Very." He set up the pins in a triangle a ways from the base of Sammy's chair. "I made the ramp adjustable. Sammy's chair looks like a good height for it the way it stands right now. But I figured not all kids would have chairs the same height. Or some kids might have longer torsos or whatever. Bottom line is, they need to be able to sit high enough to throw the ball down the ramp." He picked up the lightweight ball and handed it to Sammy, who didn't waste any time hurling the ball down the ramp, knocking over a majority of the pins.

"I good bowler," Sammy stated, pride in every word.

"Really good," Mac said, picking up the pins and ball, getting them all in position again. "Of course, we'll need several volunteers to help set up the pins and so on. And I do plan to paint the ramp and make it look decent. I also just put this wood down as a platform." He stomped on the sheets of plywood beneath their feet. "I figured I'd see Sammy in action first, make sure everything works before I get a cement guy out here to pour a slab and so on."

"I can't believe— I can't fathom you did all of this, Mac."

"It wasn't that big of a deal. I have time. And a barn where I set up a work table. Just did some measuring, hooked up a saw, and—"

"Didn't it hurt your elbow?"

He shrugged. "Not really."

"Do again?" Sammy asked.

Mac didn't know how many times he retrieved the ball and set up the pins for Sammy. Sammy's delight made it easy to keep at it, not noticing the minutes clipping by at all.

"My turn," Megan finally said. "You take a rest."

"No, it's okay. I can do it."

"Got it," she said firmly, grabbing the bowling ball from his hands. Then she smiled, letting him know she was only mimicking the way he'd taken over, grabbing up Sammy's wheelchair earlier.

She kept smiling, too. Every time Sammy knocked down the pins, she clapped for her son, and then looked back at Mac, thanking him with her smile before she set up the pins all over again. And as

Sammy and Megan's laughter rang out across the fields, Mac couldn't think of anywhere he'd rather be. Somehow it all felt so much better than other days he'd spent in the sun, even the days with thousands of fans cheering his name.

Chapter 10

Megan couldn't believe how nervous she'd been on the drive out to Mac's place. Now she couldn't believe how relaxed she felt, sitting on a patchwork quilt on his lawn, the length of his long, lean body stretched out beside her.

Mild rays of sunshine dripped languidly from the sky like rich golden honey, sweetening their spot on the grass below. A gentle June afternoon breeze ruffled the leafy limbs of the maple tree overhead, partially shading the faded blanket that looked like it'd seen many a picnic in its day. Letting her head fall back on her shoulders, Megan marveled at how peaceful she felt soaking in both the warmth of the sun and the caress of the breeze.

"It's wonderful here, Mac." She sighed.

"It's a perfect day, isn't it?" He looked around the grounds appreciatively before nodding down at Sammy who was sleeping soundly, his head nestled in her lap. "I think the bowling wore him out." His mouth curved with surprising tenderness at the sight of her sleeping child.

"Yes, the bowling and Bitty." With a gentle touch, not wanting to wake him, she brushed aside the hair from Sammy's forehead. "He really enjoyed playing with Bitty."

Her eyes settled on the gray-and-white barn cat that had wrapped itself into a curlicue and lay napping by Sammy's side. Such a sweet sight, Megan didn't bother to mention how excited Sammy had been the night before—so excited he hadn't gotten to sleep until late.

Of course, she didn't dare say that she hadn't slept well either, worrisome thoughts about spending time alone in Mac's company busying her mind into the wee hours of the night as well.

"I don't think I've ever seen him eat so much pizza. I haven't either, come to think of it." She laughed. "It was delicious, Mac. You really made it all by yourself?"

"Would this face lie to you?"

Her gaze shifted to his smooth-shaven jawline, still uncomfortable with the way her cheeks involuntarily warmed every time she looked at him. Though she knew his question was rhetorical, inwardly she automatically responded anyway, calculating all she'd seen—and felt—in the past couple of hours.

After all, as much as she wanted to believe it was only the tranquil setting responsible for their special outing, looking at Mac, she knew it wasn't true. There was no denying he had gone to a lot of trouble to make her and Sammy feel welcome and at ease—starting with his insistence on getting Sammy's wheelchair out of her car. Then there was the surprise of the bowling ramp he'd built. Along with the pizza he'd made from scratch. And the quilt and picnic basket? Somehow he'd managed to find them somewhere or another.

Plus, there were no news cameras around to record his hospitality. No reporters taking notes. Was it foolish of her to believe there was no deception in his motives?

"What made you think of the bowling ramp?"

"I'm not sure." His broad shoulder crooked upward. "About a week ago, I woke up around three a.m. and couldn't get the idea out of my head."

"Do you always wake up in the middle of the night with things on your mind?"

"Yeah." His brow tilted. "Yeah, actually I do."

She'd been referring to the after-midnight whittling incident Mac had told her about, but the way he steadied his eyes on hers. . . well, it made her think he was referring to something quite different. Something that might have to do with her. Causing her breath to hitch as she struggled to look away from him, out onto the acres of sun-soaked fields and woods. Exactly where they needed to get going to, she reminded herself. That *is* why she'd driven all the way out to the farm in the first place.

"I think we should go have a look around your property now, don't you?"

"I can carry Sammy into the house if you want," Mac offered. "He can nap on the couch or in my bed."

"Oh." She straightened. "I think he'll be okay here. Can we just keep a watch on him?"

"We'll make sure not to walk out of eye range."

Sammy barely stirred when she lifted his head from her lap and settled him gently on the quilt, making sure the shady limbs covered him. Mac held out his hand to help her up, and though she was reluctant to grasp it at first, not wanting to think about his fingers closing around hers for even an instant, she did anyway.

He pulled her to her feet and she was acutely conscious of his tall, athletic physique—taller than what she usually felt comfortable around. Even still, she noticed that his powerful, well-muscled body moved with easy grace through the grassy field. All around them was land as far as the eye could see, and on the outskirts of that, copses of trees which hemmed in the property on all sides. A small pond broke up all that green with a glittering blue where a few ducks lazily glided across the water.

Wildflowers grew in clumps every so often, dotting the earth with golden yellows and royal purples. But even though he had ownership of all that land and beauty, Megan noticed Mac seemed more excited by it rather than proprietary.

"Your uncle lived here all of his life, didn't he?"

"Most of his adult life. It was great for me, coming out here to visit him."

"Did he ever get lonely? I mean when you weren't around?"

"I don't think so. Uncle Jake had a lot going on, and he was married for a while, you know."

"Oh? There was a Mrs. Lochen?"

Mac nodded. "She passed when she was fairly young, and they hadn't had any children. I don't remember her very well; I was so young at the time. All I know is there was no other woman Uncle Jake ever talked about after Aunt Emily died."

She let the information sink in. Funny, how she'd known there was a Lochen Farm owned by Jake Lochen and had passed the place more times than she could count, but she hadn't known Mac's mother's brother or realized his ties to Mac. She also had no clue as to how pretty the Lochen property was beyond what she could see from the road.

"Are you sure you want to host the event here? I mean, aren't you concerned it might make a mess of your land?"

"It's nothing that can't be cleaned up." Mac shrugged. "And it's for a good cause, Megan. Of course I want to host it."

"What about parking? Where do you see the cars going? You don't want them to damage any of the grass and all."

"They won't," he said easily before turning to look back from where they'd come. "I'm thinking the area up where Sammy's napping would be best for the parking—in the lawn that lays in the front of the house and to the sides. That's a few acres and can easily fit hundreds of cars."

"You've actually been thinking about this. I'm surprised." The realization caught her off guard and so did her words, blurted out with no filter.

"Of course I've been thinking about it. Why wouldn't I be?" His brow furrowed quizzically, but only for a split second before he continued, "There are eight events, right?"

"Maria is chairing the Events Committee, but, yes." She nodded. "I think at last count there were eight. Oh, and now the bowling ramp makes nine."

"Nine events, which can be spread over this expanse of fields."

He waved his arms wide, visibly excited to be offering his property to her. She felt her excitement growing along with his as they scanned the acreage together.

"We need to make room for bleachers at each event," she noted.

"Bleachers, definitely. I'll get out the tractor and get this place mowed. I'm also planning to have a temporary fence put up around the pond. I don't want anyone to fall in. Or try to jump in."

"We'll find the money in the budget for that, Mac," she assured him. "You shouldn't have to pay for it."

"Not necessary. It's on me."

"Thanks, Mac, that's really nice of you, but. . ."

"You know. . ." He picked up a clump of dirt from the ground with his left hand, flinging it off into the distance. Turning to her, his words slowed to a lazy drawl, making each sound more emphatic. "You were doing really well till you got to that 'but' part. How about just saying, 'Thanks, Mac, that's really nice of you?' "

He gazed into her eyes, and she caught a flicker of humor twinkling there. But even more, she sensed an invitation. An invitation for them to come to terms with one another. To be friends.

Or more?

She wasn't sure as his lips curved in that irresistible MacNeill Hattaway grin, causing her heart to flutter against her will. Causing her to concede to his wishes, even though she didn't want "something for nothing" from him or anyone else.

But for the sake of moving ahead without contention and just to get out from under that smile of his that could blind more than the June sun, she swallowed hard and answered him.

"Mac, thanks. That's, um, really nice of you."

"You're welcome, Megan."

Grateful for an excuse to tear her eyes from his, she glanced over her shoulder to check on Sammy. He and Bitty were still cuddled up together, fast asleep.

"Looks like they're down for the count." Mac chuckled. "Want to walk some more?"

She nodded, and both mindful not to stray out of eyesight, they surveyed more of the farmland, discussing which event would fit which part of the property best. Again, Megan felt mildly shocked at how much thought Mac had put into the planning already and felt even more ashamed than she had earlier. Had she really misjudged him so badly?

"You—you really do want to help, don't you?" Her thoughts tumbled out loud again, and though she hoped they sounded complimentary, especially compared to what she had been thinking about Mac just weeks. . .actually only hours before, evidently it didn't sound the same to him.

Suddenly his jaw clenched noticeably, and she'd never heard his voice so harsh as he replied, "I wouldn't have signed up for the job if I didn't want to, Megan."

So much for the peaceful, unspoken truce they'd established just minutes before. "Well, I mean—" He stopped her before she could blurt out an explanation.

"I can tell you exactly what you mean." He paused for a moment, and when he spoke again his voice took on a calmer tone. "You think I'm doing this for myself, don't you? You think that I'm trying to get back into the good graces of the public again. That I figure they'll forgive me, and then I can turn around and do the same irresponsible things all over again. Right?"

"Well, I. . ." She bowed her head. It was true, everything he said was true. She'd judged him for his past and would barely let his present actions count for anything. But, oh, how she was sorry for that now. If there's anything she remembered from her Christian upbringing it was not to judge others—and she usually wasn't hard on anyone—but herself.

"Mac, I'm sorry. I really, truly am. I've been unfair."

With the crook of his index finger, he gently lifted her chin. "Don't be sorry, Megan. Really. It's all right."

But it wasn't all right. She'd sat in judgment of Mac because it had been so easy. After all, the newspapers and tabloids had already done the work for her. She'd rolled her eyes when most of the locals stood behind him, even with her parents and the volunteers. Most of them had gotten past his former indiscretions. They were thrilled to be working with him and giving him a second chance.

But not her. Oh no. She couldn't let it go, could she? She couldn't because—

She gasped at the realization. It was because she was afraid. Afraid ever since that rainy night when she'd jumped out of her car shaking her finger at the tall, good-looking guy whose concern showed all over his handsome face. Ever since then she'd felt the need to protect her feelings. To protect her heart.

Oh yes, she'd made up a whole list of reasons in her mind why MacNeill Hattaway was so awful. Why he couldn't be trusted. But at the core of that was her heart, and in her heart she hadn't been feeling that way about him at all.

The truth was, the more she was around him, the more she couldn't stop thinking about him. She couldn't stop blushing when he looked at her. And she hadn't wanted him to help chair the event partly because just the thought of standing next to him made her stomach go all jittery and. . .

"Mac, I—"

Ever so softly he pressed a finger to her lips. "Megan, listen, it's okay. You're right. You are," he repeated. "I am helping out with the All-Stars Sports Day event for me. I am doing it for myself."

She felt her eyes grow wide as she gazed into his narrow ones, his admission sending her emotions into a jumble all over again.

He could feel his temper rising at Megan's question, but it wasn't because of her or what she asked. It was because of him. He just wanted to be with her. To share the perfect day in the present. But it wasn't that easy—not with his past dragging everything down again. Not that he didn't deserve it of course.

Still, he hated seeing the way the distrust appeared so quickly again in her eyes. But then, he did set her up for that, didn't he? He needed to explain exactly what he meant, once and for all. Then maybe she'd believe him. Then maybe her eyes would reflect the trust and appreciation he'd caught a glimpse of earlier.

"Look, I don't blame you for your speculations. But what I'm saying is, it's not in the way you think, Megan." His voice softened. "Yes, I'm doing this for myself. I am. But only because I don't want to be the same insensitive, self-involved guy I was before."

He paused, looking away from her, watching a blue jay flit from one tree to the next while working to gather his thoughts before he spoke. "I felt honored, blessed, when Ted asked me to help with the special-needs kids. Honestly, I felt lucky he'd even talk to me again."

She crooked her head upward. "You and Ted? I got the impression you two were friends."

"Yeah, well, Ted and I played knothole as kids. He was the only person I stayed in touch with from Loveland all through my growing up years. But that was mostly because our moms stayed friends after our move."

He searched for the blue jay again, wanting to look anywhere but at Megan, hating to admit what he was about to. "I was never that great of a friend to Ted though. I missed out on his wedding. Our team was playing out in L.A. at the time and of course, I was scheduled to pitch."

"It's not like you could help that, Mac."

"No, but I didn't even acknowledge his big day with a present and. . ." He shrugged, not in a big rush to tell the worst of it, the part he felt most guilty about. "The thing is, the Hawks were in town years later when I got news that Ted and Wendy had a little girl with cystic fibrosis. Yes, I was here, and I could've easily made a phone call or gone to the hospital for a show of support. But it seemed too hard. Too hard for me. That's all I thought about. Myself. It was easier to go out and party after our series than to think about what was going on in Ted's life. I didn't feel like I had any words of wisdom to share with him and Wendy, so I took the easy way out. I just didn't show up."

The light, consoling touch of Megan's hand on his arm made him turn to face her.

"I'm sure it was an awkward time for them as well, Mac. It can be unbearably difficult at first—when you find out the precious baby you've come to love so completely for nine months—or in Sammy's case, seven months—is born physically or mentally challenged."

He started to ask her questions, but then thought better of it. Maybe, like him, she just needed to explain herself.

She slid her hand away and continued rubbing the material of her dress between her fingers like she might a worry stone. "Your emotions are totally jarred. There's so much you can't comprehend. All the while you're carrying your darling little baby, all you can think about is them and their future. And then the baby is born and all of that isn't a reality anymore. You're so unsure of everything, so worried about any possibility of a future your child might ever have."

"So, you didn't know about Sammy until he was born?"

"Not at all. His development was proceeding just fine. My pregnancy was textbook perfect. And then, seven months into it I began having problems that forced Sammy to be born prematurely. The cerebral palsy is a result of that."

He couldn't imagine how hard that must've been, to think everything's fine, and then suddenly not turn out like that at all. Obviously, the only thing he had to compare it to was being ahead in runs going into the bottom of the ninth and then having the last batter up hit a grand slam. But how banal was that? Having a life— your baby's life and livelihood at stake—was something he honestly couldn't fathom.

"I was a mess. I didn't want to see anyone. I was ugly, blaming myself. Blaming God. And blaming myself again when my husband, Sammy's daddy, walked out on us months later, thinking how I should've never married him in the first place."

Megan shook her head and fingered the wisps of hair around her face and at the back of her neck, tucking them all back into place. Almost like she had said too much and was trying to pull herself together again.

"That sounds like a normal reaction," he offered, wishing he'd been there with her. But then that was a dumb thing to think. Six years ago, he'd been a mess, for a whole other set of reasons.

"It wasn't pretty. But, oh, what a handsome little guy my Sammy was!" She brightened at the mention of his name. "When I'd see him sleeping or laying in his crib it was so hard to believe there was anything less than perfect about him."

"And that's probably all you see in him now. Perfection."

"You're right." Her smile warmed him, a reward for his insight. Not that he'd had to think very hard about it. Pride for her son was written all over Megan's face.

"So I guess what I'm saying is that in the beginning—I mean, even if Ted knew about Hannah's condition—it may not have been a good time to visit him and Wendy anyway."

"I could say that if I'd even tried, Megan. But fact is, I didn't. Thanks for your absolution though."

All that being said, it felt like time to move on, now that they'd put some remnants of their pasts to rest. Walking in comfortable silence, they came to shorter patches of grass, where a white oak tree that appeared to be as old as the settlement of Loveland itself stood with its branches stretching out in every direction like points on a compass.

"What a great tree." Megan stopped to admire the oak before

moving closer to lean against the massive, solid trunk.

"I climbed it more than a few times back in the day." Mac rubbed his hand over the lowest branch, noting how the bark had smoothed over time.

"What's that over there?" She pointed to the corner of the field where he'd spent a considerable amount of time as a kid. "It looks like there's a fence or— Oh, is that a baseball diamond or something?"

He laughed. "A little hard to detect it's so overgrown. But yeah, that's where my uncle taught me all about baseball. Well, baseball and life—and all about God, too. That's why I couldn't ever let anyone else buy this place when Uncle Jake passed. I had to have it for myself. There are too many memories here. A lot of good memories."

"Better memories than your World Series win?"

"Different for sure. Richer in a way."

"So. . .did you always like baseball?" Megan squinted into the sunlight that flickered through the limbs of the tree, looking so pretty with her face turned up at him that it took him a second to process her question.

"Like it? Uh, no. I loved it. Always did. Loved everything about it, even the history and trivia of baseball. For example, did you know before the first catcher's mask was developed in the late eighteen hundreds, catchers wore rubber bands around their teeth to try to protect them?"

"Really?" She smiled. "I've never even thought about anything like that."

"Yeah, well, I probably did because I burned to know about every aspect of the game. I loved the tools of the trade. Always cleaned off my bats, and I'll never forget how good it felt when my parents bought my first real baseball mitt for me." He shook his head remembering. "I really loved the smell of that thing."

She giggled at that, the sound drawing a smile to his face. "The smell of your mitt?"

"Oh yeah." He chuckled with her. "The smell of a leather mitt always got to me."

"That's funny."

"Not really. You're the same way."

"The same way? Uh, I don't think so. I do not go around sniffing baseball mitts." She laughed.

"No, but you take in the aroma of what you love."

She scrunched her face at him.

"It's true. I've seen you smell an apple before you bite into it. And many times I've seen you sift your fingers through Sammy's hair, and then take a whiff of it before you kiss him on the head."

"Ha! That makes me sound like some kind of mother dog or something."

"You do have sort of floppy ears now that I'm noticing."

"Floppy ears?" She gave a playful shove to his shoulder. "I don't have floppy ears."

"I'm kidding. You actually have very cute ears." He watched as she fingered one of her tiny pearl earrings. *And a cute nose. And sweet lips. And. . .* "I'm just saying you can't get enough of your little guy you love him so much. Even the scent of him."

Her expression sobered instantly. Suddenly she looked at him as if she was seeing him for the first time. "And that's—that's how much you love baseball?"

"That's how much I loved baseball." He nodded. "I'd fall asleep with my mitt covering my face at night, and I'd have it sitting on the table near my cereal bowl each morning. I read everything about the game I could. Played every day, even if I'd have to toss the ball up against the side of the house by myself. There was nothing, not one thing, I wanted to do more. Not one thing I loved better."

"You keep—you keep saying loved. As in past tense. . ." She hesitated before she asked, "Are you afraid you won't play again?"

He smiled. "No, it's not that. I can feel my elbow is improving all the time, and God willing, it will heal completely. I still love baseball, trust me. It's still deep in my blood."

He could tell she wasn't about to press him, yet he continued anyway. "But I've learned success can take something that you love—something simple and pure like throwing a ball over a plate—and make it all complicated and twisted if you let it. And of course, over time, I let it. I let everything get to me. The ups. The downs. The money. The fame. The simple thing I loved got tainted in the process. If I get the chance to play again, I hope I'm smarter than that this time around. I hope I've learned my lesson."

"I bet your uncle enjoyed sharing that success with you though. I bet he was really proud."

"He was. But, knowing Uncle Jake, I think he'd be even more proud of me today. Now that I'm trying to get back to the basics he taught me. Especially back to the kid-like faith I used to have."

He couldn't believe how much he'd said. Things he'd never told anyone else before. Things he'd never felt comfortable sharing. But it seemed in the short walk around the property, they'd come a long way.

And suddenly he realized there was another scent he was falling in love with. The scent of Megan. Sweet as the blossoms on the purple bush that blossomed outside his bedroom window all through the month of May. Fresh as the sunshine warming the back of his neck as he stood facing her. Megan, so wholesome and pure, like no other woman he'd ever known. Megan, with eyes he wanted to get lost in, who went through every day not seeing how beautiful she was inside and out.

Like the young boy who wanted to know everything about the sport he loved, he was a grown man who wanted to know everything about the woman in front of him. He wanted so badly to touch her face, her hair—to know what those lips that drove him beyond crazy would feel like pressed against his.

Placing his hand on the trunk of the mighty oak tree, next to her shoulder, he started to lean toward her.

He'd never asked permission to kiss a girl before. Women had always given themselves up willingly to him. But Megan wasn't just any woman. With her, it felt only right to ask for such a perfect gift.

Her lips seemed to part in expectation as he stepped closer still. Her hands came up, covering his chest.

In every way she appeared as ready as he was. Still, he wanted to be sure. He wanted to ask.

"Megan, may I. . ."

But before he could get the rest of the words from his mouth, she screamed. She pushed hard at his chest, shoving him away.

Chapter 11

W hat do you think, Meg?"

Later the next afternoon, Megan gazed at her mom who stood outside the dressing room in a glittery, pearl-white gown, balancing herself on her tiptoes.

"This dress? Or did you like the blue one better?" Her mom worried her lip, but even as she did so, she couldn't contain the excitement bubbling up inside her. "Oh, I can't even remember the last time your dad and I had a black-tie affair to go to," she said, sounding as giddy as one of the high school girls Megan imagined her father counseling. "Whose idea was it anyway? To have a black-tie fundraiser for your sports day event? Wendy Slater's? I've told you the story, haven't I, how we gals at We Do! got Wendy and Ted together?"

Megan could not only see her mother clearly from where she sat in the mauve retro-round accent chair in Sophisticates Boutique, she could hear her plainly, too. But focusing on her mom's words was a whole other matter. And trying to decipher which of her mother's questions to answer first, even more challenging. Her mind was still far away, high up in the clouds. Still trying to wrap itself around the fact that she'd almost kissed MacNeill Hattaway.

Almost. Kissed. Mac.

Her mind wouldn't stop repeating the news to her heart—as if her heart needed any more reminding. As it was, it felt like it'd been positively beating out of her chest all day long.

"Megan, are you feeling okay?" Her mom came down on the balls of her feet, the gown swishing as she leaned forward. "Your cheeks look so flushed, honey, and you don't seem to be very 'with it' today. Have you been taking your vitamins? How's your sleep been lately?"

"I'm fine. Really, no worries, Mom. I'm good."

Even though, no, she hadn't gotten much sleep. Again. But there was no way she was going to mention that to her mom, who would only ask why. And what would Megan tell her? That she'd been awake most of the night, wondering about Mac once more? This time, imagining what it might have been like to actually kiss him?

Her mom would be so thrilled she'd want to throw a party for all of Loveland—or assemble a parade, complete with a marching band to traipse down the main street of town.

So, no, the almost-kiss with Mac had to remain a secret for now. One she could barely believe herself.

"Well, if you're sure you're okay. . ." Her mom tilted her head.

"I'm sure," Megan replied as convincingly as she could, not wanting to cause any worry. After all, her mom was so excited for them to be spending an afternoon together. Her dad had taken Sammy for the day, giving her and her mom time to have a leisurely salad at Paxton's and to visit with Allie before wandering into Sophisticates a few blocks over. Even though the fundraiser dance was still many weeks away, Mom was determined to make the most of their excursion.

"Well then, which dress works best?" Her mom poised a forefinger thoughtfully to her cheek. "Your dad really likes me in blue. But I don't know. The blue dress was more elegant. This dress is more glitzy."

"Can you try on the blue one again so I can make a better comparison?"

If truth be known, Megan had been daydreaming so much, she hadn't really zeroed in on the blue formal the first time around. Luckily, her mom hadn't noticed and looked more than happy to oblige. "Good idea!" She headed back into the dressing room.

Good idea. . . . Megan settled back against the throw pillows once more. *Really, had it been a good idea?* To let Mac get so close to her?

But then. . .it had all happened so quickly. One minute she was leaning up against the tree and they were talking, and the next minute he was moving closer and closer.

And she didn't do anything to try to stop him because—well, because during the hours they'd spent together he'd been so tender and sensitive. So much so, she found herself crazily wondering if his lips would feel that way, too. And then, when he started to ask permission to kiss her, it was so sweet. A side of Mac she never knew existed. In response, she couldn't help but tilt her head up toward his. As she did, that's when she heard the rustling in a patch of trees just off to the side of where they were standing.

That's when she spotted a man through the trees holding a camera, aimed in their direction.

That's when instead of kissing Mac's lips, she screamed bloody murder right into his ears.

She cringed at the very thought, then straightened abruptly as her mom slipped out of the dressing room.

"Here I am in blue again." She rose up on her tiptoes once more. "I'm just not sure." She smoothed the front of the satin gown. "Are you?"

Sure? Megan wasn't sure about anything these days. So confused that she'd actually prayed the night before—for herself. Something rare for her. But she needed some kind of clarity. Badly. She wasn't sure what to think at all about the feelings washing over her heart lately. Where was it all coming from?

After Mac's attempt at kissing her was interrupted, he went chasing after the intruder, and she went running to make sure Sammy was all right. She really wanted to believe it when Mac came back out of breath, apologizing for her having been frightened. She really wanted to trust him when he told her he'd had the same thing happen a couple of times since he'd lived there, but he hadn't done anything because he didn't like the idea of putting barbed wire around the property. Deep down, she really wanted it to be true that he hadn't hired someone to take a picture of them together—that it wasn't a part of some crazy publicity stunt.

Yes, she wanted to believe him, and the weirdest part was, she wasn't even sure why. The only thing she knew for certain is that after the awkward incident she doubted Mac would ever want to try to kiss her again. He probably thought she was some kind of excitable nut case. And who could blame him?

On a simpler note, the other thing she could be sure of—now that she was forcing herself to concentrate—was the best dress for her mother.

"Dad's right, Mom. Blue is definitely your color. That gown makes your eyes pop, and it's a great style for you. You're such a young-looking nana."

"Wow! Do you really think so? I guess it's worth every penny then."

Her mom beamed as she headed back to the dressing room, but before she slid back the curtain, she turned. "Are you sure you don't want to try on a few dresses while we're here?"

"No, I'm fine."

"Oh, come on. We have time. How often do you and I get to shop like this?"

Megan knew her mom was right and didn't want to disappoint her. Especially not on their rare mother-daughter day. Plus, she had spied a few dresses she wouldn't mind trying on.

While her mom changed back into her street clothes and a sales associate took the blue gown they'd decided on up to the counter, Megan sifted through the racks, studying the dresses and price tags. After selecting several possibilities that matched both her criteria, she headed to the dressing room while her mom switched places with her, settling into the mauve chair.

It reminded her of the past, of shopping for homecoming dresses and sorority formals the way her mom oohed and aahed over each selection. But when she tried on a one-shoulder, red satin gown, the look that came over her mom's face confirmed what she thought.

The dress was definitely the one.

"It's really pretty, isn't it?" She ran her hand over the expensive-feeling material.

"*You're* really pretty. I love how striking it looks with your dark hair. That dress looks like it was made for you, Meg." Her mom got up from the chair only to crouch down and smooth out the slightly flared hemline. Then she stepped back, her arms crossed over her chest, her eyes skimming Megan up and down, up and down, appraisingly.

Megan was sure her mom was considering what shoes would look best with the gown. So it stood to reason her tuna melt lunch did a flip in her stomach when out of nowhere her mom asked, "What about Mac?"

"Mac?" Her cheeks tingled just saying his name. "What about Mac?"

"Is he wearing a white tux or a black one?"

A tux? She almost gulped aloud. Nearly the last thing she wanted to think about was Mac. And the *very* last thing she wanted to think about was Mac in a tux, and how handsome he'd look in one. "I have no clue, Mom."

"You mean you're not going together?"

"Going together? I don't know. The dance isn't for weeks."

"Well, I just assumed you might, being you're both the co-chairs."

"Yes, but. . ."

"I'm just thinking the press and everyone will be taking pictures of the two of you together. But black or white, either color of tux will work well with the red."

Black or white? Megan wished it was all as simple as that. But just thinking that Mac could be taking someone else to the dance suddenly made her stomach drop, leaving her feeling all topsy-turvy like a silly young schoolgirl with a crush. That was exactly why she didn't want to get all caught up in feelings for him or anyone else. She had enough things in her life that she needed to keep under control. Her son and his happiness and welfare. Her job. Her standing in the community. Who had room for anything else? For things like crushes. And kisses. And—she shivered. . .

"Whatever. I love the dress. I'm getting it."

"Good. While you get changed, I'm going to check out the evening bags. I haven't had a new one in eons." Her mom nodded toward the display of purses by the window. "Wait a minute. Is that—?"

"What?" Megan stepped down from the mirrored platform, peering in the same general direction.

"Is that Janey?" Her mom pointed toward the window.

Instantly, Megan spotted the person her mom was talking about and just as quickly she understood the reason her mom had such a puzzled look on her face.

"It does look like her, doesn't it?" Megan stuck out her neck to get a better view as the Janey look-alike, pausing to put on a pair of sunglasses, resumed her brisk pace down the sidewalk.

"Exactly like her."

"But with long red hair. Hmm. That's weird."

"Yes. . .weird."

She and her mom turned to each other and shrugged, neither able to put the pieces together. Clearly, nothing really was as simple as black and white.

Mac cut the power on the riding lawnmower the moment he caught sight of Bill Helmsley standing in the driveway. Evidently Bill had finished putting together the estimates Mac had asked for.

Sliding off the mower, he brushed some dry blades of grass from his faded jeans as he walked toward Bill, already having a fairly good idea of what the man was about to say before he said it.

"How's it look?" Mac tipped his baseball cap back on his head.

"Well, I went through the whole house, and I tried to make the estimates as reasonable as I could. But…" Bill sucked in some air and slid several papers from a clipboard, handing them to Mac. He shook his head as he continued. "There's just not much way around most of the improvements you want to make. It's an old house, you know? Narrow halls and steep stairways. It's going to take some money and creativity to make your house wheelchair friendly. That's all there is to it. But I guess you already knew that, didn't you?"

"I figured as much." Mac took the papers and without looking at them, folded the estimates in quarters before tucking them into his back pocket. He liked the remodeling contractor Ted had hooked him up with the minute he'd met him, sensing he was honest and straightforward, so he didn't hesitate to ask, "When's the soonest your crew can get to work?"

"Yesterday."

Mac crooked a smile. "That sounds good. Just give me a day to look over the estimates to see if I have any questions. Then I'll give you a call and you can get started."

"Sounds great, Mr. Hattaway."

"Mac." He held out his right hand.

"Yeah, Mac. Thanks." Bill shook his hand. "I'll look forward to hearing from you."

As Bill's pickup backed out the driveway, Mac turned to look out into the fields. He'd walked the grounds earlier in the day with a sales rep from a local company who said they could supply materials for a rubberized walkway. Luckily, it wouldn't be any problem to put the rubber pathway over the grasses to construct a temporary sidewalk for the wheelchair participants and their families on event day.

But just like hours earlier, his eyes veered from the grassy meadows and caught sight of the oak tree where he'd nearly kissed Megan. And for the second time that day, he didn't know whether to laugh or frown about his near-kiss miss.

It was just his bad luck, wasn't it, that a stranger would be lurking on his property at the very moment he was about to become acquainted with Megan's sweet lips? Scaring her half to death. At least scaring her enough that she just about busted his eardrum with her scream.

Or maybe. . .

He squinted at the formidable oak and could almost see Megan leaning up against it in her pretty yellow dress again. Could almost hear the brave tremor in her voice as she recounted the circumstances surrounding Sammy's birth, including the way her husband walked out on their family. That must've hurt to the quick, he imagined. But Megan squared her shoulders as she spoke about it, and her courageous front only made him respect and care for her even more.

So, yeah. . .

Maybe it had been a good thing that they hadn't kissed after all.

Not that he liked dwelling on that. Not that he didn't still want to kiss her in the worst way. In fact, kissing Megan was pretty much at the top of his mind every time he saw her. And he hated to admit it—couldn't even believe he was thinking it—but there it was: Kissing Megan was on his mind all the time he wasn't near her, too.

Even so, maybe it would be better to slow things down. *Let her know I'm sincere. Not try to push her into something she might not be ready for.*

Ah, man. . . He groaned inwardly, his insides protesting at the thought. *Do I really want to do that?*

Watching long shadows blanket and retreat from the fields over and over again as the sun drifted in and out of the clouds, he stood weighing his options.

Yeah. . .I'll take it slow, he finally resolved to himself. *Take my time,* he vowed. *And be sure not to look at that big old oak tree anymore, reminding me what I missed out on.*

It sure wouldn't be easy. He shook his head. But if he won Megan's heart as a result then his restraint would be worth it.

In the meantime, he was still going to go forward with his plans to make his house wheelchair accessible. He had to do something to make himself feel hopeful, like he was moving ahead in a relationship with Megan. He had to do something that would hold some kind of promise that she and Sammy would stay a part of his life.

What else was there to do? Except maybe have another talk with God.

Oh Lord, this isn't easy. Putting my pride aside and being patient where Megan is concerned. Not even knowing where it's all leading. Or if it will lead anywhere. But, as uncomfortable as it is, Lord, I'll try because Megan and Sammy are the best things that have ever happened to me. I have these deep feelings for them. Feelings like I've never had before—and, well, I thank You for this chance, Lord, I do. And if it ends up Megan and I are just friends, I guess I'll have to put up with that. But I hope that's not what You want, Lord. He looked up at the wisps of clouds stretched across the sky.

I don't think that's what You want. Do You?

Chapter 12

A nd these are my parents, Laura and Kurt O'Donnell."
Mac extended his hand as Megan introduced him to
the couple sitting in the matching lawn chairs on the Nisbet Park
ground. Wearing bright neon runners' gear, they fit right in with the
sportive backdrop of the park, which was decked out with colorful
balloons and banners for Loveland's Amazing Race festival.

"It's nice to meet you both," he said sincerely.

"It's *really* nice to meet you, MacNeill." Megan's father hopped
up from the chair, pumping his hand.

"Excuse us if we're a bit sweaty and disheveled from the race,"
her mother added, her blue eyes and welcoming smile reminding
him a lot of Megan.

"Are you kidding? I think it's great you both signed up for the
Amazing Race," Mac told them.

"They've been participating since the initial event years ago,"
Megan chimed in.

"Yeah well, it's a fun event." Kurt chuckled. "Even if I will be sore tomorrow."

"I know I'd be," Mac agreed. "It sounds like a grueling triathlon."

"Ah, it's not so grueling. And it's not really a triathlon either." Kurt shook his head. "Even though you are on foot, traipsing through downtown Loveland. And then, you're on a bicycle on the bike trail. And you even do some tubing on the Little Miami River. But what's different is all along the way, they have these challenge stations set up. Kind of loosely based on that TV show."

"Very loosely," Laura added.

"That's what I said, honey." Kurt raised a brow. "Isn't that what I said?" He glanced at Mac who then glanced at Megan who only shrugged and smiled.

"Yeah well, I'm sure it's a good time," Mac replied. "I wasn't even aware Loveland had an event like this until Sammy mentioned it."

He had hoped maybe Megan had put Sammy up to inviting him to the after-race festival when the two had been out to visit his farm the week before. But when all was said and done, he doubted it. Sammy had probably done it all on his own. But, whatever. He wasn't going to be picky about where the invitation had come from. He was just glad to be there. After all, it felt like a month of Sundays since he'd spent any time with Megan and Sammy, even though it'd been closer to seven days.

He'd been glad, too, that Sammy had noticed his new truck by the side of the barn the week before and asked for a ride in it. Megan had reprimanded Sammy for being so forward. But for Mac, it wasn't an inconvenience at all. It gave him the perfect excuse to pick up Sammy and Megan for the festival.

"Well, I'd say you were probably busy with more important things in past summers than our Amazing Race. Like traveling around the country striking out batters, right?" Kurt asked, a wide grin spanning his face.

"I don't know how important that was. . ." Mac shrugged. "But yeah, that was the objective."

He felt Megan lay her hand on his forearm, trying to direct his attention to the other folks seated around them. "And this is Allie and her husband, Greg. But I'm guessing you may already know them from Paxton's."

"I do." He nodded at the couple spread out on a blanket with their daughter and son. "I can't stay away from the place."

"And we're glad." Allie smiled.

"Definitely." Greg nodded. "Thanks again, Mac, for all your help with our Major League night at the grill a few weeks ago."

"Not a big deal. Just signed some autographs."

"You helped out at the grill?" Megan turned to him, her face registering surprise. "Where was I that night?"

"I don't know. But Mac's being humble. It *absolutely* was a big deal," Greg replied. "Your being there that night brought in a slew of people, Mac," he reconfirmed. "We made a lot of money for the community peewee teams, which we wouldn't have done without you."

"Ahh-hem. Ahh-hem."

The woman, sitting in a lawn chair next to a man close to her age, audibly cleared her throat. Donning a lavender visor over her blond-highlighted hair, she also wore a teasing smile.

Megan laughed and reached out to pat the woman's shoulder.

"And, Mac, last but certainly not least in my heart, these are Allie's parents and my second parents, Pam and Jim Matthews. They always sign up for the race with Mom and Dad."

"Nice to meet you, Mac." Pam reached out. "I work with Megan's mom."

"Oh yeah?" Mac shook her hand. "What do you all do?"

"You don't want to go there," Greg called out.

Mac turned to Megan who only blinked, suddenly seeming slightly uncomfortable. He held out his hands, not understanding. "What?"

"Oh, Greg's just being silly." Pam waved a playful hand in her son-in-law's direction. "Megan's mom and I plan weddings. We've been friends forever and so have our girls. Allie and Megan practically shared the same pumpkin seat."

"Pumpkin what?" Again, Mac was having a hard time understanding.

Jim laughed as he stood up to shake Mac's hand. "Pumpkin seats. Don't worry. We've heard it a thousand times, Mac. The girls have been together since they were wee little and cute as pumpkins sitting in their pumpkin seats."

"Ah—well. I believe it," he said, still wondering if they were actually talking about a pumpkin-shaped seat.

"So, how's the pitching arm doing?" Mac got the sense Jim was trying to segue to more manly topics.

"It's uh. . ." He started to say he was due back to the team doctor soon to see about clearance to play again. But he really didn't want to get into all of that. Not right now at least. Instead he shrugged. "It's doing pretty good, I think."

"Megan is a physical therapist, you know," Kurt piped up.

Before he could answer, Megan gave him a look that said please-excuse-my-parents then tilted her head at her father, her lips curling into a sweet, patient smile. "Trust me, Dad. He does know that."

"Just thought I'd mention it." Her dad shrugged.

"So, it was a good race then?" Mac seized the opportunity to steer the conversation away from the topic of his elbow. "For the four of you?"

"It gets bigger and better every year," Laura exclaimed.

"Oh, you like it because you get through the challenges so easily." Her husband pretended to sneer.

"I do like puzzles and matching things, what can I say?" Laura grinned.

"I'd think running, biking, and tubing on the river would be challenging enough," Mac quipped.

"You would think so, wouldn't you?" Allie tuned in, while re-tying her daughter's gym shoe. "But supposedly the challenge stations make it even more fun. At least that's what these guys have to say about it." She stopped what she was doing for a moment to point in either direction at both sets of parents.

"I plan to sign up for it one of these years," Megan chirped. "It sounds like fun to me."

"It's nothing awfully strenuous," Kurt explained to Mac. "Or I wouldn't be able to do it. Like at the Loveland Stage Company—that was Challenge Seven, I think, you had to 'dance a bit or spell a hit.' And I still know a few disco moves, so. . ." He flung his arm up and down John Travolta style, making everyone laugh, including the kids.

"Hey, I don't mind admitting it's nice to sit down and rest at some of the challenges," Jim added.

"No kidding." Pam laughed. "I didn't think I'd ever get you back on your feet after the challenge in the parking lot of the Loveland Massage Center."

"The one where we got to sit and feed each other water from baby bottles?" Jim chuckled. "What can I say? I was really thirsty."

Everyone laughed again, and as their merriment died down, Sammy spoke up and filled the void.

"Pap-ee, Mac bring us in new truck."

"Is that right?" Kurt turned from his grandson to Mac. "I thought I spotted you driving around town in a shiny new Ford."

Mac nodded. "I loved my uncle's old truck—a '77. But it wasn't safe anymore. In fact, the brakes were so bad on the thing, I almost ran into Megan and Sammy the night of the initial All-Stars Sports meeting. That's how we first met actually, down on West Loveland near Paxton's."

"Really? Did you tell me that, Megan?" Mac noticed Laura trying to make eye contact with her daughter. "That's quite a coincidence, isn't it? And really very ro—"

"Mom!" Megan cut her mother short. "Aren't you going to be too tired to cook out tonight after you've been in this race all day?"

"Definitely," Pam spoke up. "Which is why we decided that you kids are going to do the barbecuing. Your mom and I made all the side dishes yesterday. The brats and burgers are at your mom's house just waiting to be cooked."

"That sounds more than fair," Megan answered before turning to him once more. "I sure hope you like brats and burgers, Mac."

Everyone turned their eyes on him.

"Of course I do. Burgers. Baseball. A Ford pickup. It all goes together, doesn't it?"

"And Ize," Sammy chimed in.

"Ize?" Mac looked at Megan.

"Oh, that's right. Ice. I promised the kids shaved ices," Megan explained. "But I also promised to hand out these cards for Janey." She pulled a pack of postcards from her backpack. "To announce the contest she's running."

She bit her lip, looking apologetic and of course, Mac felt an instant desire to make everything right for her. But it was Greg who jumped up from the blanket and began to take charge.

"Well, if it's okay with everyone. . . Allie and Megan, you two go ahead, feel free to pass out the cards," he suggested. "Meanwhile, Mac and I will take the kids for ices. That'll give the parents a chance to relax and bask in the glory of having another Amazing Race under their belts." He smiled at their elders. "Then later we'll head to the O'Donnells' to barbecue."

"Sounds good to me." Kurt settled deeper into the lap of his chair, closing his eyes.

Eyes drooping, Jim didn't look far behind him. "Me, too," he agreed.

"How about you, Mac?" Greg asked. "That okay with you?"

"I'm in." Mac nodded, shuffling behind Sammy's wheelchair. "Sounds like a plan."

"Are you sure, Mac?" Megan leaned close, laying a hand on his forearm again. "You don't mind taking Sammy? And being with my family all evening?"

"Mind it?" She really had no clue, did she? "I'm all over it," he said, feeling warmed he could make her grin. "Ready, kids?"

While Megan and Allie headed in one direction, he and Greg started off in the other. As he pushed Sammy's chair and Justin and Carrie held their dad's hands, their group made their way through the crowd of race participants and curious observers. It reminded him of a time when he and his family belonged to this town. Making him feel like he belonged to a place—this place—again.

I should give Mom and Dad a call down in Florida tomorrow, he thought as they strolled across the bike path to the Hawaiian Ice Hut. *Wonder how they're doing? It's been awhile. . .*

Megan watched the full moon play hide-and-seek, flickering in and out of sight between the trees, as Mac eased his truck over the winding road leading to his farm. The breeze coming in the window felt slightly cool on her face after being out in the sun the entire day, but not enough to have to put her sweatshirt on. Or to worry about Sammy being chilled.

It was way past his bedtime, as a matter of fact, and she couldn't believe she'd said yes to yet one more activity before Mac dropped her and Sammy off at home. The three of them had already packed so much into the day, spending the afternoon at the Amazing Race festival, and then all evening at her parents' house, barbecuing and visiting while the kids played. But she was as intrigued as her son was when Mac mentioned he could bring the moon to Sammy.

Oh, please! Who was she kidding? Truth was, she was more than intrigued with Mac, too.

Even now, she couldn't help from turning to look at him, his angular profile lit up by the bluish glow of the dashboard lights. He appeared so serious and purposeful as he gripped the steering wheel, intent on getting them to the place he'd promised. And he looked so handsome. . .making her suddenly conscious of what a mess she must look like after spending an entire day outdoors.

Her white shorts and gauzy white top had been a mistake to wear, no doubt. Clearly neither was spotless or fresh at this point. Plus her hair! She didn't even want to imagine what it looked like. It'd gotten wavy and out of control in the first hour in the sun. She'd pulled it back into a ponytail without even looking, and it'd stayed that way the rest of the day.

But not so with Mac. The outdoor activities and sunshine had only made his complexion more golden. His mussed hair and day-old-whiskers only made him more rugged-looking and attractive— and hard not to look at.

To her embarrassment, he must've felt her staring because he turned, and even though it was only for a moment, he gazed at her in a way that made her think he hadn't noticed that her shorts were less than white and her hair more than messy.

"What a great day, huh?"

"Yeah, it was, wasn't it?" Her cheeks flushed in the wake of his attention.

"You've got a really nice family," he said, his eyes turned back to the windshield. "And good friends. Really easy to be around."

"They're keepers, for sure. Sometimes they try to help a bit too much, but—"

"That's better than having it the other way, don't you think?"

She nodded in the dark, not really wanting to explain at that exact moment that though his logic was sound, it wasn't that easy for her to accept all the help. Or any of it actually. "Sometimes. Probably. Yes," she answered, indecisively and was glad when he changed the subject.

"You look a lot like your mom."

"You really think so? People always say that, but neither of us sees it that way."

"You're kidding. There's a strong resemblance in the shape of your eyes. The way you smile. You have a great smile," he complimented. "It's so. . .bright."

"It's our family secret."

"Yeah, what's that?"

"Teeth-whitening strips," she told him honestly, and he chuckled at that.

"No, seriously. I don't mean just white. I mean bright. As in happy."

Oh, that was how she had been feeling lately. Happy. At least she felt that way when she wasn't also feeling confused and scared about the way she was feeling.

"I'm sure you hear that a lot though, don't you?" he asked, refocusing his eyes on the road. "About your smile?"

"Actually I do. Usually once a week."

"Yeah?" He did a double take. "That often, huh?"

"Uh-huh. When I see Dan. Dan always tells me that." Did she actually see him flinch? *Seriously?* She was only being playful, teasing. She didn't mean anything by it.

His hands tightened around the steering wheel. "Do I know Dan?"

She nodded in the dimness. "Actually, yes you do. He's really a great guy and very mature."

"Mature? I'm not sure how to take that."

"Mature, meaning he'll be seventy-two in August."

That news seemed to ease Mac's shoulders. "Hmm, I think I like this Dan guy already."

"You do like him." She smiled. "Dan Hoffman? He's one of the volunteers?"

"Oh yeah. Dan. He told me he's one of your patients. He was also a good friend of my Uncle Jake's." He paused and shook his head. "You really had me going there for a minute."

They both laughed, and she couldn't believe he'd reacted so possessively. *Really? MacNeill Hattaway? Who could have his pick of about any woman in the universe? Jealous?* She had to wonder if it was because he really did have feelings for her. Or was it just because he didn't like to lose—at baseball or anything else?

She found herself hoping it was for the former reason, not the latter.

"What funny?" Sammy asked from the bench seat behind them.

"Your mom's funny, that's what," Mac told him.

"Funny? Maw-mee?" Sammy's voice registered disbelief.

"I know. Hard to believe, isn't it, sweetie?" Megan glimpsed at her son in the backseat. "Mommy's not always so funny, am I?"

Sammy shook his head vehemently, making them laugh, which only made him shake it all over again.

"You nice, Maw-mee. Buh not funny."

"Yes, she is nice," Mac agreed, his comment causing her to look his way. "Pretty, too."

Mac gave her a sideways glance, and she didn't know how he managed to do it, but his grin widened in approval at the same time his eyes narrowed in seriousness, causing her heart to race in her chest.

Thankfully she managed to escape his gaze when they came around the bend to his farm, and he had to divert his attention to turning his new truck ever so gently onto the gravel driveway.

Slowly pulling all the way to the end of the drive, Mac turned off the engine. Before she could find the door handle in the dark, he was out of the truck and around to the passenger side of the vehicle. It wasn't like she needed any help, but there he was anyway opening her door, helping her descend gracefully. Then he grabbed the wheelchair from the bed of the Ford before hoisting Sammy down from the back cabin.

"You take me to moo-n, Mac?" Sammy asked while Mac settled him into the chair.

"No, I said I'll bring the moon to you."

"Oh."

Either way, Megan knew it didn't matter to Sammy. As long as he could be with Mac, his idol and new pal, her son didn't have a care in the world. The thought suddenly niggled at her that the day the three of them had shared felt too perfect. Too wonderful. A day with MacNeill Hattaway that she would've never believed could be true. So, why was she thinking it was for real? A tingle of warning prickled at her cheeks.

What if she and Sammy were just something to keep Mac amused while he was healing? What if he didn't care for Sammy as much as she thought he appeared to? Or maybe not for her either? Or what if—

Oh stop it! she commanded her mind. *Just stop with the "what-ifs,"* a voice inside her pleaded. *Things have been great today. So easy and natural. With just the three of us. And with family and friends. Mac even said so. Don't ruin it all. Not now. . .*

She tried to look beyond the thoughts in her head to the sky far beyond her reach. "The moon does look pretty big out here."

In the wide open space, far from town, with no competition from street lights or house lights, the huge moon looked as white as ever and so did the stars, abundant against the purplish night sky.

"You haven't seen anything yet," Mac promised from behind the wheelchair.

"Where are we headed?"

He pointed to the left. "To the barn."

"Barn?" A hint of glee permeated Sammy's voice. "I like barns."

Megan didn't bother to remind her zealous and easy-to-please son that he'd never been in a barn. Instead she let Mac push him along and lead the way, much like he'd been doing all day.

She noticed Sammy didn't say a word but rather sat in awe as Mac unlatched the barn doors and slid them to each side.

"This is a nice barn," Megan said, following behind them. "Not that I've been in a lot of barns. But this one's so clean, really nice."

"I had it redone when Uncle Jake was still alive. He had a few horses for a while until he got too sick to take care of them and had to put them up for adoption. He liked to spend a lot of time out here whittling in their company."

Mac stepped to the side and turned on what looked to be a small battery-powered lantern before pushing the wheelchair deeper into the barn. "I don't want to turn on a bunch of lights. It'll ruin what I want to show you."

"Smell funny in here," Sammy remarked.

"It smells like a barn, honey." Megan chuckled.

At the sound of the voices, Bitty sauntered out of nowhere, meowing her way toward them.

"Bitty!" Sammy extended his arm over his chair.

"How about you let your mom hold Bitty for a minute until we get to where we're going?" Mac suggested.

Megan scooped up the cat in her arms and followed along behind Mac and Sammy until they reached the middle of the barn. She was still puzzled about what Mac was up to even as she watched him pull at a dangling rope, and a makeshift staircase descended from the rafters.

"Ladies first." He motioned for her and Bitty to head up the steps in front of him and Sammy.

The air grew warmer and the lantern's light dimmer as Megan made her way up the ladder to the loft, Bitty nestled against her chest. Settling down onto a bed of hay, it was only seconds later when Mac and Sammy's heads popped through the opening.

"Hey guys."

"Mac carry me," Sammy stated the obvious as Mac deposited him onto her lap and Bitty hopped off, finding a place to curl up near her feet. "He nice. And strong," Sammy added.

"I think I should hire you to do my PR work, Sammy." Mac chuckled before moving closer to the barn wall. "Now. . ." he paused. "Are you two ready?"

They both nodded, Megan for one wondering what they should be ready for. But then they couldn't have imagined it anyway. Because as Mac opened the large wooden window that ran most of the length of the loft area, so much light flooded in that she and Sammy both gasped.

The moon that had seemed a galaxy away when viewed from the ground now suddenly looked so close. Close enough to reach out and touch, just as Mac had promised. And surrounding it were so many stars, glimmering and twinkling before their eyes, Megan thought it'd surely take till dawn to count them all.

Mac settled in next to them then, and all at once she was totally aware of how close he was. The scent of him, musk and soap blended together, was familiar to her now. So was the pleasant feeling it awakened in her. His shoulder leaned against hers in the dark, connecting them in an unspoken way, feeling easy. Comfortable.

Cuddled together, they all sat in awed silence looking out into the vast sky until Sammy rasped his thoughts out loud.

"God is big!" he said, his voice full of amazed wonder. "He very big!"

"And good," Mac said, low and reverent. "God is good."

Then, as if he hadn't surprised her enough that day with all his tender ways, he surprised her again by reaching for her hand. Gently. Softly. He covered his large, strong hand over her smaller one, making it feel like a perfect fit. His clasp warmed her. His touch assured her. And the words he spoke never felt so true as they reverberated through her. Because suddenly in the veil of night there seemed to be so much light in her life. So much to be thankful for, that tears sprang to her eyes.

There was family. . .and friends they'd spent the sunny day with. There was the welcome weight and warmth of Sammy's body leaning against her chest. Sammy—her son—who could not walk through the world, but who could send her heart on trips of bliss. There was Mac—oh, sweet, heartthrob Mac—wanting to share time with them, becoming a part of them, making her feel things she hadn't felt in a very long time.

And there was God. God who Sammy talked about as if he knew Him, as if He was his friend. God, who really did feel like He was everywhere these days. So, so close.

Oh yes, it all felt right. So right that she couldn't help but squeeze Mac's hand in reply. So good that she couldn't stop the unseen tear of joy, escaping down her cheek.

Chapter 13

I'm Jason. I'll be your server today." The waiter wiped his brow then steadied a pen over his ordering pad all in one motion. "Did you want to order lunch now? Or wait for your friend to get here?"

"I think I'll wait." Megan squinted up at him, shading her eyes from the sun. "He should be here any minute."

"Take your time." Jason slipped the pad back into his pocket. "I'd sit out here all day if I could. I'll stop back when I see him."

"Thanks."

Megan already knew Tano Bistro's menu by heart, so there was no need to look it over one more time. Instead, she settled back into the rattan chair and checked out the scenery along the sidewalks of downtown Loveland, wishing she, too, could sit outside forever on such a gorgeous day.

The humidity was almost non-existent after the rain the day before. Quite a rarity for summer in southwestern Ohio. Even so, she couldn't sit and enjoy the outdoors for all that long. Her next patient was due to arrive in an hour and fifteen minutes, and she needed to be back at the clinic a few minutes prior to that.

Still, it was nice Mac had suggested they meet for lunch in the middle of the week to discuss event details. Such a different change of pace, it almost made the obligations of the day fall away for just awhile. Making her feel like she was on a mini-getaway. To somewhere other than Loveland, Ohio. To some faraway place. Where she'd be having lunch at an outdoor café. *With Mac.*

She couldn't believe the way the crazy image danced around in her head, instantly making her stomach feel all fluttery. And make her heart feel the same way. Even a drink of her ice water didn't help at all to cool her flushed cheeks. Or to distract her thoughts from the image of the two of them that kept coming to mind.

But then. . .she wasn't used to thinking about lunches with men. Or thinking about men in any kind of romantic way at all. For years, the only males she'd longed for in her day-to-day thoughts included Mr. Clean and a grocery deliveryman. Both of whom she'd hoped would come along and make her everyday life a bit easier.

But hard as she tried, she couldn't conjure up those imaginary characters now. Those mundane daydreams had disappeared into thin air like the fuzzy white flowers of a dandelion blowing in the wind. Leaving only more thoughts. . .more daydreams of Mac. And her. Together. Sitting under an umbrella at an open air café in— hmm. . .maybe Paris? Rome? She tilted her head trying to envision it all. But she'd never been abroad. And even for a daydream those places felt far too extravagant.

But what about, say, Hilton Head Island?

Sliding her elbows on the table, she cupped her chin in her

hands, gazing out at the passersby ambling up and down the sidewalk. Letting her mind drift for a change.

Yes. . .she really could see the two of them in South Carolina. She really could imagine them in Harbortown, to be exact. With Sammy safely stowed at his grandparents' house in Loveland. Or no. Better yet, Sammy would be in Hilton Head with them, and her mom and dad would be there—one big, happy family. They'd all stay together in a four-bedroom condo. A really plush one with three bathrooms and a terrace off her bedroom. Why not, since she was daydreaming anyway?

After a day at the beach, her parents wouldn't have any qualms about watching Sammy while she and Mac slipped out for a few hours in the evening.

The two of them would head over to South Beach, walking through the shops there, holding hands—just like he'd held her hand the night before. Not really buying anything—oh, well, except for maybe a Hilton Head T-shirt for Sammy. And then, they'd stop for ice cream on the pier at an outdoor café. They'd sit and talk some. Laugh a lot. People-watch a little. Marvel at God's exquisite sunset. . .and hold hands some more.

Mac's nose would be pink from the sun and his hair even blonder than when they'd left Loveland after just a couple of days on the beach. He'd be wearing a yellow T-shirt that would bring out the amber in his brown eyes and accentuate his tan. So relaxed in his khaki shorts and Reefs, his long muscular legs would be stretched out languidly and crossed at the ankles.

She'd have on a sundress of course. Or no, she'd be in her white ruffled skirt and a tank top actually. A fun and feminine summery outfit very similar to the one the girl strolling down the sidewalk toward her was wearing. And she'd throw on some breezy, brightly-colored bangle bracelets like the girl wore. Which looked very cute along with the straw hat over the girl's very red hair, and—

"Janey?" Megan blinked. She sat up straight.

Her incognito friend stopped dead in her high cork-heeled sandals, sliding dark, trendy Ray-Bans down her nose.

"Megan?" Janey leaned over the bistro's wrought iron railing. "How did you know it was me?"

"Um, well, because you look like you."

"I do?"

"Only with red hair."

"It's a wig," Janey entrusted.

"So I gathered," Megan answered, not letting her friend know it was the second time she'd laid eyes on her that way.

"Do you think most people would know who I am?" Janey leaned over even more, lowering her voice. A lock of red synthetic hair fell to her cheek. "I mean, with the wig on?"

Megan could tell her friend wasn't searching for the most honest answer, so she tap-danced around the question. "I've known you for forever, Janey. So, of course, *I'd* know you no matter what color hair you have."

Standing up straight, Janey appeared to be considering her answer. "Yeah, I guess that's true," she finally said. "You're probably right."

Removing her sunglasses, Janey dangled them from the rounded neck of her tank top. It pained Megan to see the frustration clouding Janey's usually bright eyes. "Is everything okay, Janey?"

"Okay? You mean as in, why am I wearing a wig?"

"Well, I mean. . ." Megan shrugged. "Your hair's been looking so good lately with all those pretty highlights you've been getting. Are you experimenting with a new look or something?"

Janey nodded. "Yeah, I just thought. . ." At first her friend's body stilled as if she were ready to deliver a sound explanation. But then her face crumpled and her voice faltered as she blurted out the truth. "Oh Megan, I can't lie to you. I can't. And it's so good I bumped into you because I need to tell someone. I do. And who else would I tell, but you?"

Breaking through the bistro's metal enclosure, Janey apparently was so wrapped up in her own issues that she didn't even notice the gate closing with a crash behind her. But several diners did. They looked up from their plates at the intrusive noise as she plopped down into a matching rattan chair across from Megan. "I can't keep carrying this secret around inside of me, Megan. It's starting to drive me crazy!"

"You have a secret?" Megan pushed the glass of ice water meant for Mac across the table suddenly aware—and feeling slightly guilty—that her friend wasn't the only one who hadn't been dis-3 closing things lately. Certainly she hadn't been very forthcoming with Janey about all the feelings she'd been having for Mac recently.

Janey's bracelets clanked on her arm as she took her time sipping at the water. "Yes. Yes, I do." She nodded, like she was unable to stall any longer. "It's—I've—well. . ." Janey's shoulders slouched. She let out a long, defeated-sounding breath. "Megan, the truth is, I've been spying."

"Spying?" Megan could feel her brows knit together instantly as if someone had pulled a loose string, tugging them tight. "Seriously? On who?"

Nibbling her lip, Janey answered meekly, "On Sean. Sean Shaffer."

"Ohhhh." Megan's eyes widened involuntarily as Janey's confession sank in. "Ohhhh," she repeated.

"No, not 'ohhhh' like that. It's not like some guy thing." Janey shook her head, her fake wavy red locks swaying. "I'm not really spying on him. On Sean. It's more like I'm spying on his dough-nut shop, the Emporium."

"Seriously?"

Eyes downcast, Janey nodded, looking dismayed. "And do you know I actually saw some of my regular customers there? At least I thought they were *my* regular customers—*not Sean's*. They come to Sweet Sensations for lattes and cheese Danish, and then they turn around the next day and go see him for black coffee and jelly doughnuts. I mean, it might sound silly to you—but it kind of hurt to see that." A pouting frown pulled at her lips. "You know what I mean?"

"It doesn't sound silly," Megan replied. Whether she wanted to admit it or not, she'd probably feel the same way if some of the families she'd come to know over the years decided to go to another clinic for their therapy treatments.

"I just don't know what I'm doing wrong."

"Doing wrong?" She leaned over the table, closer to her friend. "Janey, you're not doing anything wrong. You have great product." She tried to assure her. "It's just sometimes people get a taste for something a little less than perfect, I guess."

"A *little* less? You're saying Sean's cookie-cutter right-next-to-the-gas-station doughnuts are just a *little less* tasty than mine?"

Janey's eyes narrowed like darts of accusation, penetrating Megan's resolve. Feeling like she was suddenly on the witness stand, she fumbled to come up with the perfect answer. "No, no, of course not. I'm sure we're talking *a lot* less. Way less. I'm just saying—well, like, do you always want steak? No. Sometimes you just want a regular hamburger, you know?"

"I'm a vegan, remember?"

"Well, you know what I mean, Janey. The same thinking applies to your situation."

Megan tried to hide the frustration in her voice. But attempting to comfort her friend was never an easy task, and Janey's doughnut problem had certainly spoiled the wistful daydreams she'd been enjoying about Mac.

"There's always going to be competition. That's just the way it is," she said, hoping to end the conversation, knowing Mac would be there—in real life and not just a daydream—any minute.

"I know—I know. . ." And instead of the usual spark Janey got at the mention of the word *competition*, she uncharacteristically sank deeper into the chair, perplexing Megan even more. Surely Janey wouldn't stay and sulk when Mac arrived, would she?

"So how's the contest been going?" Megan tried to steer Janey's thoughts toward something concrete, and hopefully, positive. "Did you get some interest last weekend? I saw a lot of people coming and going from your place."

"I did get a lot of the Amazing Race traffic." Janey nodded. "I hope you and Allie got my e-mail thanking you guys for handing out the postcards. The cookie jar is almost filled to the top with entries."

"Well see, that's a good thing, isn't it? And proof that a whole slew of your customers have a Sweet Sensations favorite." She paused, still thinking about Janey's trips to the Donut Emporium. She hoped Sean hadn't recognized her. It'd be so embarrassing if he had. "Did Sean know it was you?"

"Sean?" Janey shook her head. "Oh no."

"Really?"

"No, not at all."

"How do you know?"

"I just know."

"But how?"

"Because if you must know, he flirts with me when I visit his shop. Would he ever do that if he knew it was me?"

Megan wasn't sure how to answer that question, so she ducked it with an indirect response. "Well, regardless, he must think you're pretty if he's flirting with you. Right? How's Sean looking these days, by the way? Still have that baby face of his?"

Before Janey could answer, the waiter was back at the table again.

"So what do you think? You ladies ready to order?" he asked, pad in hand once more.

"Oh," Megan spoke up. "This isn't my friend."

Janey blinked at her, baffled. Megan noticed Jason react the same way. "Well, I mean she's my friend. But she was just passing by. She's not the friend I was expecting," she explained.

"Oh yeah, That's right. You said your friend is a 'he.'" Jason slid the pad into his pocket again. "No problem. I'll be back."

"He?" Janey quizzed as Jason walked away.

"Mac."

"Ohhhh," Janey replied in the same singsong way Megan had a few minutes earlier. "A sweet little lunch at Tano's with Mac. Nice!"

"Actually, we're just reviewing some things for the Sports Day event."

"Uh-huh. You really need to catch me up on things, Meg."

"I have been keeping everyone up-to-date. I sent out an e-mail just last week, talking about Volunteer Day and how we need volunteers to head out to Mac's farm to do some preliminary set-up work. But it'll be on a Saturday, so I figure you'll be working, right?"

"No, I mean you need to catch me up about you and Mac."

"Well, we—he's—I'm—" Megan stammered, not sure where to begin and what it would all mean in the end anyway.

"Hold that thought," Janey teased, and then laughed when Megan couldn't manage to put together a sentence. "I can't wait to hear everything. But I'll give you some time to gather your thoughts. I have to get back to the bakery anyway. Lucy loves baking but she's not fond of waiting on customers, and I've been gone longer than I said I'd be."

Her bracelets jangled again as she took one last sip of water. "I can't believe the dance is coming up so quickly!" Standing up, she slung her cloth tote over her shoulder. "Megan. . ." She paused, removing her sunglasses from her tank top then settling them into her mane of fake hair. "Can I ask you a favor?"

"Sure. But I hope it doesn't involve borrowing dressy shoes for the dance. Most of mine are dated. I don't even know which shoes *I'm* wearing yet."

"Oh no, not that. Your shoes wouldn't fit my big old feet anyway." Janey waved a hand at her. "No. . .I just—I'm wondering if you'll stop in."

"To Sweet Sensations? Of course I will. I always do, don't I?"

"No, I mean to Sean's. To the Donut Emporium. Will you stop in and do a little looking around?"

"You want me to spy?" Megan could barely believe her ears. "And wear a red wig like you?"

"Of course not. You don't have the coloring for a redhead at all." Janey looked at her blithely. "No, just be yourself. Stop in and check out things for me. I need your perspective. Will you? Please?"

Megan moaned. "Really, Janey?"

She loved her friend, but loathed the thought of getting involved in her spying drama. Actually she tried to refrain from getting involved in most of her dramas. Though the two of them had been close for forever, listening to Janey was as far as she usually liked to go.

"You know Sammy loves jelly doughnuts. You know I won't get out of there without buying him one or two." Megan tried to discourage the idea, playing on Janey's typically competitive nature.

"As long as Sammy doesn't start liking Sean's better than mine, it's okay. I can deal with it." Her friend's voice softened. "Please, Megan," she begged, her brow furrowing. "It would really help me to know what you think."

"I already told you what I think, Janey. Remember, my steak and hamburger theory?"

She tried not to look directly into Janey's pathetic, pleading eyes. Without a doubt, her friend was going to the extreme to come up with the poorest, most pitiful expression ever. But even if Megan didn't get all the way sucked in by Janey's pouting face, there was no escaping her incessant, imploring voice.

"Puh-lease? Pretty, pretty please?" she repeated.

"Oh Janey!" Megan sighed at her relentless friend. "Okay." She finally gave in. "Okay. I'll *try* to get over to the Donut Emporium."

"Promise you'll try hard?"

Megan couldn't make herself say yes. But she couldn't force herself to say no either. Not with the way a glimmer of light began to shine in her friend's eyes. Not with the way a smile tugged at Janey's lips for the first time since she'd sat down. Instead, Megan simply smiled back and gave her red-haired friend a little wave good-bye.

"Yeah, sounds good." Mac stood on the downtown sidewalk, holding his cell phone to his ear, trying to wind up his weekly chat with his agent. "Of course you'll be the first to know what Dr. Kline says, Hal. But my appointment's not for weeks."

"I know I'll be first." Hal half-chuckled and half-harrumphed in Mac's ear. "Because I'll be calling you the minute you leave Kline's office," he promised. "And be careful with your elbow in the meantime, will you? None of that heave-ho, manly manual labor stuff you can't seem to get enough of on that farm of yours."

"No worry." Mac glanced up at the We Do! Wedding Planners sign. "Not tackling anything too manly and physical today, Hal," he said, as they exchanged good-byes and he opened the door of the shop.

Besides the sound of soft chimes that greeted him, the first thing Mac noticed about the inside of We Do! was that it was very, very pink. The direct antithesis of any stadium locker room he'd ever been in.

The second thing he noticed is that all of the women there grew quiet the moment he walked through the door.

Lord, I need Your help here, he prayed as he stepped farther into the establishment, which somehow instantly reminded him of colored Easter eggs and Pepto-Bismol all rolled into one.

He hadn't thought it through at all when he'd decided to pay a visit to Megan's mom at her place of business. From the overall reaction he was getting, it was obvious males didn't typically drop into the shop. Except for maybe a UPS man now and then. Or, other than that, maybe when an intended groom accompanied his bride-to-be for a scheduled appointment. But beyond that, he could pretty much tell a male's presence was a rarity.

Luckily though, Laura O'Donnell seemed to be the type who could smooth over any uneasy situation easily. Handing her client a photo album to browse through, she excused herself and came sailing over to him.

"Mac!" She glided around the reception desk, a warm smile gracing her face. "It's good to see you." She laid a welcoming hand on his arm and, leaning in closer, lowered her voice. "Please excuse all the gaping mouths. It's not often a baseball superstar comes wandering into We Do!"

Already feeling awkward enough, he brushed off the compliment. "Or any man, I imagine. Sorry I just showed up like this. I should've called first. Or made an appointment." He scratched his forehead, chiding himself. "I was just going to meet up with Megan over at the bistro and thought I'd stop in here on my way to ask you a question. But I can always give you a call later. . .when you're not busy."

"Oh no, it's fine. I can take a moment. Ask away." She leaned against the reception desk, crossing her hands, as if she had all the time in the world.

"Well, I've been wondering. Can Sammy keep a secret?"

"Sammy? Hmm. . ." Laura's face contorted. "Well, he certainly kept a secret about his pappy's new fishing rod at Christmas last year. For several months actually. So, I think I'd have to say yes."

"And how about you?" Mac tilted his head. "Can you keep a secret?"

She laughed, her eyes twinkling. "Most of the time." She nodded. "It depends on what it is, I suppose. Care to tell me what you have in mind?"

"Well, I know Sammy is in day care this summer while you and Megan are working. But I also know in the evenings, if Megan has to go out, she depends on you and Kurt to watch Sammy."

"Reluctantly she relies on us, yes. But only because Mrs. Biddle, her regular sitter, still isn't up to watching him."

"I've heard." Mac nodded. "Well, what I was thinking is that Sammy really liked the bowling ramp I built for him. I'm in the process of making a few more in case it's popular with the kids on event day. Right now, one of the ramps is sitting over at a warehouse that Ted's brother owns. Anyway"—he shifted on his feet—"I thought it'd be fun for Sammy to get some practice on it. Then on Event Day he could surprise his mom with how good he's gotten."

"Oh Mac!" Laura clapped her hands together. "That sounds like fun—and like a secret I can keep." She laughed. "So you'd pick up Sammy at our house when we're watching him and take him over to practice?"

"Well yeah, on nights when I know I have enough time to get back and forth without bumping into Megan."

"I love it! Count me in!" Her eyes sparkled with gratitude. "Thanks so much for thinking of this, Mac. Sammy will be so excited. Oh, and Kurt may even want to join you and Sammy sometime."

"The more the merrier," he said, realizing how much he meant it. After all, having Kurt's help with Sammy would make things go quicker and smoother. Plus, he had enjoyed talking to Megan's dad the night of the barbecue. They'd talked about a lot of the baseball greats and even baseball history. Few men knew the sport like Kurt did.

"Let me give you my cell number." Laura was already looking for her readers. Finding them, she slid a business card from a holder on top of her desk and took her time writing out the seven-digit phone number. "Do you know if you all have sold many tickets for the fundraising formal?"

Mac blinked at the change of subject. "Uh, I think last I heard Wendy said we're about sold out."

"That's wonderful!" Laura turned from the desk, holding the card in her hand. "It should be a great night. I can't believe it's coming up so soon."

"Yeah, you're right. The summer is flying by." Mac held his hand out for the card. But Laura acted as if she didn't see his hand there at all. Instead, she smiled, tilting her head thoughtfully.

"It is, isn't it? And such a nice thing to do this summer. The dance. Are you asking a certain someone?" She finally relinquished the card to him.

"Asking?" He took out his wallet and slipped the business card inside. "Uh, I assumed Megan and I would be going together."

Laura didn't say anything. But she didn't have to. The way she peered over her glasses at him, eyebrows arched, said it all. He'd have to be blind not to pick up on what she was getting at.

"But I shouldn't assume that," he said slowly. "I should ask her at lunch today."

Her slight smile instantly blossomed into something even more special and genuine. "The bistro has great food, don't they? You two will enjoy your lunch, I'm sure," she said, ushering him to the front door. "Oh, and Mac—about Sammy. I'll talk to him. Mum's the word." She put a finger to her lips.

Mac had to grin to himself as he left the wedding planners' shop, suddenly aware of what had just transpired. Megan's mom must be really good at her job with soon-to-be-married couples. Easygoing, but somehow direct, she undoubtedly had an uncanny ability for organizing people and guiding them toward the right decisions without them really realizing it—until afterward.

As the noon traffic stopped for him at the crosswalk, Mac caught a glimpse of Megan already seated at the bistro. Even in her red work polo, she still looked so pretty, a sight that could make his heart hum. But that wasn't the only thing that added an extra lift to his step as he crossed the street. It was the realization that in Laura O'Donnell's own subtle yet effective way she'd just given him her stamp of approval.

Well, that's one lady in the O'Donnell family, he thought. Although from the way things had been going with Megan, he got the sense her feelings for him were growing, too. At least it certainly seemed that way.

But I can sure use Your help to fan the flame, Lord! He appealed to his Father in heaven just as Megan spotted him. And with a smile he'd grown to love, she waved.

Chapter 14

Megan wasn't quite sure what made Mac ask her to the dance when they'd had lunch at the bistro over a week ago. All she knew is that she was glad he did. Or at least she *had been* glad, until she started getting ready for the special night. That's when reality struck and the idea of being on a date with Mac—a formal date—made her so nervous that her hands began to shake.

Which didn't help a bit as she attempted to put on her makeup. And didn't help either when she was trying to do such a meticulous job of it, especially when applying makeup wasn't something she felt very adept at to begin with.

Oh, just calm down. She tried to comfort the reflection staring back at her in the bathroom mirror. *Calm. Down. He's just a man.* She brushed eye shadow on her lids. *Just a—*

Okay, maybe Mac's maleness wasn't such a good topic to dwell on, she decided as her stomach began to flutter. Better, instead, not to think about him at all. *Best to think about the details of the dance,* she thought as she fished through her makeup bag for her mascara.

But drawing the mascara wand from its tube, she swiped at her lashes realizing that there wasn't much to think about in that department at all. Once she had helped Wendy pick out the spot for their dance at the Oasis Golf Club and Conference Center, Wendy's four-person fundraising committee had taken care of most of the details for the evening. So no issues there to contemplate.

Sammy. She forced her thoughts to switch gears. She could always think about him, she thought, putting the mascara back in its place and digging out her berry blush.

But, actually, everything was also fine in the Sammy department. Lucinda, a cousin of Allie's husband, happened to be in town and offered to watch Sammy along with Carrie and Justin for the night. She was someone Megan had met before, and she had no reservations about leaving Sammy with her, so. . .

That left her mind drifting back to Mac again, and—

Oh, could it be any hotter in here?

Cheeks reddening under the rosy blush, she hurriedly applied the finishing touch, covering her lips with a soft, creamy cherry color. She couldn't wait to get out from under the globe bulbs burning bright above the bathroom mirror.

Thankful to exit the master bath, she stood in her bedroom fanning herself and glimpsed at the clock on her nightstand.

Eight minutes! Eight minutes until Mac was due to arrive! In an instant her heart was racing in her chest, partly because she needed to hurry. And partly because that meant she'd be seeing him soon.

Or is it "mostly" because I'll be seeing him soon?

The thought teased at her as she swooped up her gown from

the bed and then made herself slow down to delicately step into it. Thankfully, the red satin material felt smooth and cool, non-clingy against her skin. Zipping it up the side, she plucked her new silver strappy heels from their box and slipped them on. Then she stopped for a moment to have a look at herself in the mirror, and decided— not bad.

Not bad at all.

The jeweled silver ring on her one-shoulder gown worked perfectly with her shoes, and she swayed her hips just slightly, loving how gracefully the skirt of the dress fell from the four-inch wide inset waistband that hugged her snuggly.

Surprisingly, she'd done her hair herself and it actually turned out looking good. Not wanting to hide the gown's one-shoulder feature by wearing her hair down, she'd gone online and taught herself how to make an elegant ponytail—far unlike the haphazard way she usually pulled back her hair into a rubber band without even consulting a mirror.

I think I'll be using this new technique again. She turned her head left to right and left again, checking out the result, still shocked she'd managed such a feat.

She'd also had another nice surprise—well, actually three of them—when she was trying to figure out accessories for the evening. Hoping not to have to spend more money, she'd gotten her jewelry box out of the closet and dusted it off. Inside, she rediscovered a diamond bracelet and matching earrings that her parents had given her when she graduated college. Neither had been worn for forever—or at least long before Sammy had been born.

Yes, overall, assessing herself from head to toe, she'd done a good job of pulling her look together for the eventful evening. Smiling at her reflection, she was feeling pleased and confident. That is, until she heard the unmistakable rumble of Mac's Corvette pulling into her driveway.

Her breath hitched as she tiptoed over to her bedroom window quietly, as if he could hear her heels creeping over the carpet. Barely pulling the dusty-blue curtain aside, she peeked out surreptitiously and watched as Mac's tall muscular body unfolded from the small car, making the vehicle almost appear toy-like. So handsome-looking in his black tux, he paused, as if he'd remembered something. Then he reached back into the car, bringing out a bouquet of ivory roses. It made her smile to see the way he stopped and straightened his jacket and tie with his free hand before he proceeded up her walk and rang the doorbell.

Even though she knew it was coming, the sound still gave her a jolt, causing her fragile heart to beat in unison with the click of her heels as she crossed the hardwood entryway to open the door.

"Hey." She smiled up at him. "Come on in. It's still hot out there, isn't it?"

"Sure is." He ducked in the door, and right away his slow grin melted her the same way the evening sun caused beads of perspiration to dot his hairline. "These, um, these are for you."

"You didn't have to bring me flowers, Mac. But thank you." She sniffed at the flowers, taking the bouquet he held out to her. "They're—"

"Beautiful," he said.

But the way his eyes shone as he gazed at her, she knew he wasn't talking about the flowers at all.

As the band played another familiar-sounding song, and she and Mac slow danced across the ballroom floor, Megan couldn't help but think back to a Fourth of July when she was ten years old. That particular summer her dad had bought packages of sparklers and handed them out to every kid on their street.

She'd always thought the houses up and down their block were somewhat special, and she never tired of looking down the lane at the eclectic group of homes. Some residences had sprawling yards surrounding their low, lengthy ranches. Other lots featured Victorian two-stories or cottage-style homes with postage-stamp-sized yards and wildflower gardens on each side of the house.

But that night—with kids waving dozens of wands of crackling yellow and gold. . .with fireflies twinkling across all the lawns. . . and bursts of color shooting into the sky—their street transcended its everyday kind of special. Instead, it was transformed into an enchanting, magical kingdom. A place right out of a fairy tale.

And being in the ballroom at the Oasis again, Megan couldn't help but feel that same way again.

When she'd made the trip with Wendy to check out the center for their fundraiser dance months earlier, the room had appeared fine for their purposes. Clean. Doable.

But now, glancing around its perimeters, her eyes caught every glimmer and sparkle here, there, and everywhere. The shimmering light from the gold wall sconces. The twinkling crystal centerpiece vases filled with orchids. The glittery gowns that draped the women as they glided across the dance floor. Even the sheen from the men's ebony tuxedos seemed to capture the light and shine.

All of it blended, illuminated so breathtakingly, transforming the ordinary rectangular room into a magical setting.

Or maybe. . .it wasn't any of that at all.

Maybe. . .it was just the feel of dancing in Mac's arms that had her thinking that way.

He felt so tall and solid against her, yet he moved so easily. Effortlessly, actually, he glided them across the dance floor until finally she had to look up at him. She had to look up to make sure he was real, and not some Prince Charming. To make sure the moment was real because she wasn't used to that kind of fairy tale feeling in her life.

"What is it?" He gazed down at her, his smile as smooth as the lines of the tux that fit every part of his body. . .perfectly. So perfectly across his broad shoulders. And down the strong arms that held her close.

"What's what?"

"What are you thinking?"

"How can you tell I'm thinking?"

"Oh, I can just tell."

Probably because she wasn't jabbering a mile a minute, she figured, like she had been during their first dances. But she hadn't been able to help herself. She'd been nervous. Being so close to Mac sent tremors through her that were both delightful and disturbing at the same time. It didn't matter that she was a mom of an almost seven-year-old and that she was too old to be acting semi-giddy, she had been anyway. Unlike her usually reserved self.

"I'm thinking about the Fourth of July."

"Ah. Fireworks, huh?" His brows arched with interest. "I like how you're thinking. You are feeling fireworks? Yes?" he teased, adding the last part with a slight Italian or French or whatever kind of accent. A very bad, but funny, imitation of an accent.

She laughed. "Not those kinds of fireworks. That's not what I was thinking about."

"No?" He looked disappointed, or if he wasn't, he was doing a fine job of acting that way. Better than his accent. "Really?"

"Well, yes. But, no."

He chuckled. "Ah well, a guy has to try, doesn't he?"

But no, Mac didn't have to. Not really.

Because you're gorgeous and every woman in this room can't keep their eyes off you, she thought, but before she could come up with some cute response, she felt the pressure of his hand on the small of her back. Felt the way it intensified as he added, "And I'll keep trying."

His words, like his touch, warmed her, and as he held her closer, she finally laid her head on his shoulder and let her eyes close. Let his strength and grace lead her. Let a wave of calm wash over her. Let go. So rare and trusting. Aware of nothing but the feel of her cheek against his solidness. Wishing she could stay that way forever, and she did, until her eyes fluttered open at the sound of his voice.

"Hmm. . .that's not good."

"What's not good?" She looked up from his shoulder.

"Wendy's waving to us." He paused. "But. . .I have an idea. I'll act like I didn't see her." He suddenly swung their bodies halfway around, sped up their tempo, leading them away from where Wendy was standing by the tables, beckoning them.

"Mac!" She giggled, trying to catch her breath from that and their dart across the dance floor. "We can't just ignore her. It's probably time for us to introduce the volunteers and everyone."

"Aw. . .can we not be the co-chairs for one night?"

She laughed at the pouting little boy face he pulled. "Hey, I was going to chair the event all on my own, remember? But then you had to push your way in and save the day." She needled him with a smile.

"Well, of course I had to. But you're glad I did, aren't you?" His lips suddenly went from a frown to the lopsided Hattaway grin no woman could resist.

But, unfortunately, she had to try to at the moment. Because now Wendy was waving her arms, not just her hand, attempting to get their attention. "We really need to go see what Wendy needs."

"I know," he grumbled. "But we need to finish this dance, Ms. O'Donnell."

"That's not a problem, Mr. Hattaway."

That promise made, he released her from his arms and took her hand, leading them off the dance floor.

Not a problem at all, her heart sang out.

Truly, if anyone would've told her six years ago, even six months ago, that she'd be dancing in MacNeill Hattaway's arms all night long, laughing with him, teasing him, not wanting to be anywhere else except with him, she wouldn't have believed it.

And yet there she was. There he was. It was happening.

Oh Lord, is this really You doing all of this? Is it? Because it seems too unreal to be true.

Oh, how she wanted to trust in a plan for her heart designed by God. How she wanted to believe there was something between her and Mac—something more than one magical, fairy tale night.

And just as much as all that, she wanted to trust in love again. Because in that instant she realized that was exactly what she was feeling.

Mac turned left out of the Oasis parking lot, veering the 'Vette toward Megan's place, trying to remember the last time he'd driven a date home and had to go through the whole say-goodnight-on-the-doorstep sort of thing. In high school maybe? After some big dance perhaps?

Of course, he also couldn't recall the last time he didn't want an evening to end.

It wasn't lost on him how right and good it felt being with Megan. And how different his feelings were for her from any woman he'd ever known. In his former life she would've been the girl he shied away from. Big baseball star that he was, he still wouldn't have felt "worthy enough" to be with her. Not someone like Megan whose values were so on target. Someone who was a loving mom, a dedicated physical therapist, and also a member of the community everyone admired. A woman who he felt he might taint with just the touch of his hand.

But things had changed now. He had changed.

"I will repay you the years the locust hath eaten." The verse echoed in his head.

When he'd first been hospitalized after his accident, a nurse named Chantel had prayed over his life as he lay there in those first hours wishing for an end. Wishing he were dead.

No doubt, the angel of a woman had heard about his off-the-field antics as most people had. But instead of judging him, she prayed to God for him, repeating that verse from the book of Joel, petitioning for restoration of his body and soul, over and over again.

At the time, he didn't quite know or care what the words she mumbled over him about locusts and all that meant. But little by little, as he started healing, and mostly as he began to seek God on his own, he began to realize more and more how Chantel's prayers had been answered. And how his prayers were being answered, too.

The hollowness he'd felt for so long—the shame that always burdened him—those feelings all began to fall away. And in their place was God's love and grace, filling an emptiness in him—a void—he'd attempted to satiate in so many other ways for so many years.

And then, he met Megan. And in his heart he couldn't help but sense that Megan was a part of his renewal as well. Another gift that God had given to bring him to fullness and victory over his past.

He was thinking about it, mulling it over on the way to her place. So much so that he barely knew how they got there, and was almost surprised when the 'Vette puttered up her driveway nearly on its own.

Helping Megan out of the car, together they took the short yet long walk up to the door. *Her* front door. Lord, help him! After an evening of being the suave date in a tux, he suddenly felt unprepared and self-conscious about what to do or say next.

He scratched at his chin. "I, uh. . .right this minute I feel like such a—"

"I know. A schoolgirl." She finished the sentence for him.

He chuckled at her sincerity. "I was going to say a rookie." He smiled. "Pretty much the same thing though. You, too, huh?"

"Uh-huh."

His palms suddenly felt sweaty. Like bases were loaded, and it was a full count. Only before, he could rub his clammy palms on the legs of his baseball uniform. Now he rubbed them together in mid-air.

"Awkward," he admitted, his MacNeill Hattaway womanizer persona nowhere to be found.

"Somewhat." She nodded.

"Yeah, well. . ."

He gazed into her eyes then silence fell between them. The glow from the porch light lit her face, and the way she looked back at him had his heart thumping in his ears, blocking out the sounds of the summer evening he'd been aware of just moments before, the crickets chirping in her yard, barking dogs echoing down the block, cars whooshing down the street with open windows leaving trails of voices, laughter in the air.

For him, there was only her. . .and of course, his desire—wanting to kiss her so much. But he bit down on the inside of his mouth instead, that pain not even close in comparison to the way he ached from wanting to kiss her. But he'd promised himself he'd hold back. Promised.

A June bug flitted from the porch light, buzzed around his face, seemingly trying to remind him of the same thing. He whisked it away, and with that wave of his hand the moment he and Megan shared seemed to fly off to somewhere, too.

"So. . ." He finally spoke. "It was a really good dance."

Megan glanced down at her silver shoes, just barely sticking out from her red dress. She sighed. At least he thought he heard her sigh. Because the moment between them had passed?

"Really good." She looked up at him, nodding agreeably. "People were very generous with their bidding and donations. Wendy and her group make a great team."

"Yeah. We make a pretty good team, too. You think? You and me."

"Yes. We do, Mac." She blinked, new warmth entering her eyes. "We do."

"Megan, I—"

You were going to take things slow, remember? A voice reminded him, once again cutting him off from sharing what was on his heart.

"Yeah?" She sounded expectant.

"I, uh. . ." He practically winced out loud, trying so hard to tamp down the urges he was feeling, wanting to reach out and take her in his arms. Instead, he took her hand, but afraid he'd pull her into his arms, he held it loosely. "Can I give you a call tomorrow?"

"A call?" For a moment she looked like she couldn't decide. The thought that she might say no caused his jaw to tighten. "Sure," she finally said, much to his relief. "Sure."

She slid her hand from his, crossing her arms over her chest.

"Okay. I'll do that," he promised, backing down the porch steps onto the sidewalk. "I'll call you," he said, but she'd already turned and had taken her key from her little silver purse and was starting to unlock her front door.

Another few seconds and she'd be gone. Gone from him, except for in his thoughts where he was sure she'd be all night, and he'd be kicking himself for letting the evening end without her in his arms. And for not spending every last minute he possibly could with her.

Halting in his tracks, he spun around. "Megan?"

She turned, tilted her head.

"I was just thinking."

"Yeah?"

"You owe me the rest of that dance."

"What?"

"We didn't finish our dance. We got interrupted, remember?"

Finally. . .a smile. The smile he'd become accustomed to. The smile that made him feel lighter. That made him smile, too.

"I do remember. But—"

Before she could say anything more, he strode across the walk to the bottom of the porch steps. He held out his arm, reaching up to the top step where she stood.

"You want to dance here? Now?" She giggled like she thought he was crazy. But he could tell she was pleased.

"Is that okay?"

She didn't answer. Instead she took his hand, descending the two steps as poised and graceful as a princess descending a winding staircase leading to some mansion's grand ballroom.

Only she wasn't icy or pretentious or aloof as some royalty might be. No, God—King of kings—had made His Princess Megan warm and caring, and had crowned her with a beauty that was far more than skin-deep. And then, He'd done another thing, Mac realized as Megan stood before him and he pulled her close. God had also made her a woman—the woman—who fit perfectly into his arms. Like no other woman ever had in his life.

Holding her in the circle of his embrace, he started to take a step to dance, but his feet would barely move. Instead, immersed in the moonlight, they swayed to the melody of their beating hearts, his yearning for her growing with each moment. Until finally, he couldn't stand it any longer.

Lifting her chin with his hand, he brushed a gentle kiss across her forehead. A feathery kiss to her cheek. But, of course, it wasn't enough for him. And not for Megan either it seemed. He felt her yield to his touch, and so he claimed her lips. At last. Pressing his lips against hers, he covered her mouth and devoured the softness there. And felt a rush of pleasure when, thankfully, she returned his affection with a passion that matched his own.

Chapter 15

Megan placed the gas nozzle back into its slot and tightened the gas cap before glancing at her watch.

Nine forty-five. Still plenty of time before her eleven o'clock patient. She'd thought Sammy's dentist appointment would run much longer than it did so she hadn't scheduled her first patient until later in the morning. But, in a way that was good. At least now she'd have some free time to spend with him before running him to day care on Route 22 and 3 before her workday started.

Scooting back into her SUV, she turned around to Sammy, who was staring out the rear window. "Hey kiddo, what do you think about a jelly doughnut this morning?"

The mention of his favorite sweet pulled her son's attention from the shiny silver and red motorcycle in the gas line opposite them.

"You kidding, Maw-mee?" Surprise widened his sweet eyes.

"No, I'm not kidding." He always had a way of making her laugh. "Is that a yes?"

"Yeh! Buh don tell Doctor Bell. He get mad."

No doubt, it was slightly crazy to be indulging in a serious amount of sugar only minutes after Dr. Bell's hygienist had finished cleaning Sammy's teeth. But Sammy's report had been good—great actually. No cavities and double stars for pink gums and proper brushing, something Megan helped him with each morning and night.

And besides, with the Donut Emporium right there at the gas station, she was thinking she could kill two proverbial birds with one stone. She could also visit Sean's place for Janey and tell her friend all about it when they met up for dinner later that evening.

"Don't worry, Sammy. I won't tell," Megan promised, as she started the engine and drove all of twenty feet or so across the parking lot that the station and doughnut shop shared. "And we'll brush your teeth with the new brush Dr. Bell gave you once we get to day care, okay?"

"Yeah, brush 'em," he agreed.

Luckily there was a handicapped space open, giving Megan plenty of room to get Sammy out of the car and into his wheelchair. The space happened to be closer to the gas station than the Emporium, but that was okay. The sun felt pleasant as she pushed Sammy's chair along the sidewalk the two businesses shared—not unbearable the way it'd be feeling in another couple of hours. Its early morning glint bounced off the cars and the storefronts where she happened to catch her reflection in one of the windows.

At first it startled her to see herself. Sometimes lately she didn't recognize the woman smiling back at her. In the past, she'd made a point of smiling, always wanting to put on a happy front. She didn't want anyone to think for a minute that she didn't feel blessed to have Sammy as her son—that she didn't feel honored to be his mom.

But truth was, the incredible fatigue that came from caring for a special-needs child could really zap the life out of her. Often that smile was over-the-top and forced.

Yet since Mac. . .

She felt her cheeks heating thinking about their first kiss. And how it felt to dance in his arms. Thinking about the way he often looked at her. How his smile would go all the way to his eyes, which made her smile more. Yes. . .sometimes she'd catch a glimpse of herself in a mirror or window, and it would absolutely surprise her. She looked so happy. Genuinely happy. Scarily so! Because of Mac, things in life were so much lighter for a change.

"Here we are, Sams. Our first visit to the Donut Emporium." She started to grab for the door, planning to prop it open with her foot while she wheeled Sammy inside. But the door opened on its own accord.

Well, that wasn't exactly true.

"Welcome. My name is Rachel." A nine-or-so-year-old blond wearing a beaded headband, jean shorts, and a lavender T-shirt with sparkles, held the door for them. "We're glad you're here."

Hmm. A four-foot greeter! Now that's something Janey doesn't have at Sweet Sensations.

"Thank you, Rachel." Megan grinned, pushing the chair over the threshold into the bakery where a heavy smell of sugar hung in the air like a cloud of fog.

"We glad we here, too!" Sammy said a bit loudly, causing

several customers hovered around the bakery case to turn to look at him. But if Rachel noticed, she wasn't embarrassed. Instead, she nodded at Megan's hands clenched around the wheelchair's handles.

"I can do that for you."

"Yeah?"

Rachel nodded.

Megan sized her up quickly and decided she looked strong and capable enough. She leaned down to get her son's permission. "Sammy? Would you like Rachel to push your chair?"

Sammy nodded vigorously, as she thought he would, his eyes twinkling, already entranced by his new acquaintance.

After getting in line, it was only a matter of minutes until the customers in front of them had cleared out. And there was Sean Shaffer staring at her from behind the glass case.

She really didn't know how Janey could act so nonchalant about seeing Sean again. He was even better looking than he had been in high school. His baby face had matured into easy-on-the-eyes, all-grown-up, good-looking features. It was a warm and friendly face, and his body wasn't so bad either. He was average height, shorter than Mac. But still, even with an apron on, you could tell he had a good physique. Obviously he wasn't much tempted by all the doughnuts he was around every day.

Tilting his head, he squinted. "I feel like I know you, but I'm really bad with remembering names. Sorry."

"Megan." And when he still didn't recognize her, she added, "O'Donnell."

"Right! Your dad was my guidance counselor."

"Probably. He had that last part of the alphabet. *P* through *Z*."

"And this is your little guy?" He nodded to Sammy.

"He sure is. And Rachel is your—"

"Niece. I'm just helping my sister Tammy out. I told her Rach could come and hang out at the shop on days that she works. Helps her save on babysitting money."

Something Megan could relate to. "That's really nice of you."

"It's just until school starts. And she's really been a help. Haven't you, Rachel?"

But Rachel was more interested in Sammy than the adult conversation.

She squatted down to get even with Sammy's face. "What's your name?"

"Sammy."

"Sammy, cool." She spoke to him as if they were equals in age and every other way. "I like your chair. A chair on wheels is a good idea. I could use a chair on wheels when I get tired of standing at the front door."

Megan noticed Sean frown. "Rachel honey, I told you. You don't have to stand at the front door all day."

"That's okay. I don't mind," she answered her uncle.

"Women in my family. . ." Sean shrugged. "They're a hardworking bunch." His lips slid into a proprietor's friendly grin. "So what can I get you, Megan?"

"Actually we just need one jelly doughnut."

"Coming right up." He grabbed a sheet of waxed paper from the dispenser. "That's all?"

"Oh, and I could stand a cup of coffee."

"No problem." He moved in swift motions behind the counter, retrieving the order. But after she'd handed Sammy his doughnut and got her wallet out to pay, Sean paused.

"Wait a minute." He clicked his fingers. "You were good friends with Janey Saunders, weren't you?"

Megan's hands stilled like she'd been caught stealing a handful of doughnut holes. "Uh, yeah. Yes," she admitted.

Sean harrumphed and rolled his eyes. "I still never got why she told everyone I dumped her at prom senior year. What an imagination! But. . .whatever." He shook his head. "A buddy told me she's the owner of Sweet Sensations bakery."

"Uh, yeah," Megan repeated herself. "Yes, she is. She's had the place for a couple of years."

"Good for her. That's great." Megan noticed his obvious sincerity. "Hopefully she doesn't twist things around and think I'm after her business or anything. Truth is, I finished college with a business degree but then wasn't happy with that, so I went on to culinary school before I moved back here. I'd love to own my own restaurant someday and not just be a doughnut man. But it's all a process. . . ." He grabbed a rag and swiped at the glass counter. "But anyway, back to Janey. Hopefully, she's cool with everything. She still can't be as delusional as back in high school."

"Janey? Ha!" Megan groped for a few dollars from her wallet. "She's uh—Janey's fine. So how much do I owe you?"

"Two dollars."

She couldn't wait to get out of there, her cheeks burning, but Sean took the money and asked, "Anyone else you run into from school?"

"Not really. But you know, I mean, plenty of people are still around. It's just I'm busy with Sammy and work and. . .stuff."

Like sneaking around to doughnut shops for my friend who really still is a bit delusional. She dropped her wallet into her purse and zipped it up, hoping to hurry out of the shop. But Sean had more things on his mind.

"Hey, come to think of it. Do you remember a redhead in our class? There's a woman who's been coming in here, and well, she reminds me of someone. I just can't put my finger on who. I've gotten to talk to her some, but just when I'm on the verge of asking her name, she scoots out of here before I can find out."

"A redhead?" Megan could feel her face going into a full-fledged burn. "Um, the only *real* redhead I can remember from school was Melanie Ellis." Well, that was a version of the truth.

"No, definitely not her. This woman is taller. Usually has on a sunhat and sunglasses. Really great sense of style and, I don't know. Just something about her."

He had a misty look in his eyes that made Megan want to die on the spot. No doubt he was taken by the mysterious redhead and maybe even wanted to ask her out.

It was the same starry-eyed expression her almost-seven-year-old had on his face, she noticed, as he stared at Rachel. Sammy, her special-needs son, who was pretending to be especially needy and intentionally messier than usual, getting jelly all over his shirt so Rachel would continue to wipe it off.

I'll never get those stains out! Megan sighed.

Oh, did she have a lot to say to Janey tonight. An entire earful. Or two.

The morning hadn't been going anything like Megan had planned, and the trend continued when she arrived at the clinic.

"Your eleven o'clock just called and had to reschedule." The receptionist worried her lip. "I tried to reach you."

"Oh." Megan moaned. "I had my phone on silent and didn't even think to look at it. But thanks for trying, Ellen," she tried to say brightly even though she felt her shoulders slump in disappointment. If only she'd known she had more time, she and Sammy could've visited Mrs. Biddle, whose recovery had been going remarkably well. Or she could've taken Sammy to nearby Montgomery for a really nice breakfast at First Watch or the Pancake House. Instead of ending up at Donut Emporium where she'd evaded the truth, and was still feeling bad about it even though she only did it to protect her "redheaded" friend.

"It looks like your next patient isn't due for another thirty minutes or so."

"Well, in that case I think I'll try to get caught up on some paperwork," Megan said. But as soon as the words were out of her mouth, she remembered that Mac had a radio interview. His first radio interview to promote their All-Stars Sports Day event. And, glancing at her watch, she figured he might be in the midst of it right at that moment.

Bypassing her office, she walked down the hall to the employee lounge where a portable radio sat on the kitchen counter. One of the other therapists had brought it in at the beginning of baseball season so they could tune into games in between patients. Turning it on, Megan switched it to the correct station, feeling an instant gush of warmth when she heard Mac's voice.

"Yes, Trista, that's true," he was saying as Megan settled into a cushioned chair. "A lot of people in Loveland and many local businesses have been working together to ensure All-Stars Sports Day will be a true success."

"And now, tell us, what kind of activities will be on hand for the participants?" the interviewer—Trista—asked.

"All sorts of things," Mac told her. "Whether a child is wheelchair-bound or not, we'll have outdoor bowling, croquet, basketball, and all kinds of fun races just to name a few activities. Also, luckily, some of my baseball buddies from the Hawks will be there that day to play ball along with a handful of volunteers. Whoever wants to challenge them should go online and sign up. We plan to rotate players if we get overloaded."

"You're obviously pumped about this, huh, MacNeill?"

"I am. It's one of the most exciting things I've ever been involved with in my entire career."

"And speaking of your career, some people may wonder how you got from there to here—to heading up an event like this."

"I don't think it's much of a stretch really. I've always loved sports, especially baseball. This event gives me the opportunity to help disabled kids play, or even discover some sport that they might enjoy."

The interviewer giggled in a way that sounded out of context, causing Megan to frown. Why did she have the feeling the woman was fishing for something?

"Uh-huh. Oh sure, I get that part, Mac." Trista's voice suddenly sounded sweeter than Sammy's jelly doughnut. Plus, she'd gone from MacNeill to a friendly "Mac" fairly quickly in Megan's opinion.

"The bottom line is, you like games, right?" the interviewer cooed.

"Well, sure. Sure I do."

"And it seems you've played your share of them. On the field. And off the field."

What on earth? Megan shot up straight in the chair, stunned. Staring at the little silver box, she willed Mac to come back with some brilliant response. Something to defend himself. Or a segue to change the subject entirely. But he stammered and hemmed and hawed, sounding as caught off guard as she was.

"I—excuse me?" is all he managed to get out.

Trista, however, didn't skip a beat.

"Is that why you've never been able to settle down with one person and take a relationship seriously?"

"Hello!" Megan jumped out of the chair. "Is this an interview or an inquisition?" She shouted at the inanimate radio, wishing so much she could come to Mac's aid. Luckily, for the sake of their All-Stars Sports event, Mac was doing a better job of keeping his composure than she was. He simply laughed. It was a forced sort of laugh, she knew, but at least he maintained his cool.

"You know, Trista—" he started slowly, his voice even.

Ever the expert, Trista cut him off deftly before he could fully recover. "On another note sounds as if you have some news you may want to tell us about."

"Some news?" Mac asked.

Some news? Megan repeated in her head.

"About the rumors."

Megan blinked once at the radio, and then once again, waiting to hear Mac's reply. *Rumors? Really?* Was there something he'd failed to tell her? Something everyone else knew?

"I'm not sure what you're referring to," he finally said, allowing Megan to let go of a pent-up breath she didn't even realize she'd been holding.

Trista prodded on. "Isn't your agent talking to other teams?"

"Agents are always talking. That's what they're good at."

"Oh, you sure are the coy one, MacNeill Hattaway, aren't you?" Trista's tone had gone all gooey again. "Well, if you won't tell our listeners then I will. Rumor has it that once you get that elbow of yours healed you could be playing for the Mariners or the Miners."

The Mariners or Miners? Seattle or Sacramento? Megan felt her heart sink all the way to her toes. *Thousands of miles from Loveland, Ohio? Really, Mac?*

"Like I said, agents are always talking. I can't comment about that, Trista."

"But it is a possibility then?"

Megan crossed her arms over her chest, feeling like she was about to get hit with some unsettling news. But Mac's answer was vague.

"In major league sports, anything's a possibility, Trista."

"Of course." Trista sighed at the ambiguous answer, and Megan did, too, for a whole other reason. "So, MacNeill, since we're running out of time here," Trista began to wrap up the interview, "is there anything you *would* like to comment on?"

"Sure. I just want to remind folks that they can go online to get all the details about the All-Stars Sports Day games at. . ."

Megan didn't need to hear any more. In fact, as she edged up to the counter to turn off the radio, she almost wished she'd never turned the thing on in the first place.

It had been hard enough to be reminded about Mac's past dealings with women. To have it publicly restated that the man she'd fallen for had never, ever been involved in a lasting relationship before.

But then the other issue—the news that he might be traded! Just the idea of it caused her knees to go weak. Grabbing onto the counter for support, she stared at the white tiles behind the sink, Mac's words playing over and over in her head.

". . .*anything's a possibility*. . ."

That definitely left a lot of doors open. And was it true that he couldn't comment? Or that he wouldn't?

She wished so much she could've seen Mac's face to gauge his expression because she certainly couldn't read anything into his voice.

Oh dear Lord, what have I done? She buried her head in her hands. *What have I been thinking?*

Somehow she'd let down her guard because of Mac's attentiveness to her and Sammy. She'd succumbed to all of his sweetness. . .his charm. . .and ultimately—his kiss. Somehow, yes somehow before she knew it, she'd come to love the man!

But the guy she loved was the Mac she'd seen riding his tractor through the fields when she pulled up to his driveway. It was Mac, the co-chair she'd been so reluctant about at first, whose fervor to create a special day for the disabled kids was unrelenting. The man who knuckle bumped the volunteers and kept them charged up and smiling.

And then. . .when the time was right, it was the man who could make the world go away when he held her in his arms and drew her close to his chest. And who used those same strong arms to lift Sammy up time and time again. Who would swing her son in the air till Sammy giggled in a way—so free, so gleefully—that she had to swallow back the lump of gratitude in her throat and blink away the tears from the corner of her eyes.

That was the Mac she knew. That was the Mac she loved. She didn't even know the baseball-playing Mac. Wasn't acquainted with the World Series-winning pitcher. She'd only read about that Mac in newspapers and tabloids.

And if Mac started playing ball again, traveling, having women falling at his feet—what then? Even if he could handle that, could she? Could she really handle having a relationship with a celebrity? Someone who could possibly get uprooted, moving from team to team, year to year? Is that the kind of life she wanted for herself? More than anything, is that the kind of life she wanted for Sammy?

And what about Mac? Could she ask him to give it up?

"You okay?" Ellen breezed into the lounge and grabbed a bottled water from the refrigerator.

"Stomach's just a little queasy," Megan answered truthfully. Probably because she felt like she'd just fallen from the cloud she'd happily been drifting along on for the past few weeks.

But it's all my fault. All my fault. Sammy and I were just fine. For so many years we've kept it together. I've kept it together, all under control. And then I did what I said I'd never do. I had to let a man into our lives. And not just any man—but a pro athlete for goodness' sakes!

"I probably just drank a lot of coffee without enough food." She shrugged an excuse to her concerned-looking coworker.

"There's a box of saltines in the cabinet." Ellen pointed over Megan's head. "Or I have some yogurt in the fridge. I hope you're not getting a summer bug or anything. Those are the worst." Ellen scrunched her nose sympathetically.

Megan sucked in a deep breath. "No, no bug. I'll be fine." She drew herself up straight.

She had to be fine. No matter what, for Sammy, she had to be. But, oh, how her chest ached! Everything in her heart wanted Mac. . .wanted to be close and stay close to the Mac she knew. But doubts and fears weighed in heavily, warning just the opposite. Cautioning her to take a step back. Before it was too late.

Chapter 16

Even hours after the interview, while driving to the team doc's office for his appointment, Mac was still berating himself for the turn his talk with Ms. Newmark had taken. He sure was out of practice, he thought, as he guided his truck up Columbia Road.

He'd never been that crazy about interviews to begin with. Had never cared for the spotlight much—which he figured most people would probably find hard to believe, considering how much media attention he attracted. But even so, he used to be more adept at steering an interview in the direction he wanted it to go.

Typically, with most female interviewers, he could use his swagger and any number of compliments to get off a sore topic and onto a more palatable one. And with guys, it was generally easy to buddy up and banter about games and statistics till time ran out.

Plus, a lot of interviews were done over the phone now and not at the stations, which didn't help. It was always better to see who you were facing. Who you were dealing with. Like this Trista Newmark woman.

He stopped at the next intersection and turned the air conditioning down to low, mulling over the woman's name in his head.

Trista. Trista. Newmark. The name sounded more than vaguely familiar, but he couldn't fathom why.

Aw well, maybe it's good I didn't lay eyes on her. Maybe the woman would've turned me to stone. Undoubtedly, she wanted to make things uncomfortable for him for some reason. And she had!

He pushed on the accelerator and at the same moment his cell phone vibrated in the drink holder of the console. He picked it up, glancing at the screen. Hal. He clicked on the phone and didn't even bother with a hello.

"You were listening, huh?"

"Yeah, obviously Ms. Newmark isn't a fan of yours."

"Uh, that's putting it mildly." Mac chuckled. "It's okay though. I'm a little rusty fending off touchy subjects. But I'll get my chops back. Plus it didn't help that she caught me off guard the second time around with that business about getting traded. Wonder where that came from?" he asked—as if he didn't know.

"It never hurts to leak a rumor here and there, Mac."

"Rumors. Aren't those sort of like lies, Hal?"

"No. Look it up in the dictionary. A rumor is an unverified story, and stories are fiction. It's the nature of the game. Keeps your name in the news."

Good old Hal. He never gave it a rest. "You could've warned me."

"Yeah well, even so, you pulled it off. You were getting your act together by the end there. . ." Hal's voice drifted momentarily. "You on your way to Kline's office?"

"I'm pulling in as we speak."

Making a right turn into Dr. Kline's lot, Mac parked his truck in the reserved section alongside the red brick medical building.

"Let me know how it goes," Hal requested. "Actually, I'll call you back in an hour to hear what I'm already programming to be fantastic news, okay?"

Mac half smiled. "Sounds good," he assured him before clicking off the phone and cutting the ignition. Sliding out of the truck, he scuffed over the pavement in his sandals, realizing for the first time that morning that his stomach felt nervous.

Who knew what news Dr. Kline would have for him? He thought his elbow was feeling better. Feeling fine actually. But it really wasn't up to him whether he'd be okayed to play ball again. And that's what the appointment was all about.

It is what it is, right, Lord?

He had all the faith in the world that God would see him through any answer the doc gave him. Still, he paused on the sidewalk a moment, rolled his shoulders back, and inhaled deeply before he slipped into the side entrance of the facility designated for Hawks players and other pro athletes.

Immediately, a receptionist welcomed him and ushered him into an examination room reserved for pro athletes under Dr. Kline's care. It was only minutes before the orthopedic surgeon bustled into the room.

"What's up with those Hawks?" the doctor asked, by way of a greeting. He extended his right hand, and Mac reached out to shake it, always appreciative of how the busy Dr. Kline made sure to make eye contact.

"They're doing fairly decent."

"Yeah, decent is the word for it. But not great."

"Ah. There're some new guys on the team. Young ones. But they'll get it together."

"Let's hope." The doctor rolled his eyes. "So how's the elbow?"

"That's what I'm here to find out."

Mac extended his arm again, and this time the doctor took a few minutes to examine it thoroughly.

"Everything feels good. And looks good. How does it feel to you?"

Mac shrugged. "I've been whittling and doing some work at the farm. I feel like the physical labor has been building it up lately, not breaking it down."

"Farm work, huh?" The doctor smiled, clearly amused but also looking at Mac more respectfully than Mac had ever noticed before. "Think you might want to leave the cow pasture behind and get back out on the mound again?"

"Are you asking me, Doc? Or telling me?"

"I'm telling you, Mac. Considering all that arm of yours went through in the accident, I didn't know if I'd ever be able to say this—but you're cleared to pitch again." Dr. Kline patted him on the back. "You're good to go, number sixty-one."

"Thanks, Doc. I mean it. Really, thanks," he kept repeating, stunned. Excited. And relieved.

In fact, all the way out to his truck, it didn't feel like his feet touched the ground. He couldn't believe that in less time than it had taken for Trista Newmark to drag him through his past, Dr. Kline had given him hope for his future. A chance to play ball again.

He hadn't bothered to tell Megan about his appointment, not even knowing if anything would come of his visit to Dr. Kline, figuring he'd deal with it on his own. But now, hopping into his Ford, he reached into the console for his phone and started to call her, wanting to share the good news with her. And her alone.

But then he stopped himself.

She'd be working and most likely wouldn't pick up her phone anyway. And besides that, he decided, getting his elbow cleared was big news. Really big. The kind of news you tell in person. To a person you care about.

He'd try to keep quiet about it until he saw her the next time, although he wasn't sure when that would be. She'd be busy having dinner with Janey later and he'd be busy, sneaking Sammy out to practice bowling.

Still and all, there was another someone he needed to talk to, wasn't there? A conversation that couldn't wait. So he drove to the nearest church he could find and luckily found its doors unlocked. He wanted to get down on his knees and give thanks and praise. He wanted to ask for forgiveness once again, too.

Because while sitting in Dr. Kline's office he'd finally remembered why Trista's name sounded so familiar. And why she probably had been harsh with him. Trista had a younger sister named Trina whose heart he *had* played games with years ago. But those weren't the kinds of games he wanted to play again. No, not anymore.

Megan eyed the row of blue umbrellas topping Paxton's outdoor café tables. "Do you want to eat dinner inside or out?" she asked Janey.

"Oh, let's try outside. I've been inside all day. Or, no." Janey changed her mind. As usual. "It's still kind of hot out here. Why don't we go in?"

"In is good," Megan agreed wholeheartedly, pulling open the old-style wood door of the grill.

She was more than glad to escape the oppressive heat of the evening. Her head had been pounding for hours as if Colonel Thomas Paxton's entire eighteenth century militia had been marching across it. After the day she'd had, to say she was plain worn out emotionally and physically was an understatement. She was more than ready for any creature comforts and could feel her body relax a bit and go "ah" at the cool feel of the restaurant's air conditioning. The cushioned booth she and Janey settled into felt heavenly to her tired limbs.

More feelings of well-being spread through her when silver-haired Geneva, who'd been serving at Paxton's since Megan was a teenager, came to the table bearing two icy cold glasses of water with lemon. "Hot out there, isn't it, girls?"

"I hope the weather lady is right." Janey nodded. "I hope we get some of the cooler weather she's been promising."

"It's getting closer to back-to-school time." Geneva slipped two straws from the hip pocket of her khaki capris and laid them on the table. "Things should be getting cooler soon," she said as her eyes lit on Megan. "So. . .do you know what you want, hon?"

"I—I. . ." Megan could feel her mind still reeling from the events of the day. For a moment she almost forgot Geneva was asking about food and not something more philosophical as in what she wanted out of life and love in her pursuit of happiness. But then the question clicked. "I'll just have the usual," she finally replied.

"One grilled chicken Caesar salad coming right up." Geneva nodded before turning to Janey. "And are you trying another wrap tonight?" She winked knowingly.

"Why not? I'm almost through the list. How about the Big Veggie Wrap? That sounds good."

"They are good." Geneva's eyes widened reassuringly.

"Is Allie working tonight?" Megan asked before Geneva could slip away. No doubt she needed some ibuprofen for her headache. But a dose of Allie's company could always work wonders.

"Yeah, she's in the back." Geneva pointed toward the kitchen. "Covering for our dishwasher who has the flu." She rolled her eyes as if she might not believe that excuse. "I'll tell her you gals are here. I'm sure she'd like an excuse to take off her rubber gloves and say hi."

As Geneva walked away, Megan pulled her purse onto her lap and reached into the deep pocketbook, feeling around for her container of ibuprofen.

"Are you trying to tell me something?" Janey asked when she pulled out the plastic bottle. "I know I can be a real pain."

"Oh no, it's not you." Megan gave a soft smile at her friend's self-deprecating humor. "It's just—it's been a day."

Not only had she endured Mac's interview, but an hour later,

Dan Hoffman had come in singing Mac's praises throughout his entire therapy session. Everything he'd had to say was true, but she'd been trying to get Mac off her mind by working instead of being reminded of him every second of work.

But that hadn't happened. Not even when Dan's session was up. Someone else tuned into the Hawks' afternoon game, which led to more chatter about baseball and their fellow Loveland-ite Mac. By the time she'd seen more patients, picked up Sammy from day care, and driven to her parents' house, all she wanted to do was take a few minutes to put her feet up on the couch before meeting up with Janey. But her mom had rushed her out of the house as if she couldn't wait to get rid of her.

She sighed, opened the ibuprofen, and shook out a pill. It wasn't until then that she remembered how the entire day had started—with her crazy trip to Donut Emporium. How could she have forgotten that?

"By the way, I did it," she told her friend.

"Did what?"

"I dropped into Donut Emporium for you."

"You did?" Janey's eyes darted from side to side as if someone nearby might hear what they were talking about. Of course, Megan could've told her that no one did hear, and no one cared to hear either. "What did you think?" her friend leaned forward, looking overly conspiratorial.

"About the place?" Megan lifted a shoulder. "It's, you know, it's a doughnut shop. I mean, it's super clean and he had his cute little niece Rachel greeting people. And I suppose it's in a good location. I mean, if a person needs to stop and get gas, too. But again, Janey, when it comes to your bakery, it's like I told you before—they're two different things."

"Was *he* there? Did you see him?"

"He, Sean? Oh yes, my dear friend, *he* was there."

Thinking back on the conversation with Sean and how she'd evaded the truth made her head hurt even more. She shook out another pill. Placing the tablets on her tongue, she gulped them down with some icy water.

Meanwhile, Janey's lips pursed together tightly. A look of ill ease contorted her face.

"Janey, I really can't imagine that you don't think Sean's cute."

"Cute?" Her friend's eyes grew wide. "How can I think he's cute? He's the competition, Megan. And that's the only way I need to see him—as the competition."

Megan shook her head. "He's not really, you know. He's not actually trying to compete."

"How can you say that?"

"He's just a guy with dreams." Megan shrugged, recalling her conversation with Sean. "Just a guy who would like to open a restaurant but had to settle for a doughnut shop for the time being. It's really not that complicated."

"You're siding with *him?*" A pouting lip immediately erupted on Janey's face.

"Of course not. If I were, I certainly wouldn't have evaded his questions this morning."

"You told a lie?"

"Well, I didn't tell the whole truth, that's for sure. He asked me if I knew a redhead who'd been coming into his shop. And then he described you." Taking a packet of crackers from the condiment basket, Megan tore at the wrapper. "I have to warn you, he had that funny look in his eyes. Like he'll probably ask you out if you ever go in there again, Red. So you'd better be careful about traipsing into the Emporium. Or be prepared with a reason why you can't date him."

Megan bit into a cracker, brushed away some crumbs that had fallen on the table, and then looked up at Janey—whose cheeks were unusually flushed. More like on fire. "Oh my gosh!" The realization hit her. "That's your plan?" She sputtered cracker crumbs into the air. "You *want* him to ask you out? So then you can stand him up the way you think he stood you up at prom?"

Instantly her friend scooted back from the table, looking sheepish. But it took a few moments and some direct staring into her eyes before Janey came clean. "Okay, yes. Yes, it had crossed my mind to pay him back. But then I realized that's just silly and petty, and that it's about more than that. It's about business. It's about Sweet Sensations."

"Hmm. All about business, huh?"

Even that didn't ring true to Megan. She knew her friend would never intentionally harm anyone, but she also knew the girl had a penchant for winning. Janey Saunders hated to lose at anything— whether it was a game of tennis, making muffins, or having the upper hand in a relationship.

If Janey wasn't deliberately trying to even an old score with Sean then it could only mean one other thing. Something Megan should've recognized in her friend much sooner. Especially considering she'd done pretty much the same thing with Mac, protesting wildly about him to anyone who mentioned his name when he'd first come into her life.

"And you're sure it's not about any other 'sensations?' " She stressed the word long and clear. "Maybe some you're feeling for Sean?" Megan cracked a smile at her friend.

But Janey only frowned. And groaned. "Oh Megan. . .what have I done? Even if I had some, well, interest in Sean—I mean what do I do at this point? Whip off my red wig and say, 'Surprise! It's me, Janey!' He'd think I was crazy."

"He already thinks you're—" Hurriedly, she stuffed the uneaten half of the cracker in her mouth to stop from saying more.

"Already thinks what?"

Megan worked to swallow the dry thing. "That you're—c–cute."

"You mean he thinks the redheaded girl is cute."

"Oh. Yeah. Yeah, you're right."

With that sad epiphany and the rest of the day still weighing on her, Megan slumped back in the booth. Rubbing at her temples, she wished the ibuprofen would kick in quickly. "Oh Janey. . .this guy stuff isn't easy, is it? How did we get ourselves into these situations?" She let go of a deep sigh.

"Situations? What situations?" Allie suddenly appeared with their tray of food and a bright smile.

"Allie! It's so good to see you!" Megan knew she sounded over the top. But she couldn't help it. Seeing Allie, her spirits lifted immediately, like the cavalry had suddenly arrived.

"Sit and we'll tell you everything." Janey scooted over to make room.

"Wish I could, but it's one of those nights around here." Without having to ask, Allie correctly set their plates down in front of them. "I'm filling in for the fill-ins."

"How are the kids?" Megan asked, ignoring her salad for the moment. "Everyone good?"

"Great. They're coming with me to help with the Volunteer Day out at Mac's farm." She paused, scanning the table. "You all need anything else? Extra honey mustard or anything?" Allie glanced between the two of them.

Megan shook her head along with Janey. "We're fine." She unrolled her napkin in her lap. "I'm so glad you're bringing the kids out."

"Yeah." Allie nodded. "I think it'll be good for them, although they probably won't last very long."

"That's okay. It'll just be fun to have you guys there for however long."

"So. . .how's everything going with Mac?" Allie plopped her hands on her hips, looking bent on cutting to the chase. "He's not one of your 'situations,' is he?"

Megan should've known her intuitive and inquisitive friend wouldn't let her earlier question go unanswered. Glancing from Allie to Janey and back to Allie again, she finally found her voice and 'fessed up. "It's—it's a long story. I just think maybe— I don't know, I'm thinking I should take a step back."

"Back?" Janey jumped in. "Like back to under a rock?" She looked at Megan like she'd gone crazy.

"Excuse me, *Red?* You should talk."

Allie leaned over the table, spreading her hands referee-style between them. "You two are beginning to sound like sisters. I don't know what you all are talking about, and I wish I had time for the details. But the thing that I've found works best with Greg is honesty. Pure and simple honesty." She paused thoughtfully. "And well, peanut butter cookies. Those work great. Oh—and foot rubs. He really likes—"

Allie must've realized that she and Janey were staring at her because she stopped there. "Well, maybe you just want to start with honesty."

Straightforward and sensible. No wonder she and Allie had always been the best of friends. "Sure you can't sit? For just a minute?" Megan asked again, hoping more chatting with Allie would help clear her head. But Greg was waving to his wife from the kitchen, and after a round of hugs, Allie went back to work. Meanwhile, she and Janey let the subjects of Sean and Mac rest while they ate dinner, which was probably better for their digestive systems anyway.

Once they finished and the table was cleared, Janey got out her publicity folder and started going through the papers inside.

"This is the press release Mary Duncan wrote up. I'll be sending it to the *Enquirer* and the *Loveland Herald*. It's an update, giving more details about the activities now that we have that information. Oh, and this"—she pulled a mint green paper from her stack—"is another flyer advertising the event. It'll probably be the last one to go out."

"I love the All-Stars Sports logo you came up with, Janey. It looks great in print and I can't wait to see it on the T-shirts."

"Thanks. It did turn out good, didn't it?" Her friend preened. "Mary and Beth Hermann have offered to take the flyers to

Maineville, Montgomery, and Milford and put them up on bulletin boards in Starbucks and places like that."

"That'll be great."

"Oh, and thanks for sending this to me also." Janey slid a photo from the folder. "Do you have the disc for it? I'm not sure just yet where or how we might use it. But I'm glad you had someone take it. It's a darling picture of you and Mac and Sammy."

"Me and Mac and Sammy? From Amazing Race day? Or what?" She couldn't imagine what Janey was talking about. "Can I see?"

Janey handed her the photo and Megan's heart stopped still in her chest. "I—I didn't send this to you."

"You didn't? It came without a name. That's why I assumed it was from you. Honestly, I was wondering why you didn't just drop it off to me at the bakery."

"Oh, this is. . .this is creepy." A new pain shot between her eyes.

"You didn't know anything about it?"

"No, not at all. Well, I mean that day Sammy and I went out to Mac's farm for the first time, there was a man there with a camera. He ran off as soon as we noticed him. Mac went chasing after him, but never caught up. And. . .well, I guess I didn't realize he'd taken pictures of us." She sighed. "Or at least I'd hoped he hadn't."

She stared at the photo in her hand. It would've been a great picture of the three of them on the blanket enjoying each other and the sunshine, if it hadn't been taken by some person lurking in the shrubs. It would've been a nice way to remember the day, if it hadn't been taken by someone who'd been stalking them. "I don't understand why someone would do this. It's not like they're making money from it."

"Yeah, not true paparazzi, I suppose." Janey reached for the photo and folded it in half and in half again as if she clearly meant to discard it later. "I'm sorry I upset you." She shoved the bent-up photo back in the folder.

"You didn't do anything. I just don't understand. . .who?"

"I don't know. You and Sammy were in Sweet Sensations before you went out to Mac's that day. Someone could've overheard us talking about it." Janey bit her lip. "Maybe?"

"But why?"

Janey shrugged. "Probably because Mac's a celebrity. I mean, it's just like that Trista lady this morning during the radio interview. Who knows why she went after him?"

"You heard that, too?"

"Yeah." Janey sounded solemn for a change. "That's why you said what you did earlier? About backing off? Is it true you think he'll get traded from the Hawks?"

"I don't know what to think. Or what I think." She looked into her friend's sympathetic eyes. "But I know I need to stop wondering and go ask Mac."

And that was the honest truth.

Chapter 17

Mac had barely gotten home from his bowling practice with Sammy, locked up his truck, unlocked the front door of the house, and flicked on the outdoor lights when he heard a set of tires hit the gravel driveway.

Seeing Megan's white SUV wind its way up the drive by the light of the half moon, he hustled out onto the wraparound porch, quickly grabbed the whittling knife he kept in an antique milk case by the front door and a birch limb he'd been working on resting up against the case. Plopping himself down into one of the weatherworn wicker chairs, he leaned back and propped his feet up on the wide wooden railing that ran the length of the porch.

As if on cue, Bitty came meowing out of the evening darkness and curled up by his feet, making it look like the pair of them had been sitting there together for hours that way. Which happened to be a good thing, since he'd implied to Megan that he'd be hanging out at the farm all night while she was out to dinner with Janey.

Knife and tree limb in hands, he pretended to be engrossed in his whittling. But, of course, his mind was a hundred miles from that, happily focused on Megan instead.

He was surprised that she was dropping by instead of heading over to her parents' to pick up Sammy, but glad, too. His time practicing bowling with Sammy had been really special, and now the chance to spend a few hours with Megan would be even more so. Altogether, both activities made him feel privileged, like he'd won the lottery or something. And the other good thing—he wouldn't have to wait any longer to tell her the big news about his elbow.

But after he heard her cut the engine, noticed the headlights go off after a bit, and then watched her amble slowly up the sidewalk with her head bent down, he sensed something wasn't right.

Immediately his legs dropped from the rail with a thud. He laid the whittling paraphernalia aside and got up from the chair, wanting to go toward her. But the way she wouldn't even look up at him paralyzed him. He froze in step as Megan paused on the second porch step and wouldn't come any closer. Felt his stomach instinctively twist when she didn't bother to reach out and pet Bitty like she usually did.

"Did I interrupt anything?" Megan finally looked his way, but managed to avoid his eyes.

"Are you kidding? I'm glad you stopped over. Want to sit?" He pointed over his shoulder at the pair of once-white chairs.

"No. I have to go pick up Sammy. Just thought I'd drop by on my way."

He knew her parents' house was in the complete opposite direction, but didn't mention it.

"How was dinner?" he asked instead.

"Good."

"Paxton's is always good."

"True. It always is."

And there it was—an awkward silence. They rarely had those anymore, not since they'd first met. But they sure were having one now. Mac felt pressed to fill the void.

"Sure you don't want to sit down?" Maybe if he could just keep her near him, close in his camp, he could unravel whatever was suddenly tangling up things between them.

"No." She fidgeted with the keys in her hand, barely looking at him. "I just— Well, I needed to talk to you is all."

"Okay. No problem."

But it wasn't okay, and the way she was acting was a problem. He tried to soften his expression, making it easier for her to speak. But his jaw clenched instinctively, as if preparing to get struck by who knew what. "I'm all ears."

"Well, I—I was thinking. . ." She rubbed at her forehead as if it was paining her to do so. "Tomorrow all the volunteers will be out here, and well, next week is the big event and—"

"Oh yeah—and don't forget Thursday they'll be announcing the event at the Hawks' home game. We're still on for that, right? I wanted you to meet some of the guys. They're characters. But underneath it all, they're okay guys." He forced a chuckle, despite the unease he felt between them. "You'll like them."

"Yeah. . .that's one of the things I wanted to talk about." Megan paused, bit her lip. "I—I don't think I can go with you."

"Yeah? You have to work? Need a sitter?" She really hadn't

planned ahead for the game? That stung a bit.

"No, I. . ." She shifted on her feet, causing the shadows around her face to shift as well. The light caught her features, and he had a clearer sight of the gripping consternation there. How had that happened when the last time he saw her she only had smiles for him—and what he thought was love shining in her eyes?

"That's—that's what I was going to talk to you about, Mac. I mean in a week this'll all be over, you know? Sports Day will be over. And well, when it is, we won't exactly be tied together anymore."

Not tied together anymore?

"What?"

"Well, if it wasn't for the All-Stars Sports Day event we would've never met. Even you said that at one point."

"Yeah, but I just meant—"

She talked over him, noticeably intent on cutting him off. "And you're right, we wouldn't have met. So now that the sports day is almost over—well, next week—there's no reason you—we—need to keep seeing one another."

"No reason?" In a millisecond, his chin hardened. Anger surged up into his head, making it feel as if his brain could explode instantaneously. Despite that, he worked to control his voice. "You really think there's no reason?"

"I'm just trying to be honest with you, Mac. I mean, it just makes sense that we'd back off. You know, now that we're not going to have anything to connect us together anymore."

What was she talking about? Where was all of this coming from? *Nothing to connect them?* That was like a bullet to the heart.

He clenched his teeth. Okay. Well. If she couldn't see all the things they had in common to connect them, he sure wasn't going to stand there and enumerate them all.

And if she truly didn't feel connected to him in all the ways he felt attached to her, what was he going to do? Beg her to feel differently?

He couldn't believe the humiliation, the hurt. He'd never had to beg a woman for anything before. His pulse pounded in his temples as he tried to contain his temper. His fists clenched at his side.

"I don't know why you're suddenly acting this way," he ground out. "Aren't you even going to tell me why you changed your mind?"

He lifted his jaw, prepared to take whatever comments she dished out. His insides in turmoil, he tried to make eye contact, ready to see the truth for himself in her eyes.

But she turned her face away, looking out past the glow of the porch light, into the dark night instead. When she didn't answer him at first, a trickle of hope seeped in. Tempting him to reach out to her. But it was obvious she'd made a decision not to stand within his reach. He shoved his hands into the pockets of his jeans instead.

"Megan? Aren't you going to answer me?" So frustrated, his words came out in a bark. "Is this really what you want?"

She turned at the sound of his voice, and he thought he saw tears coming from her eyes. But she backed down the steps into the blackness before he could be sure of what he was seeing. There was no denying what he heard though.

"Yes, it's—it's okay with me," her voice hitched on the words.

He stood stunned as she fled down the sidewalk to her car.

Megan could barely see through her tears well enough to make the turn-around by Mac's barn and to head out of his driveway onto Route 48. Luckily the dark, winding part of the country road had become more familiar to her over the past several months. She'd driven it often lately, easily sailing over the once-foreign curves on her way to the farm. And every time she did, the drive and just thinking of where she was headed gave her that warm, excited feeling of coming home.

Just like Mac had.

Oh, what have I done? She sobbed into the darkness.

"What have I done?" The words echoed back at her. So did her remorse. The talk with Mac hadn't gone anything like she'd wanted it to. It hadn't gone at all the way she'd planned it would.

On her drive over to see him, she'd decided she'd do exactly what Allie had suggested. That she'd be honest and open and tell him everything that was on her mind. How she really wasn't sure she could handle being involved with a professional baseball player. How she liked control and didn't do topsy-turvy all that well and didn't know if she could take being in a relationship with someone who would always be traveling. Or who could get traded to a city across the country.

And the whole celebrity thing. She'd really wanted to talk with him about that. Sure, there were countless women out there who might find Mac's star factor attractive and alluring. But it didn't hold much appeal for her. In fact, it frightened her more than anything.

Especially where Sammy was concerned. And especially after Janey showed her that photo of the three of them. To think that being in a relationship with Mac could put her and Sammy in the limelight—make them targets for gossip and subjects for sneaky thrill-seekers who wanted to get a picture of them all—scared her. Point blank.

She was going to say all of that. Get it all off her chest. And from there, she'd imagined they could sit and talk, sort things out. Truly, in her heart of hearts, she thought just seeing Mac would ease much of the fear she'd been feeling about the two of them being together.

But then she'd pulled into his driveway.

And right before she turned off her headlights, she looked across the field and saw it—the practice diamond where Mac and his uncle had spent so much time together.

Baseball. It truly was Mac's first love. He'd told her that. And the thing was, he didn't even have to tell her. She could see it in his eyes. In his whole being. He came to life just talking about it.

She'd felt so much closer to him the day he'd shared that with her—all about his love of baseball.

Funny though, how now the realization of how important the sport was to him made her feel so distant from him.

Baseball was what Mac was meant to do. He was great at it. It was his calling. Others might still be wondering if he'd ever play again. But from all she'd seen and all she knew about elbows, she didn't know any reason why he wouldn't be out on the mound next season.

Which was nothing short of a miracle.

But then miracles do happen when they're supposed to.

"And Mac is supposed to play ball," she whispered to herself.

The reality of it felt like a stab to her gut, making her crumple in the car seat. It hurt so much, realizing she shouldn't get in the way of that with all her reservations. Her hang-ups. And fears.

She loved him. Yes, she loved him too much for that to happen.

And, no, he shouldn't have to give up his first love. Shouldn't have to compromise or choose. And by backing out on their relationship the way she had, she'd made it easy for him. He wouldn't have to make choices or concessions.

Of course, he hadn't looked happy about it. But once he started playing ball again, he'd be fine. Everything would be okay again. For him.

A block from her parents' house, she paused her car at a stop sign, sitting there awhile wishing in some small way that knowing that gave her some sort of solace. At the moment though, her heart ached intensely. And it seemed impossible and improbable that it would ever stop.

Finally pulling into her folks' driveway, she grabbed a tissue from her purse and blotted at her eyes. Took a few final sniffles, tried to pinch some pink into her cheeks, and put on a fresh dab of lipstick.

Hopefully, her mom wouldn't notice she'd been crying. The last thing she needed was to listen to her mother right now. But. . .as she shut the car door and walked up the drive, she wondered if she should've listened to Allie.

True, in the end she'd done what she thought was right—what first came to her heart. But oh, how it hurt. Oh, how it felt so wrong!

Chapter 18

Even with all the people swarming around his farm for Volunteer Day, and even though he was bent over a makeshift worktable involved in making a wooden booth from scratch, Mac could still sense exactly where Megan was at all moments.

They'd barely said a polite hello to one another when she'd first arrived with Sammy and her parents. Quick as they could manage, they'd gone their separate ways busying themselves with all there was to do with All-Stars Sports Day just a week away. The problem was, even hours later, he could still feel her presence as if she were tethered to him.

Unfortunately, where Megan was concerned, he had a natural sixth sense about her. Similar to the sixth sense he'd had on the pitcher's mound where he could easily pick off runners who were trying to steal bases behind his back.

Only with Megan, it was far worse. There was no reprieve. No three strikes and batter's out, with a time to rest during the next half inning. Instead, the feelings didn't stop. Making it super difficult to concentrate on all the pieces of wood strewn around him while he could perceive her traipsing across his property, helping out the groups of volunteers. And making it much harder than it needed to be to construct a simple, last-minute balloon stand, especially when all he really wanted to do was reach out for her—which apparently was exactly what she didn't want from him.

Much as he couldn't stand it, as he bent over his work his mind was totally focused on her and clearly not on the task at—

Hand!

"Ah, for the love of Pete!" He shot up straight, flicking his hand in the air, trying to shake the pain from his thumb.

"It works a lot better when you hit *the nail* with your hammer. Not your thumb," a male voice came up from behind, razzing him.

Mac craned his neck around to see. "Thanks, Dan," he grumbled, too irritated to greet the older man any other way. "I'll have to remember that."

"Hurt much?"

It hurts something awful, he wanted to say. But, of course, Dan was talking about his thumb and not everything else that was aching inside of him.

"Only when you keep talking about it." He slung back a gruff retort. Too gruff. But Dan let it slide. He only chuckled.

"Place is crawling with volunteers, Mac."

"It is at that," Mac agreed. He rubbed his sore thumb on the leg of his jeans before bending back over his project. "Lots of them here today." And he was particularly glad there was assigned staff to coordinate the entire group so he could be off working on his own projects, on his own time, and in his own space. As it was, he wasn't in any mood to have to act diplomatic and pleasant with the rest of the world.

"You and Megan have done a great job organizing this event. I can already see it's going to be tip-top," Dan complimented. "Next Saturday is going to be unforgettable for a lot of kids and their parents. Yeah. . ." Mac glanced up from his hammering for a moment to see Dan looking around, sizing up the surroundings where many of the booths and activities were already in place. "You and Megan make a good team for sure."

Good team. Yeah, right. . . He'd said the same thing to her the night they'd first kissed. So much for that kind of thinking.

"Whatever." He shrugged and turned back to something far simpler for his mind to figure out—the two-by-fours and nails. But Dan wouldn't let it go.

"Well, you do," he insisted. "You two are a perfect pair togeth—"

"Oh jumpinjehoshaphat!" Mac yelped, dropping the hammer, grabbing onto his throbbing thumb once again.

Dan sniggered. "Lucky for me, I was just about to offer to hold the board for you. You're kind of dangerous today. You okay?"

"Of course I'm okay. It's just a hammer."

"I mean you and Megan. Are you and Megan O'Donnell okay?"

"Me and Megan?" Shaking his head, Mac bent over to pick up the hammer he'd thrown on the grass. "Don't know what you're talking about."

"Really? Because I saw Megan the other day at the clinic, and she was doing the same thing. Trying to avoid talking about you the same way you're trying to avoid talking about her. So, what did I do?" Dan cocked his head, tucking his thumbs into the brown belt holding up his baggy blue jeans. "I put one and one together."

"You mean you put two and two together."

"No. I mean, one and one. Making two. You two. You and Megan. I've seen the way you act around each other at the meetings. First there was this rivalry between you both." He chuckled. "That was amusing to watch. But for a long time now, things have been different. I definitely think there's something going on between you and Megan. In fact, I know there is. After all, I might be growing old and senile—but I'm not an idiot."

Mac felt his insides uncoil a bit at Dan's self-deprecating comment. "Nothing senile about you, Dan. You're one of the smartest men I know."

"Yeah. I know, I know." Dan laughed. "I was only saying that to try to get you to smile. But. . .since that didn't work, maybe I can get you to talk. Would you rather talk some?"

"Trust me, Dan. There's nothing to talk about, and I've got to get this booth built pronto. There's a crew of volunteers waiting to paint it."

"Okay, you don't want to talk? Fine. I'm here. I volunteered. I can risk my life and stand and hold the boards for you. We don't need to talk."

But that promise didn't last long. As soon as Dan shuffled around to the end of the boards Mac was nailing together, he started up again.

"What do you think about the Hawks?" he asked over Mac's pounding. "They're doing pretty good in this series with the Sox."

"Haven't been following it."

"Haven't been following the Hawks?" Mac detected amazement in Dan's voice even over the noisy clash of the hammer.

"Nope. Not really."

"Why do you think that is? Because you still have a bum elbow? Because you don't think you'll be playing again?"

"No. My elbow is perfect. No pain while I'm hammering. See." Mac stopped long enough to stretch his arm, twisting it every which way. "It's fine."

"Well, now." Dan's chest inflated and a genuine, broad smile filled his face as if he had something to do with Mac's recovery. "That's something to celebrate!"

"Yeah. Yeah, I thought about celebrating," he said, his mind trying hard to block out thoughts of Megan again. As if it was possible.

"But then?"

"But then. . ." He puffed out a disgusted sigh. "Okay. You're right about Megan. Yeah, we've been, well, together. Really together. I've never met anyone like her. I've never felt this way, and. . ." He stopped, suddenly wondering why he was telling the old man so much. Wondering why, too, it felt good to be doing it. "Bottom line, I was going to tell Megan. She was the only person I really wanted to tell."

"And then. . ." Dan urged him on.

"Nothing 'and then.' She came by last night and pretty much said we were over. Just like that."

"Hmmph." Dan's white-tipped, wiry eyebrows narrowed into one long stripe. "She threw you a curveball, huh?"

"Seriously, Dan? A baseball pun? Not really in the mood for baseball puns right now."

Dan's shoulders scrunched upward in apology. "I didn't mean

for it to be a pun, Mac. It's more of a saying than a pun, I think. A colloquialism." He paused, as if to consider that fact before he pried more. "Did you try to call her and ask her why?"

"Are you kidding?" Mac grabbed the joined boards, laying them aside. Reaching for the next pair of boards to be nailed, he could feel the anger—and well, hurt—surging through his veins again. "Look, I've done everything to show her I care. Everything. For her and for Sammy. And if she can't see it or feel it—or whatever—I don't know what else to do."

"Oh, I get it." Dan nodded. "It's the pride thing."

Mac ground his teeth. "No, not the pride thing," he objected, even though everything inside him was working to tamp down the idea that it might be a 100 percent true. "It's the right thing," he argued instead. "She wants me to leave her alone? Fine, I'll obey her wishes. Even took her number out of my phone so I wouldn't be tempted to call her."

"So after you got mad, and deleted her number from your phone, then what did you do?"

"What did I do?" Mac felt his jaw drop a foot. "Dan, are you not hearing me? I did nothing. That's what she wants. That's what I did. Nothing. If she wants to talk to me, she'll have to call."

What else could he do? He'd woken up two mornings ago like he'd been waking up for months now, thinking of Megan. And of Sammy. Thinking the three of them were—a team—a pact—a *something*. Thinking they were on their way to becoming a unit. A family, hopefully. And then to find out Megan wasn't feeling the same way. . .it left a hole in his heart, far bigger than the entire Hawks' baseball stadium.

Oh great. He shook his head at himself. Now he was conjuring up stupid baseball references. Lame! He dug into his work apron for a half dozen nails.

"Well, you could've at least prayed," Dan piped up. "Have you done that? Have you prayed about it?"

"Pray about it? Of course I've—" Mac stopped mid-sentence, his thoughts churning while a new kind of heat flamed his neck, his cheeks. Embarrassment.

He hadn't prayed, had he? He'd only kept asking why. That really wasn't much of a prayer, was it? It was more like a theme for a pity party.

"You know, your Uncle Jake, God rest his soul, had a saying."

"I think I know what you're going to say, Dan."

"The one about—if your problem is big enough for you to be troubled by, it's big enough to pray about. But if it's not big enough to pray about, you shouldn't be troubled by it."

"Yeah, I remember. And, well, believe me, I'm very troubled."

Mac suddenly sensed Megan's presence even more, as if she were so close, right behind him. Looking up toward the house, he saw her there, her form outlined behind the curtain as she stood by the kitchen window. "Of course, praying. . . I mean, it still doesn't mean she'll change her mind, does it?"

Dan shook his head sympathetically. "I don't have all the answers, my friend. I can only suggest you go to the One who does."

Megan was glad when Wendy asked her to help retrieve the

sandwiches the sub shop had donated for the volunteers' lunches from inside Mac's house. Quickly depositing Sammy with her mom, she was happy to escape the great outdoors and head in. Mostly because no matter which field she found herself in or which booth she helped with, she couldn't get far enough away from Mac and the feelings for him that kept welling up inside her.

But then, what was she thinking? Because standing at Mac's kitchen sink, washing her hands, didn't offer any relief from thoughts of him either. She had to force herself not to pull back the thin cotton curtain to glimpse at him while he hammered away at his project. Had to mindfully tell herself "no, no—and no" since everything inside her felt so drawn to him.

And, why hadn't it occurred to her how vulnerable she'd feel being in his house again, anyway? Especially in the kitchen surrounded by his familiar everyday things—his oversized olive green coffee mug, his baseball cap lying on the oak kitchen table alongside a folded morning newspaper.

And then, there were the more than ordinary things that permeated the area like lingering, taunting ghosts—the memories of being there with him sharing an evening. A meal. Laughing with him and Sammy over something silly. Not to mention how she could almost feel the way it used to feel when he'd come up behind her as she stood at the sink and he'd place playful kisses at the nape of her neck, sending shivers and tingles all the way up to her—

"The guys from the sub shop put the drinks for the volunteers over there." Wendy's slight Kentucky accent snapped her out of her reverie. Thankfully!

Megan turned from the window to see her pointing to a row of

Styrofoam coolers lining one side of the kitchen wall.

"And I'm crossin' my fingers all fifty sandwiches are in the fridge just like the sub shop guys promised me they'd be." The door squeaked as Wendy opened the refrigerator and peered inside. "Yes ma'am. They're here, all right," she said. "Plenty of room for them, too. Doesn't that poor Mac ever do any grocery shopping? Or know how to cook a supper or two?" She peered over the refrigerator door. Clearly amused, her eyes twinkled at Megan. "You need to teach that boy his way around the kitchen."

Megan was surprised the refrigerator could be as empty as Wendy was saying. It'd always been stocked when she and Sammy used to come over. "He makes a really good pizza from scratch. . . ." she murmured, wondering why she felt a sudden urge to defend him.

But Wendy barely heard her. She was already back to business, as usual. "Now I'm thinkin' all we need are some baskets. Or a couple of trays to carry the subs outside to the picnic tables."

Wordlessly, Megan moved over to the island and bent down, pulling open the cabinet doors. She sifted through the items stored there, pots and pans clanging together, making a racket until she finally retrieved two metal cookie sheets.

"How about these?" She rose up with the pair in her hands.

"Great. You want to hold 'em while I load 'em up?"

"Sure," she said lightly, even though she felt an instant heaviness come over her.

It wasn't that it was hard to stand and hold cookie sheets, by any means. It was just that it weighed on her sadly, recalling how she'd put the cookie sheets to use one rainy night. Mac had pulled Sammy's wheelchair up to the kitchen table and the two of them sat there, working on a model car together. Meanwhile, she had happily busied herself making chocolate chip cookies. It felt so right, the three of them together like that.

Luckily though, Wendy's chatting distracted her from memories again. "Is Mac doing some major renovations in here? It sure appears that way," she commented. Looking up from her task of mechanically placing subs on the tray, she nodded at the huge sheets of plastic draped through different parts of the living room. "What all is he doing?"

"He's making some of the rooms bigger and hallways wider and. . ." Megan shrugged, her eyes downcast, watching the pyramid of sub sandwiches grow on the sheet. "Just doing some general remodeling, I guess."

She and Mac had never talked in any great detail about the renovations. He'd always been somewhat vague, like he simply planned to give the place an overhaul—a facelift. She'd never really thought to question him beyond that. It wasn't her place to as far as she was concerned, and honestly, she wasn't that interested. They'd always had so many other things to talk about.

"His Uncle Jake lived here for a long time," she explained to Wendy. "So I think he wanted to make a few improvements here and there. Which is good, I guess, especially if Mac ever needs to move out of state and put the house up for sale."

The thought had come to her just as she said the words out loud. Had that been in the back of Mac's mind all along? The truth of the possibility jolted her full force, jerking her head back on her shoulders. Evidently Wendy had the same sort of reaction. Her head shot up out of the cold cavern.

"Move? Sell? Why would he do that? Now that his elbow has been cleared, he'll be back playing with the Hawks next season, won't he?"

Mac's elbow was cleared? The cookie sheet suddenly dipped from Megan's grasp, causing the stack of subs to skitter across—and almost off—the metal tray.

"Whoa. Is that thing getting heavy?" Wendy reached out to upright the sheet.

"No. It's—it's fine."

And Mac's elbow was fine. He'd been cleared. Something she'd never doubted would happen. In fact, it was exactly what was supposed to happen—Mac getting back to playing ball again. Still, the news—hearing that it was for real—threw her insides totally off-kilter.

"That's twenty-five sandwiches anyway," Wendy was saying. "I'd say we're ready for the second cookie sheet."

In a haze, Megan walked over to the island and slid the full cookie sheet off the top of the other one and onto the counter. Keeping the remaining empty sheet in her hands, she moved back over to the refrigerator, standing like a sentry once more.

"How did you find out?" she asked Wendy. "About Mac's elbow, I mean."

"Oh, he mentioned it to Ted this morning," Wendy told her, leaning into the refrigerator, pulling out handfuls of subs. "When we first got here. He also invited Ted to go to the Hawks' game with him this Thursday night. Guess he'd planned to go with someone else," she chatted, hands moving the whole time. "But the plans fell through, and—okay—" She stood up to her full height. "That's it for the subs. That's the last twenty-five." She shut the refrigerator door then paused. "Hey, wait a minute. Weren't you supposed to go with Mac? Didn't ya'll mention that at one of the meetings? They're announcing the event at the game, right?"

"Yeah, but I just—can't." Megan tried to avert her eyes from Wendy's. "I'm glad Ted gets to go though."

She didn't want to share the reason why, and Wendy was kind enough not to press her.

"Oh, Ted is thrilled. He gets to meet all the players and everything. I'm so sure I'll be hearing about it all for days and days."

For a moment, it filled her mind—the hurt look in Mac's eyes when she told him she couldn't go with him. And then, when she told him. . . Well, she didn't even want to think about it. Didn't want to remember the way he looked at her. Confused. Hurt. Disgusted. She couldn't blame him for any of it. But now he'd be playing ball again. Now it would be all good for him again. She knew it would. . . .

"Okay." Wendy clapped her hands together. "All we need are napkins. Do you think Mac would mind us using some of his?"

"I sincerely doubt it." He was only the most generous man Megan had ever met. The thought caused a cramping around her heart. She set the second full cookie sheet on the island momentarily and rubbed at her chest as she walked over to the pantry.

In the meantime, Wendy lingered by the pantry door, reading the framed embroidered message hanging on the wall there. Megan had always assumed Mac's Aunt Emily must've enjoyed doing cross-stitch because her work was all throughout the house. More than once, just like Wendy, she'd stopped to read the colorfully stitched quotes.

"'Prayer changes things,'" Wendy read out loud. "What a great reminder! So simple yet so true. Don't you think?"

"Uh-huh." Megan nodded. But even as she stepped into the pantry, retrieved a package of napkins, and closed the pantry door behind her, her insides ached, wishing she could believe to the core of her being that those words really did hold true.

Evidently never-stop-moving Wendy believed because she'd ceased movement for a moment and actually stood staring almost reverently at the cross-stitch. And Mac. . .he believed the same thing. So many others she knew did, too.

Sighing, she wedged the napkins under her arm and grabbed one of the sandwich trays. "I can get this tray if you can get the other one," she said to Wendy. "And we can have some of the guys come in and get the coolers, right? They're probably pretty heavy."

"No way we're breaking our backs over those," Wendy agreed.

And as the two of them got on with the business of feeding the volunteers, and she and Mac stayed busy trying to avoid one another, Megan still felt those words gnawing at her.

Prayer apparently did change things where other people's lives were concerned. But for her, things—even falling in love—seemed to be so complicated. Something always blocking her happiness. She wasn't sure why that was true.

Chapter 19

How many days till All-'tar Day, Maw-mee?"

Megan guided her SUV through downtown Loveland, feeling her shoulders droop when she had to stop at a crosswalk for an older couple holding hands. Everyone seemed to be holding hands these days, didn't they? Young and old folks alike?

"This is Thursday, Samster. So two more days. It's this Saturday," she answered automatically, her mind not completely tuned in to him. She was too busy trying not to let her eyes—and heart—stray to the bistro where she and Mac had shared lunch weeks earlier. Or the shady bike trail where they'd pushed Sammy along some evenings. Or Paxton's. Or the ice cream shop, or. . .

She pulled her wraparound sunglasses from the visor and put them on, hoping to at least dim some of the memories of Mac somewhat. Besides, she'd taken a couple of days off work so she could concentrate on other things that needed attention in her life. Things like Sammy's birthday invitations, getting her oil changed, some last-minute details for the sports event, and just to make herself feel better—a trip to the hair salon later that evening for a trim she needed desperately.

"We see Mac then? This Saturday?"

"Sure. You'll see Mac then." She sighed involuntarily, already hoping Event Day wouldn't be as awkward as Volunteer Day the weekend before. Not that she and Mac hadn't been completely civil with each other then. They were totally polite when they needed to be. All day long. And into the evening.

And it had felt just awful!

"An' how many days to my birt-day, Maw-mee?"

"Nine more days. It's the Saturday after this one."

"We see Mac next Saturday for my birt-day," Sammy said. Only it wasn't a question this time. It was matter-of-fact. Expected.

Megan hadn't mentioned anything to him of course, about what was going on between her and Mac. She'd hoped by only seeing Mac on the weekends at the different events, Sammy would slowly get weaned from his presence in their lives overall.

And it was so much better for that to be happening now—just the way that it was—she convinced herself. So much better than if she and Mac had kept going on the way they had been and after a year or so, he dropped out of her and Sammy's lives. That would've been twice as hard, wouldn't it?

After all, Mac could be living someplace else by then. Or be so wrapped up in playing ball and traveling with the team, he wouldn't even remember them back in Loveland. Who knows? He could even backslide, slip into old habits, turn into MacNeill Hattaway, the womanizer again.

There were so many reasons why it was better she cut the cord now, not just for Mac and his career, but for Sammy and her, too.

So many reasons. . .

Except there was no way she could explain all that to Sammy, was there? When Mac wasn't around, Sammy was still obsessed with him, forever talking and asking about him.

But then why wouldn't he? Mac had always treated him incredibly well.

"I don't know if Mac will be there or not, Sammy. We mailed his invitation earlier, remember? But sometimes people are busy," she told her son, being realistic.

Sometimes they don't want to see certain people because of certain things.

But of course she couldn't say that. Instead she opted for, "And sometimes they have other reasons why they can't—"

Her son cut her off. "We not mail Rachel's invitation. We take to her?"

"That's right. Because we don't have Rachel's address."

And they didn't even know her last name actually.

"We take to her now?"

"Yes, indeed. Right now." She crossed over the Little Miami Bridge, flicked her left blinker, then came to stop at the red light at the intersection. "Are you excited?"

"I like Rachel a lot."

"I know you do, honey."

Sammy had a short list of the people he'd wanted to invite to his birthday party. Obviously, there were his grandparents. Then Allie and Greg and their kids, Justin and Carrie. But he also wanted to ask Mr. and Mrs. Biddle, who Megan learned was improving much each day and would probably be ready to watch Sammy again in January or so. As well, he wanted to invite the Slater family. Janey was next on his list, and he hoped she would bring him a dozen jelly doughnuts. But, definitely at the top of his list were Mac and Rachel. And the more he talked about Rachel, the more she realized how much of a crush he had on the girl.

"My hair look okay?" he asked from the backseat.

"Your hair?" Megan glanced in the rearview mirror. Was he serious? When had he started thinking about his hair? Or even noticed he had any?

"Mac pat my hair down sometimes. He say, 'You a handsome dude, Sammy.' " For a moment his voice didn't sound like her son's. It took on an older, more confident tone, mimicking Mac.

More than that, it sounded full of all the loving conviction Mac had always lavished on her Sammy.

A lump rose in her throat.

"Mac—Mac says that?" She'd seen and heard Mac do and say a lot of things to Sammy. But that was a new one.

"Yeah. He says, 'Girls like handsome dudes like you, Sammy.' " He gave a half giggle. "Then he goes, 'High five.' And we smack hans. Sometimes we smack hans though, and then Mac, he take my han and he holds it. Tight."

Tears sprang to the corners of her eyes. *Oh Mac. Oh Mac.* In a million years, would she ever be over him?

The car honked behind her, and with tear-blurred vision, she glanced up to see a green arrow. She rounded the corner, Sammy unaware of the emotions that welled up inside her.

"We almost there, Maw-mee?"

"Al—" She cleared her throat. "Almost, honey."

Megan glanced back at him and couldn't believe the huge smile that lit his face. In eager anticipation of seeing Rachel again, she was sure. As if she didn't have enough to be emotional about, how it tugged on her heart that a girl was tugging on his!

By the time she pulled into the Donut Emporium lot and parked, his nearly-seven-year-old body trembled with excitement. But once Megan got him out of the car, into his wheelchair, and handed him Rachel's invitation, they made their way up to the doughnut shop door, and all of that changed.

"Where Rachel?" he asked when the door didn't open automatically with his new friend on the other side.

"I don't know, Sams."

Megan held the door open with her leg as they inched inside. But the shop was empty and she could see Sammy's instant disappointment. His shoulders sagged immediately; his hand holding the invitation fell limply into his lap.

Until Sean and Rachel came bounding out from the back room.

"Sammy!" Rachel ran to Sammy's side while Megan whispered a thanks to the heavens.

"You can't imagine how much he's been looking forward to coming here," she confided to Sean.

"You mean seeing Rachel, I suspect." He smiled. "We were just in the back finishing up lunch. How are you guys doing? Can I get you anything?" he asked pleasantly.

"We'll have two jelly doughnuts to go. And Sammy has an invitation to give to—"

But before she could get the words out, Rachel was squealing. Sammy hunched his shoulders at the sound, but couldn't quit grinning, reveling in her excitement.

"Uncle Sean! Can I go? It's for Sammy's birthday. See?" She waved the invitation in the air.

After figuring out that Rachel's mom would be working the day of the party, but that Sean could bring Rachel, Megan gave him directions to her house. She also encouraged him to stay instead of just dropping Megan off, telling him about some of the other guests he might know.

"Will Janey be there?" he asked in particular.

"Uh, you mean Janey Saunders?"

"Do you have any other good friends named Janey?"

"Not a one actually. Janey will— You know she actually hasn't gotten back to me yet."

Which was absolutely true. But it was also true that her two dearest friends, Janey and Allie, had never missed one of Sammy's birthdays no matter what. Still. . .she wasn't exactly sure why Sean was asking. Just in case Janey's being there might keep him away, and subsequently Rachel, was there any reason to mention that?

"I can't wait to come to your party, Sammy," Rachel cooed. "It'll be so much fun!" She took hold of Sammy's hands and clapped them together. Megan had to smile at the two of them, both laughing like it was the funniest thing ever.

"Mac right, Maw-mee," Sammy told Megan ten minutes later when they'd left the doughnut shop with their bag of treats.

"Mac?" Her heart leaped involuntarily. If only he knew he was killing her, bringing up Mac's name all the time.

"Uh-huh." Sammy beamed. "Girl do like handsome dudes like me."

"You right, Mac."

Mac pushed Sammy's wheelchair through the warehouse, over to the spot where he had the practice bowling ramp all set up. Fortunately it was cool inside, but he always brought a couple of water bottles for him and Sammy anyway.

"What am I right about, buddy?" he asked while glancing at his watch to see exactly what time it was. Laura said Megan would be back from her hair appointment by around seven-thirty, so Kurt would return to pick up Sammy at seven fifteen. That meant they had about thirty-five minutes to practice and rest in between. Plenty of time—

"Girls like me."

Mac erupted with a laugh. "Of course girls like you. What's not to like? Is this a certain girl you're talking about?"

He pushed the wheelchair up to the bowling ramp and came around to face Sammy. He saw the telltale glint of infatuation in Sammy's eyes when he said, "Rachel."

"Rachel. The girl at the doughnut shop, huh? Your mom talked about you two meeting each other a few weeks ago."

Mac had never known—and figured he would never know—the privilege or joy of being married to Megan. But, he sure felt the pain of being divorced from her, even outside of marriage. It didn't feel good mentioning conversations they'd had in the past, knowing their interactions in the future would be slim to none. Sometimes it didn't even feel good being around Sammy and being reminded of every good time, every quiet time, and even every in-between time the three of them had shared together.

Bittersweet. Maybe that was the word for it. He wasn't sure. He only knew that he wasn't about to give up being around Sammy. Not if he could help it. Simply put, the boy meant the world to him. He didn't want to give up on that relationship as well.

"Rachel pretty."

"I'll bet she is."

"You like pretty girls, Mac?"

"Sure." Mac shrugged. "Pretty. Nice. Smart. Fun."

"My mom pretty and nice. You like her, right?"

"Yeah, I do, buddy. She's— You have a good mom," he said, unzipping the bowling bag, trying not to dwell on that too much. "Hey, you remember what we said, right?" He handed Sammy the orange lightweight bowling ball. "We're practicing because it's fun to work at something you love. It's fun to get better at it."

Sammy hugged the ball in his lap. "An' we want to surprise Maw-mee."

"And, yes, we want to surprise your mommy." Mac unscrewed the cap on one of the waters, offering Sammy a drink first. Sammy shook his head, so Mac took a long swallow.

Well, that had been his first thought when he'd come up with this practice bowling scheme. He thought it'd be fun to surprise Megan with Sammy's new bowling skills. But honestly, he was still angry at her and his pride still bruised black-and-blue from the way she'd led him on or whatever she'd been doing. At the moment he couldn't have cared less about doing much of anything for her. Now his objective was solely aimed at Sammy. Getting Sammy better for Sammy in order to make him feel good. Practicing with him the same way his uncle Jake had practiced with him.

"You do like bowling, don't you?" The thought occurred to him that he didn't want to be pushing Sammy into something he wasn't that crazy about.

"Yeah. I show you I like it."

Sammy aimed the ball exactly the way Mac had instructed him over the past weeks. Easy as anything, the orange orb went sailing down the ramp, splattering bowling pins in every direction. He managed to repeat that move successfully time after time, calling for some high-fives and drinks of water.

Mac had helped out with some baseball clinics over the past months and had even coached some kids at the beginning of his career—long before he'd gotten carried away with other "not so positive" things.

But working with Sammy brought out something in him that he'd never experienced in those other situations. Most likely because he felt so close to the boy. In fact, he felt like Sammy could be his own son. Which hurt. But felt really good at the same time.

"I'm proud of you, Sammy. Really proud." Mac bent down in front of him. "You try harder than a lot of pro players I know, you know that?"

Sammy's face shone with a look of awe. "I do?"

"You do." Mac nodded. "How old are you now?"

"I six."

"Only six? Buddy, you've got lots and lots of years of bowling ahead of you."

"But I be seven soon." Sammy struggled to hold up the correct number of fingers. "You come to my party, Mac? Maw-mee mail you invitation."

"Your party?" Megan had mailed him an invitation? Only for Sammy's sake, he was sure. But still, it could prove to be an uncomfortable situation. For him at least. Everything was pretty much a jumble inside of him. For one, he couldn't find a place to store up all his leftover feelings for her. And just the idea that he still had those lingering feelings made him angrier than he wanted to admit. "Well, Sammy, I . . ."

Mac stood up and began to hem and haw, started to hedge and come up with any number of reasons why he couldn't be there. But then he looked down at Sammy and knew he couldn't say no to the eyes gazing up at him so expectantly. Not only couldn't he say no. He didn't want to. Despite the surrounding circumstances, despite the fact that he and Megan didn't have a future together, he didn't want it to be like that between him and Sammy. So he said what was pressing on his heart instead.

"I'll be there, Sammy. For you, I'll be there. Always."

Chapter 20

Megan stopped inside her parents' foyer and peered into the gold-framed mirror hanging above the antique chest there. Evening sun poured through the palladium window above the front door, offering plenty of light, wrapping her reflection in an amber glow.

She swished her head from left to right, enjoying the feel of her freshly-cut hair. Christy had done a good job as usual. Mac would be sure to compliment her. . .

If only he were still in her life.

"Hey, sweetie." Her mom came around the corner from the kitchen, waving a dish towel hello. "Your hair looks cute."

Mom! Forever her savior.

"Thanks, I thought I'd try something different. Go a little shorter. I needed a change." More like something to lift her spirits!

"Long or short. You can wear it both ways."

"You're my mother." Megan smiled. "You have to say that."

"Not really." Her mom slung the dish towel over her shoulder, settling her hands on her hips. Thinking her petite stance might look more formidable that way? "I tell it like it is when I have to," she said, before retracing her steps back into the kitchen. "I do, believe me."

"Oh yeah?" Megan followed behind, teasing. "And when would that be?"

"Like when I—when I—Oh. . ." She tossed a hand in the air, at a loss for an example. Reaching into the silverware drawer next to the sink, she drew out a fork. "Hey, try this for me, will you?" She pointed to a glass baking dish where Megan could barely see any cake for all the layers of whipped topping and sliced strawberries. "I just finished it up. It's angel food cake with crushed pineapple and strawberries. I wanted to bake something different for card club next week and thought I'd do a test run." She sank the fork into a corner of the dish and came up with a mouthful, which she pointed in Megan's direction.

Never one to turn down anything with whipped topping, Megan opened her mouth, happy to oblige while her mom tried to wait patiently before she asked with wide eyes, "So. . .what do you think?"

"Oh my gosh, Mom." Megan shook her head. "It's—"

"Bad?" Her mom's face crumpled.

"No, no. It's incredible."

"Oh, well good." Her mom gave a short sigh of relief then scuttled around the kitchen collecting a cake knife, plate, and napkin.

"Want to sit and have a piece?" she asked, even though she was already in the process of cutting a generous square, placing it on a plate, and handing it to her.

Not that Megan was about to refuse. She'd been eating far too many sweets recently, it was true. Anything to fill the void she'd been feeling inside. As if any of it could replace the person she was missing in her life. Even so, she sat down at her usual spot at the table, digging into her mom's newest dessert, savoring every whipped topping-laden bite. "Is Sammy with Dad? I didn't see his car out there."

"They should be back shortly." Her mom sat across from her. "Christy finished you up early, didn't she?"

With a full mouth, Megan nodded then swallowed. "Now, where is it they go again? Sammy and Dad? I can't remember if you told me."

"Oh, you know, around."

"Hmm. . ." she said, focused more on licking the fluffy sweet stuff from her fork than on her mom's answer. "This really is one of your best creations."

"I'll cut some for you to take home when you leave later." Her mom looked so pleased by her obvious enjoyment of the treat. "I'm sure Sammy will like it, don't you think?"

"He'll love it. I should also tell Janey about it."

"Oh, speaking of Janey. I meant to tell you, I saw her and Sean Shaffer together last Saturday night."

Megan halted the fork an inch from her lips. "Janey and Sean? Together? I doubt it, Mom."

But obviously her mom didn't have any doubts. She nodded vigorously. "Oh no. I saw them. At the movie last week. You know how they have the Moonlight Movies on the riverbanks? They were showing *Just Friends*. That really funny movie with Ryan—oh, Ryan—"

"Reynolds."

"Right. And, like I said, Janey and Sean were both there."

"Well, that I believe. But they couldn't have been at the movie *together*." She enveloped the fork-load of creamy stuff with her mouth, thinking she really needed the recipe. It would be great for Sammy's birthday party. Or anytime actually.

Tilting her head, her mom's lips pursed, considering. "Maybe they didn't come together. But they sure *seemed* together," she said, not letting the subject rest.

Megan was well aware of her mom's track record when it came to sensing things between males and females, but really—Janey and Sean? On Saturday? No way. She shook her head.

"Mom, I just saw Janey for dinner last Thursday, remember?" And she'd talked to Janey on Sunday, too, giving her the lowdown about Volunteer Day since she couldn't make it that day. She'd also told her friend about the breakup with Mac. But Janey hadn't said a word about Sean to her. "Sean and Janey are miles apart. Not even close to being together."

"Well, it's true that Janey was sitting on one side of the amphitheater, and Sean was sitting on the other. But I saw them meet in the middle at intermission and, trust me, those two easily looked like they could be involved. I saw it in their body language. He was leaning close. She was smiling into his eyes. They were obviously smitten with one another. And, well, they looked so cute, standing side by side."

Always great criteria for a lasting relationship. Megan wanted to shake her head but there were still at least three more bites of her mother's angel food cake concoction to focus on.

"As a matter of fact, Janey and Sean looked the same way you and Mac do," her mom continued.

"Huh?" Megan's fork dangled in midair.

"You and Mac look like a couple. Like you belong together."

Megan hadn't wanted to get into telling her mom about Mac at the moment. She had hoped to get through the event on Saturday first. But with the way the conversation was going, the time was probably right. Unfortunately. She let out a sigh. Set down the dangling fork. And pushed the plate aside.

"Is it too sweet?"

"No, it's not that. It's surprisingly light actually. It's just that there are some things going on, and I—"

"What kinds of things?" her mom prodded.

"It's hard to explain because you and I. . .we're, well, we're so different from one another, Mom."

"Different? You and me?" The animation left her mom's face. She blinked, looking like a cross between bewildered and crestfallen. "I can't imagine what you mean."

Megan's heart wrenched. The last thing she wanted to do is hurt her mom's feelings. Actually, it felt like she'd been hurting too many people's feelings lately and not meaning to at all.

"Not in a bad way, Mom. There's nothing bad about you or what you do. Love and romance, that's all a part of your business. You're a wedding planner, for goodness' sakes. That's how you always look at things. When you see two people, you automatically see a match. A couple. I don't look at love that way at all."

"I see more than two people, Megan. Even more than a couple," her mom clarified. "I see a connection. A connectedness."

"Right. Because everything about you is 'love this' and 'love that.' Which is what I'm saying. We're different in that way." Oh, how had she started down this road anyway? She'd kept these thoughts to herself for how many years? More than she could count.

"And you're not about love? That's a crazy statement, Megan," her mom chided. "What about the way you love your son? And care about other people's special-needs daughters and sons? And what you do for a living—isn't that love? Your loving, caring touch helps people heal and get better."

"That's so different. I'm talking about *your* kind of love. The romantic kind, where you fall in love and get married. Which I did. And what do you know, it didn't work out, did it?" She wasn't even sure why she blurted out that bit of past history. Sounding so snippy. And pitifully sorry for herself. As if her mom had anything to do with it.

Yet her mom's reaction was exactly what she expected. She reached over and gently touched her hand. "Megan, what's going on?" she asked softly. "You really don't seem like yourself."

Oh, how she dreaded telling her mom. How she hated having to look her in the eyes and tell her the truth. But somehow she sucked in a deep breath and let the words flow out when she exhaled. "I broke things off with Mac."

"You what?" Gone was her mother's gentle touch. And her soothing voice. She flopped back in the chair, her eyes nearly as wide as her gaping mouth. "Are you kidding?"

Megan stiffened in the chair, feeling defensive. "Mom, seriously, did you really think it could work? Me and a pro baseball player? A national celebrity? Really? That's what I mean when I say we're different. To you, it's romantic. To me, it's not logical."

"Did I think it could work?" Her mom dipped her head. "Yes, Megan, I did think it could," she said emphatically. "And do you know why I thought it could work? Because it *was* working." She leaned forward, her eyes pleading to understand. "Why did you break it off? I don't get it."

"I didn't want him to have to choose." But even as she said the words out loud, she realized the excuse sounded weak.

"Choose? Choose what?"

"Between playing baseball and being with me. I love him too much, Mom. I really do. And I don't think it's right. He shouldn't have to compromise doing something he loves so much."

"Compromise? Did he say that's what you were asking him to do?"

"No. But I thought about it, and there are so many things that could happen. What if he got traded? What if it was to some team far away and he'd have to divide his attention between doing what he loves and trying to maintain a long-distance with me? And Sammy?"

"Well, some couples do cope with situations like that, Megan. It's not that far-fetched."

"Yes, but they don't have to deal with paparazzi."

"Paparazzi?" Her mother raised her brows. "In Loveland?"

"Well, not paparazzi, but sneaky people taking pictures of us and Sammy when we don't even know it. And it's not only that, Mom, but what if women start chasing after Mac again? And what if he likes it?

Then Sammy and I will just get hurt down the road. And you know what? I don't want to be the one to stand in the way of any of that. Not Mac's career or his fame, or other women or anything."

"Oh my gosh, Megan. Do you think you've thought of enough what-ifs? Hmm. Maybe if you try real hard you can come up with more awful scenarios for the future."

Her mother's sarcasm was shocking. Never had her mom spoken to her like that. "What?" Megan's head flung back.

"Megan, can I tell you something?" Mom asked, though it was apparent she was going to whether Megan gave permission or not. "When I look at you and Mac, do you know what I don't see?"

"What you *don't* see?"

"Yes, you heard me. What I don't see is a physical therapist. What I don't see is a major league baseball pitcher. But I will tell you what I do see, and I'm not being a gushy romantic doing my 'love this' and 'love that' thing."

Megan swallowed. So much for thinking her mom couldn't tell it like it is. "Mom, I—"

"No it's fine. I can see how you might think of me that way. But let me tell you, what I see with you and Mac are a man and a woman who love each other. Love each other very much. And I also see a man and a woman who both love a special little boy. And whenever I see that between two people, that intangible thing that you and Mac have, I pray that if it's God's will for them to end up together, that they will. And I also pray that if I can be of any help along the way, I'll be able to do that, too."

"I'm sorry, Mom. I am." She hung her head.

"There's no need to be sorry. But Megan, can I tell you something else?" She touched her hand again. Wrapped her fingers around Megan's. Lifted her chin, and looked into her eyes. "There's no need to be scared either. Do you hear me? Don't be scared, my precious daughter, don't be."

Her mom drew her to her shoulder and caressed the back of her head. Megan hadn't been held like that since forever, and for a moment it felt like the safest haven in the world. The sweetest place to be. A place where she was known. And loved anyway.

Because without a doubt, her mom could always see through her. All the way into her heart. No matter how guarded she tried to be. How she tried to hide her feelings and put up facade after facade; her mom could always see through it all.

Her mom just knew.

"Oh Mom!" She burst into tears. Tears that ran beyond her control, feeling as if they'd been pent up, put away in reserve for far too long. "What if I can't do it?" She sobbed through the words. "What if the only thing I know how to be is Sammy's mom? I was okay seeing Mac and being with him, but now that I've fallen in love with him. . .I'm so afraid. What if I mess it all up? What if I've already messed it up? Or I'm just not strong enough?"

Her breaths came in gasps. "I tried so hard before, Mom. I tried to do everything right when I was pregnant and still—" She broke off, guilt weighing on her like it always did. "Sammy can't walk or run or talk like other kids. He never will. Even though I tried, Mom." Her voice broke. "I really, really tried."

"Oh Megan. . .Megan. . ." Her mother shook her head emphatically, authoritatively. But even so, Megan could see the hurt for her in her mother's eyes. She saw it in her mom's glimmering tears. "You've got to stop. You can't keep carrying that burden around, do you hear me?" Her mom reached for her hands. "What voice in your head are you listening to, child? There's nothing you could've done any better. And we've got special little Sammy in our lives. He's perfect."

"He is perfect. I know that, I do. He's the only son I want," Megan said, meaning it with all her heart. "But then I chose the wrong dad for him once. What if I choose the wrong person to love again? Bring a man into our lives who walks out? I'm just so scared. So scared." She shook her head. "If it's just me and Sammy, I know how to keep us from being hurt. I know how to control our lives."

"But Meggie." Her mother squeezed her hands. "As much as you try, and I know you do, honey, you can't control it all. Because you're not in control." Her mom leaned in, saying gently, "God is, Meg. Our Father is. And as difficult as it might be to comprehend, I have to tell you, God loves Sammy even more than you do. More than you can imagine."

Someone loved Sammy more than her? Megan looked up, startled. Not in all her years of motherhood had she ever thought of God that way. Never.

"I know," her mom said, obviously noticing. "I'm a mother, too, remember? And it's hard—oh, it's so hard to not keep digging in, not keep thinking if you can only do everything in the world humanly possible, be the Super Mom of Super Moms, that everything will be all right for our kids. I know. I've been there. . . .

"But Meg honey," she said, her voice tender, "have you ever thought that Mac may be exactly the person God has been waiting to bring into your life? And Sammy's life, too? I know giving yourself to love can be overwhelming. It can make you feel out of control. I get it," she said soothingly. "But isn't it just as frightening to think of the joys you could miss out on? Do you want to take that chance? Do you want to take the chance Sammy could also miss out on that joy?"

Stretched out on the couch was usually a good place to be. But Mac couldn't get comfortable. Or interested in the mystery he was reading. Laying the paperback on his chest, he reached for the remote by his right hip, turning up the sound on the television. But even the ESPN highlights didn't appeal to him at the moment, so he muted the TV once more.

"Maybe we should get a dog. What do you think about that, Bitty?" he asked the cat lying at the opposite end of the couch by his feet. Bitty barely acknowledged his voice. Only lifted her head slightly and then huddled back into her own fluffy ball of fur again.

"I'll take that as 'a disinterested,' " he told her.

Lately he had been letting her come into the house more often. Even so, the homestead had still been feeling lonelier than usual.

Maybe because it wasn't the cozy haven it once was before all the renovations going on, with the mess and furniture scattered about. But more than likely it was because he'd just gotten back from being at the warehouse with Sammy, and truth was, he missed being with him already. Not to mention there was a prevailing emptiness he'd been feeling knowing Sammy and Megan weren't stopping by anytime soon.

Actually, outside of Event Day, quite possibly never again.

Not that he could do much about it. Except maybe literally whittle away some of the extra time he had on his hands. He was just about ready to take his melancholia to the porch and do just that when his phone vibrated in his jeans' pocket, startling him.

Taking it out, he stared at the screen hoping to see the name of the person he missed more than anything, but of course, she'd meant what she said. It wasn't her calling.

"Hey Hal. Getting kind of late, isn't it? Isn't it past your work time?"

"Not in California."

"True, true." Mac chuckled.

"It's not only earlier in California. There's also more sun."

"But. . .we're here in Ohio, Hal."

There was a silence on the other end. Until Hal finally spoke. "Not for long, Mac."

Mac sat up abruptly, feeling as if a boulder was lodged in his chest. "Hal, cut to the chase. What are you talking about?"

"You know that rumor about you being traded?"

Mac sucked in a deep breath. "It was more than a rumor?"

"Uh, yeah. I didn't want to say more about it until I knew more but. . .being a Sacramento Miner wouldn't be so bad, would it?"

Shocked, Mac couldn't think of a reply. But as usual, Hal was never at a loss for words.

"Nothing legally binding right now because, of course, we have to wait until after the Series is over. But they'd really like you to come out next weekend for a little dinner and dancing."

"Dinner and dancing? Hal, could you be a little more serious here?" Although why should Hal be serious? It wasn't his life that was about to change.

"You're right. That wasn't funny. But they do want to meet with you next Friday evening. I had Sophie book a flight for you to leave Friday morning and return on Saturday. A little over a twenty-four hour trip and could be the best one you've ever had. They're talking big bucks, Mac. And I think the timing is great. You're healed, you're well, and what else do you have going on in Loveland after this sports day thing is over, right?"

His head spun as he said good-bye and sat staring at the muted TV. After all these months of waiting, he had a new elbow. And a new team to go to. After all these months he thought he had Megan and Sammy, too. But there was no Megan now. And no Sammy.

Is this really what You want, God? He cradled his head in his hands. *Is this the path You want for me?*

Chapter 21

The first thing Megan heard when she woke up Saturday morning was Tim McGraw's baritone coming across the hallway from the other bedroom. The second was Sammy, chiming in with Tim singing "Live Like You Were Dying."

Obviously Sammy, who'd had an incredibly difficult time settling down and going to sleep the night before, was wide awake, and McGraw's song was the perfect one to be playing when his radio alarm went off. Even though Megan had assured him she wouldn't oversleep for All-Stars Sports Day, she had to smile when he insisted she set his clock for the special day anyway.

Honestly, she hadn't had such an easy time going to sleep herself. But it wasn't only because of Sports Day and hoping after all the months of planning everything would roll out well for their first annual event.

It was also because of Mac. She lay there in the dark for hours, only glimpses of the street lamp lighting her room, thinking about seeing him again. Thinking about all she and her mom had talked about. Thinking about her feelings for him. Feelings that just wouldn't go away. And sometime before finally falling asleep with a prayer on her lips and her own alarm going off, she'd made a decision. She wanted to talk to Mac, to explain herself, to ask for his forgiveness.

Yes, she really did want to look him in the eye and profess her love, to say it all.

She wanted to take a chance at love. At loving Mac. If only he still cared about her, too.

Flipping off the bedsheet with more fervor than usual, she bounded out of bed. The clock might've said she was on time, but she felt like she was running late for something. Every part of her finally ready and hoping so much to talk to Mac, to explain herself.

However, an hour later, when she and Sammy arrived at Mac's farm after eating breakfast and donning their red All-Stars Sports Day T-shirts, she spotted him standing by the roped-off entrance talking to a volunteer and could feel her nerve waning. Seeing him again, looking so ruggedly awesome in his usual T-shirt and jeans. Knowing inside and out that he was too good to be true. Could she really expect he'd want to listen to her?

She pulled the SUV up into her pre-designated parking spot by the barn, turned off the ignition, and took a deep breath. For one anxiety-filled moment, she wished there was only a bull named Fu Manchu to face instead of Mac.

As far as she could tell, he hadn't noticed they'd arrived. But by the time she unloaded Sammy's wheelchair and got him out of the car and into it, all of that changed.

"Mac, we here!" Sammy called out to him, as if Mac had been waiting for them, and only them, to arrive all morning.

Mac ended his conversation and graciously walked toward them, his eyes glancing everywhere but at her.

"Sammy! How's it going, buddy?" he greeted her son. "You ready for this day?"

"I ready!"

Megan dared to look up at Mac but then instantly wished she hadn't. It weakened her resolve even more. Because she missed seeing the way he cared for her reflected in his eyes.

Missed the way he would've usually greeted her with a kiss. And how normally she would've had a breakfast sandwich or a coffee for him that she'd picked up on her way out to his place.

But there was little "normal" between them at this point. Now there was only an awkwardness and stilted conversation, mostly revolving around Sammy.

"He's more than ready," she said for want of anything better to say.

"I'm sure he is." Mac ruffled Sammy's hair.

"I ready to bowl!" Sammy exclaimed.

Mac chuckled at his enthusiasm while Megan reminded, "We got here early to work on some last-minute things though, remember, Sam?"

"Like what?"

"Like the booths and games and. . ." she rambled to her son, but even as she did, her face burned hot. She knew what she wanted to ask Mac. Knew what she had to ask him. "Mac, can we talk?" she said in a rush, not even qualifying the question with a time or place the way she'd meant to.

He finally looked at her, but didn't seem the least bit comfortable about making eye contact. Scratching at his temple, he glanced away hurriedly, out over the fields. "If it's about the gate on the fence around the pond, I already know what you're going to say. But you don't have to worry. I sent Jason out to the hardware for a lock. It'll be fine, trust me."

"Oh?" She blinked. "Good thinking, thanks. But actually there was something else. If you have a few minutes later when all of this—"

"Hey Mac!" One of the red T-shirted male volunteers sprinted up alongside of them. "Rick Hall, your buddy from the radio station, is on my phone. He has a question about the opening ceremonies that I can't answer. You mind?" The volunteer handed Mac his cell.

"Megan! I'm so glad you're here." Another red T-shirt emerged by her side, this time a lady about Megan's mother's age. "Can you come over to the merchandise booth? We need your help deciding on which totes to put where."

"When do I bowl?" Sammy wanted to know in the midst of the conversations.

"At one-thirty." Both Megan and Mac paused from what they were doing, answering him in unison.

For a brief moment their eyes met above Sammy's head. But just as quickly, Mac turned away.

Megan couldn't guess how many parents from Loveland and other

Cincinnati suburbs had brought their kids for All-Stars Sports Day. She had tried to count cars at one point, but lost track once she got close to two hundred.

It had been a major scheduling feat, but all the volunteers got a chance to rotate shifts so they could have the opportunity to watch their own kids participate in the activities. Sammy had already tried a game of wheelchair basketball for his age division and had cheered on some of the older kids in a baseball game when it came time for bowling for his age group.

"I like basketball, Maw-mee. And baseball. But I love bowling," he kept telling her, over and over.

She wasn't sure why he'd say that. She could only figure it was probably because he remembered the first time they'd ever visited Mac's farm and Mac had the special bowling ramp built for him.

She couldn't blame him. That day had made an unforgettable impression on her as well. Even as she pushed Sammy's wheelchair over the rubber waffled sidewalk from the baseball field, past park benches a volunteer had donated for the event from their Loveland landscaping company, it lingered in her mind. It was the first time she and Mac had *almost* kissed.

"There Nana an' Pappy!" Sammy exclaimed. "Mac, too!"

Her parents had signed up to help with the bowling event, to set up and retrieve pins at one of the four ramps. And true to his word, Mac was already at the area. Standing next to her parents, he watched the older girls finish up their round of bowling. And, of course, reached out to help when one of the girls was having a hard time of it.

He was always so good with Sammy and the other kids. He

believed in them. Actually, he believed period, didn't he? And just because she'd had trouble believing, she'd removed him from Sammy's life.

Oh, how she wanted to talk to him.

But it wasn't going to be easy. Not when he'd barely glance at her. Yet with Sammy, she could see Mac had no love lost there. His eyes practically shone when she pulled Sammy's wheelchair to a stop near the bowling ramp.

"Hey champ!" he greeted her son.

Sammy grinned widely. "Ima do good bowling, Mac."

"It'll be fun, buddy." Mac held out his hand, and Megan didn't know how Sammy knew, but the two of them went through the ritual of a secret handshake she'd never seen them do before.

Then it was time for the four boys to line up their wheelchairs at their respective ramps, nets surrounding each area in case of a wild bowling ball or flying pin getting loose. Each of the boys' families was obligated to keep score, as if they were bowling at a real alley.

Sammy was the youngest in the group, so Megan thought it was nothing but a fluke when the first ball he sent rolling down the ramp caused more than a handful of pins to topple.

But then when it happened again. . .and again. . .and even again, and she jotted down the high scores, she didn't know what to think.

She looked at Mac and her parents for an explanation. But they didn't seem as surprised as she was as they cheered him on. Twenty minutes later when Sammy won, and Mac was wheeling him over to shake the hands of his competitors, she couldn't do much of anything but stand and feel happily shocked for him.

"I bowl good," Sammy said proudly after being presented a blue ribbon for the event. "Didn't I bowl good, Maw-mee?"

"Better than good, Samster." She bent down to hug him. "I didn't know you could bowl so well."

"You surprised?"

"Well, you might say. . .yes, I'm surprised."

"I practice." He beamed.

"You practiced, huh?"

She wasn't sure what he was talking about. She'd never seen him bowl except for the day they'd been out at Mac's farm months before. But she hated to tell him his winning had probably been little more than beginner's luck, so she smiled and said, "Well, you know what they say, practice makes perfect."

"Uh-huh." He nodded. "I glad you surprised. We want to surprise you."

"We?"

Sammy nodded, uttering another, "Uh-huh."

She looked up at her parents who were standing next to Sammy's chair. Mac was still busy talking to the volunteer who had presented the ribbons. Or maybe he didn't feel right being part of the family's mini celebration, she wasn't sure.

"We who?" she asked.

Sammy's grin was extreme, as if he'd won the competition all over again. "We sneaky."

That still didn't answer the question of "we who?" She glanced up at her parents, who also wore dazzling smiles.

"I can't believe you never figured it out," her mom chirped.

"Never figured what out?"

"Well, all those times you came to pick up Sammy when I was

babysitting and he was off with your dad."

"*You* taught him to bowl?" She gaped at her father. She'd never known him to be a bowler.

"Me, bowling? Of course I didn't. Your mom's been working me over for years, trying to get me to play in a league."

"Well, then. . ." If it hadn't been her dad, and her mom was always at the house when she arrived, that only left— "Was it Mac?"

Her mom answered with a clap of her hands. Sammy giggled, and her dad let out a chuckle.

"And you were all in on it?" she asked.

"Oh yes, Meg. I've been *dying* to tell you," her mom answered all in rush, clearly eager to spill all she'd kept pent up inside. "Mac came to me months ago with a plan he'd come up with. A surprise for you. He'd asked if he could take Sammy to practice bowling on the nights your dad and I were babysitting."

"I not a baby," Sammy chimed in. "I almost seven."

"We know that, honey." Her mom grinned widely.

"So I'd run Sammy over to Ted's warehouse where Mac had everything set up," her dad explained with a lopsided grin, "and then bring him home when the two of them finished practicing."

"Oh my—" Tears pricked the sides of her eyes. She blinked, trying to hold them back. "Mac? Mac did all of that?"

"Maw-mee, why you cryin'?" Sammy frowned. "You not happy I won?"

"No, I'm very happy about that. Really I am, Samster."

"Mac, Maw-mee surprised and she crying," Sammy shouted.

Megan could see Mac's ear tilt in Sammy's direction at the sound of her son's voice. Clasping the volunteer on the shoulder, he finished their conversation then sauntered over.

"Did you call me, Sammy?" he asked.

"Maw-mee surprised an'—"

Megan butted in. "Mac, you taught Sammy to bowl? They just told me all about it," she blurted, sniffling back her tears, embarrassed for him to see her emotions running so high. "I—I don't know how to thank you."

"It's not a problem." He shrugged off her gratitude, barely looking at her. "I did it for Sammy," he said emphatically. "We're buddies, aren't we, Sammy? He's helped me immensely. I wanted to help him, too."

Her mom looked misty-eyed. Megan could only imagine all the thoughts going through her mind at that moment. "Your dad and I have to get over to relieve the Slaters," she said with a shaky voice. "Congratulations, sweetie." Her mom kissed the top of Sammy's head while her dad patted Sammy's hand. Then they headed toward their duties at the concession stand, but not before her mother had a chance to mouth, "Say something!" from behind Mac's back.

As if Megan didn't want to. But it wasn't easy when his words echoed in her mind, about how he'd done what he had for Sammy.

He may not even have feelings for her anymore.

The thought caused her words to falter as she asked, "Mac, can we—um, talk? Even if it's later, after we're through? I'd really like to talk to you."

"Yeah, sure," he said, looking more somber than excited about it. "There's uh"—he glanced down at his feet—"there's something I need to talk to you about anyway."

"Hey guys," a familiar voice chimed from behind them. "Guess who? It's your favorite photographer." Janey came around to face them.

Sammy the chatterbox spoke first. "You come to take picture of my ribbon?"

"Better yet, how about I take a picture of you, Sammy O'Donnell, the number one bowler, holding your ribbon?" Janey smiled.

"Okay. And Maw-mee and Mac, too," Sammy insisted.

"Hey, it's your picture. You can have whoever you want in it." Janey adjusted the lens on her camera. "How about it, you two?" She looked up. "You in?"

Megan felt like it was taking Mac all the time in the world to get situated behind Sammy's wheelchair. And it wasn't lost on her how he finally claimed the opposite side of the chair, at the farthest point the two of them could stand from one another. Not so long ago he would've reached out for her hand. Or had his arm wrapped around her waist or shoulder as they leaned in toward Sammy for a picture. Now it was as if he was literally repelled by her. In the midst of what was supposed to be a celebratory moment, her head dropped at the sad thought.

"Um, could you look up, Meg? And could you all get a little closer? Like the three of you know each other?" Janey peered from behind the camera again.

Megan's heart pounded wildly as she and Mac stepped nearer to one another. Especially when Mac's shoulder brushed against hers. Instantly without a conscious thought, she felt a surge of warmth rise up within her. No matter what, he would always be able to do that to her.

Standing there, cheeks on fire, trying to smile at the camera, she couldn't help but think how far they'd come since Janey had taken the first picture of the two of them together. And sadly, how far she'd managed to push them apart.

Maybe it had only been twelve hours total. But in Mac's mind, it had been a crazy-long day of trying his hardest not to look at Megan.

Especially since for the past few months, looking at her had topped his list as one of his favorite things to do.

He'd spent the day turned away from her smile, not wanting to remember how it used to lift him up. Kept his eyes plastered on Sammy, or the ground, or whatever else he could find, so he wouldn't have to look into her eyes, knowing there wasn't a place for him there anymore.

Even with everything else going on around him, with the competitions and kids and all, it'd been tough not to notice how she was prettier to him than every other girl out there in her red T-shirt, dark hair tucked behind her ears.

So it had been better not to look as much as he could. Not to notice at all.

Until now. Now he had no choice.

Because after Rick Hall emceed the closing ceremonies, giving praise and thanks for the day, and everyone had cheered about the idea of a second annual All-Stars Sports Day. . .

After carloads of participants took over an hour to pack up and wait patiently to exit the event. . .

After Laura and Kurt had driven off to take Sammy for celebration ice cream. . .

And every last one of the volunteers' cars had disappeared one by one from his farm. . .

After all that, it was only Megan and him and a setting sun, languidly spreading its pink-orange glow across the sky as if taking a long, slow bow at the end of its performance for the day. As if it, too, was about to depart.

Leaving them completely alone.

"What a day!" Megan let go of a happy sigh and sat on one of the loaner park benches. He noticed she'd positioned herself to the far right side, leaving plenty of room for him.

He felt a reckless surge, almost like he was giving in to a dare, when he decided to sit beside her. "A great day."

"Can you believe it? We did it. Well, us and dozens of huge-hearted volunteers."

He still wasn't keen on looking into her face. But he didn't have to. He could hear the pure joy in her voice when she exclaimed, "The first All-Stars Sports Day! Unbelievable."

"You've been dreaming about this day for a while, haven't you?"

"For years," she admitted. Sounding wistful, she continued, "See, somehow I thought I'd have to do it all alone. Somehow I thought I should do it all on my own. But that just wasn't true, was it? If I had worked alone, it wouldn't have turned out near as well." Her hair fell across her face when she leaned forward and turned her gaze toward him. "Mac, this entire day wouldn't have been possible without you. Without your help."

"Yeah, well." He sloughed off the compliment. "I really doubt that's true. With all your passion for the kids, I imagine you could do anything you wanted to."

And all very well without me, he wanted to add since she was the one who didn't need him in her life anymore. But he didn't say that. Why sound like a sore sport?

"Well. . .I wouldn't have *wanted* to do it without you, Mac."

So she wanted to do the event with him. Just not life. He ground his jaw. Whatever. He was trying not to hold it against her that she didn't feel the same way he did. But pride or no pride, it was still hard to believe. Hard to come to terms with.

"And now we've got the second annual All-Stars Sports Day to look forward to. I hope you won't mind helping."

Still feeling a little bitter—and more than a little put out with her—he got to the point. "Is that what you wanted to talk to me about?"

"Yes. Well, no, it was more than that. It was—" She instantly froze up. Seemed caught off guard like she needed another moment to gather her thoughts when she said, "But you mentioned you wanted to talk to me about something, too?"

"Yeah, yeah." He rubbed his hands together. "About Sammy's birthday party. I got the invitation and. . ."

Her eyes widened as she looked at him apprehensively. Did she want him to say yes? Or no? He wasn't sure.

"I'll be there, but it'll be toward the end of the party."

He noticed she looked relieved. Surely for the same reason he was even going to the party—to be sure to spare Sammy's feelings.

"That's fine. We can always wait to sing and cut the cake until you get there."

"Well, don't feel like you have to. I'll do my best to get back to Loveland from the airport as fast as I can though."

She clasped her hands together, rubbing her right thumb across the knuckles on her left hand. "You're—you said you're going out of town?"

"Yeah, I, uh—" He figured he might as well go ahead and tell her. People were going to start hearing things soon enough anyway. "A lot's happened since we talked last. My elbow got cleared, for one."

"I just heard that today, Mac. From Wendy. That's wonderful news. I'm really happy for you."

"Yeah." It wasn't the way he'd pictured telling her, but then lately nothing had been going the way he imagined it would, had it? "On the heels of that I got some other news. No one knows except for Hal, and now you, but there's a 99 percent chance I won't be here in Loveland next year to help with the All-Stars Sports Day."

"You won't?" Her brows furrowed.

"No. In all likelihood I'm being traded."

"Traded?" She frowned. "To where?"

"Sacramento."

"Cali–California?" She looked shocked.

"I know. Could they send me any farther? Obviously nothing will or can be finalized next week. But they've got me flying out for a meeting with the team heads, and Hal says they've already come up with some numbers. So. . ." He paused, took a deep breath. "That's what I wanted to tell you. I'll be back on Saturday but I'll only be able to catch the last part of Sammy's party."

She sat staring at him, not saying a word.

"Can you explain that to Sammy for me?"

"Oh." She blinked then nodded. "Of course I can. Yeah, I will. But Mac, if it's a lot of trouble. . .you've already done so much for him. I can't believe how you made time to practice bowling with him. And then, he won. You're so. . ." She stopped herself. "It's something he'll never forget, Mac. I won't either."

He didn't know what to say. Even though there was a lot he could've said. Like how it was nothing. How he'd do anything for Sammy. For her. How once he started doing for them he'd never wanted to stop. Never thought it would stop.

"I didn't mind. He's a great kid."

They sat in silence for a moment. He looked out into the fields but could feel her next to him. Now her hands were unclasped. She rubbed them over the legs of her shorts.

"So are you glad about it?" she asked. "About the trade?"

"Well. . ." he drawled then finally turned to look into her eyes. "I have to be honest, I wasn't at first. But then I started thinking maybe it'll be a good way—and a good place—to start over. Far from past history here. Fresh. New team. New surroundings. New people."

"Well. . ." She paused, sought his eyes. "Good then. I'm happy for you, Mac." She nodded, her lips curved in a slight smile. "You deserve to be happy."

He'd been fighting all day looking at her too closely. And now, having her stare at him that way, he'd thought of asking her to consider the two of them one more time. To ask what had gone wrong—or how he'd apparently misread her feelings so badly from the start. But then, why? He really didn't need the extra hit to his pride.

Instead he only asked, "So, what did you want to talk to me about?"

"Oh, that's all. Just, uh, about Sammy's party. I'll mark you down as a yes but coming late. And speaking of late. . ." She jumped up from the bench. "I bet you'd like to have this place to yourself. Mom and Dad and Sammy are probably finished with their ice cream by now anyway.

"So. Great day." She held up her hand to him like they were friends who normally high-fived, instead of like the couple they used to be who would squeeze each other's hands. Hold each other's hands. And touch each other gently. Lovingly.

"Yeah, big day." He nodded.

Part of him couldn't help but want to reach out and grab her hand, pull her into him like he had so many times before. But, of course, he didn't dare.

Even so, he hated that as he met her hand in the air, his fingers lingered on hers more than just a moment too long. Then once again, they parted. She was on her way. Gone.

Chapter 22

Ever since he'd been a toddler, Sammy had been fascinated by balloons. Such a simple thing, yet they brought out the biggest smiles in him.

That's why every year on his birthday Megan made a special point to go all-out on the balloon front. Or, actually her balloon planting began the night before his big day. That's when she'd sneak into his bedroom after he'd fallen asleep and leave a multi-colored bouquet to surprise him in the morning. Downstairs, too, she'd have another group of balloons standing ready to bob around his birthday cake at party time. And there was always one special balloon—an extraordinary sort of one—she'd choose to tie onto the arm of his wheelchair.

This year, that balloon was Party Town's number twenty-seven. A three-and-a-half foot, bright yellow Happy Face, wearing a polka-dot party hat along with its traditional plastered-on smile.

With Mac another week gone from her life. . .and thinking

about all the weeks and years ahead without him, Megan needed the Mylar smile to cheer her up. To help her get outside glum thoughts about the future. And to remind her to focus on the present. Namely, Sammy's special day.

Even so, she couldn't help but think about Mac each time the doorbell rang. Although he said he'd be arriving late, her heart involuntarily lurched in her chest—she bet as much as Sammy's did. Only she knew her son's heightened anticipation mostly had to do with Rachel.

"Think that her, Maw-mee?" he asked when the bell chimed again.

Due to sheer process of elimination, Rachel had to show up soon. Sammy's smiling face and his Happy Face balloon had already greeted most of the other guests earlier at the door—her parents, Allie and Greg and their crew, the Slaters and the Biddles. Janey, Rachel and Sean, and Mac were their only no-shows so far.

"It very well could be, Samster. Let's check it out."

Pushing his chair across the foyer, she noticed him patting his hair once more and really hoped that his first crush ever would be at the door, if only so he wouldn't have to go through the anticipation all over again.

Luckily, Megan walked around the wheelchair and opened the door to Rachel and Sean, and—

Janey?

"Hey, you guys." Trying to act as natural as ever, she hailed the three of them in out of the misty drizzle, all the while surreptitiously glancing over their shoulders out to the driveway. Janey's car had to be out there somewhere, didn't it? But she didn't see it in the drive or on the street, and though everything inside her wanted to know what was going on, she tried her best to pretend that the three of them arriving together was the most natural thing ever.

"Come on in!" she said, feeling like the Happy Face balloon's twin sister, a smile ingrained on her face.

"Happy birthday, Sammy!" Rachel exclaimed over the adult's hellos. Clamoring across the threshold like a female thoroughbred focused on the finish line, she handed Sammy a gift wrapped in Spiderman paper. As Megan shut the front door behind her guests, she didn't think she'd ever seen his eyes glow quite so bright.

"Oh Sammy," Rachel squealed, "you have the best balloon ever." She gave the Happy Face a gentle bat.

"It have big smile," he said to his new friend and crush. "Want to see my cake? It have big smile, too."

"Sure." Rachel took over the wheelchair easily. Megan always appreciated how the young girl never hesitated. How she never let the hunk of metal stand between herself and Sammy.

After a moment, Greg came up and whisked Sean over to where the men were watching the baseball playoffs. Which left her and Janey. Staring at one another.

"So, you and. . . ? You two came together?" The mere idea was so improbable to Megan, so out of the blue, that she couldn't even manage to put their two names in a sentence together.

"Me and Sean." Janey's eyes glowed. "Yeah, we came together all right. Can you believe it? Crazy, isn't it?" Purse hanging at her side, she hugged her arms around herself, shaking her head in disbelief. "Oh Megan, I've started to call you a million times to tell you. I even wanted to mention it when you called the last couple of times to tell me about Mac. But then. . .I felt so bad about the two of you and how things were going. And, I don't know. I thought maybe I'd jinx something if I started talking about how much I've been starting to care for Sean. How it feels like there's something real between us. You know?"

Megan blinked.

Janey thought there might be something real between them? Evidently a lot had happened in the past few days. She tried to process that quickly. "My mom mentioned she'd seen you two. At the movie on the banks. But I didn't really think—"

"Your mom? Really? Did she say anything? I mean, did she, you know, get a feeling about the two of us?"

Her friend seemed so eager to hear that it almost made Megan feel envious, remembering how good it had felt to have feelings like that for Mac. Evidently, too, Janey was so head over heels for Sean that she'd forgotten she'd never put much stock into what her matchmaking mom had to say. But Megan wasn't about to remind her suddenly lovesick friend of that.

"Actually, Mom said that even though you both were sitting apart during the movie, when you met up at intermission, you two looked like you were together."

"She did? Your mom said that? Well, if she can see something special, then maybe it is real." She blushed, her eyes gleaming as she looked off into the distance, into the family room where Sean was watching TV with the guys.

"But how did you two hook up? I just don't get it." Megan almost had to wave her hand in front of Janey's face to get her friend's attention.

"I know, it's crazy. But not bad crazy. I think it's good, Megan."

"I'm sure you're right. It's surprising, that's all." Two weeks ago, Janey had been lamenting about Sean. Now she was talking about a real relationship with him?

"Well, before the movie even began, I spotted Sean sitting across the amphitheater," she said, her voice barely above a whisper. "I couldn't believe he was there. I got these butterflies in my stomach. The whole thing. It even got worse when he glanced around and noticed me. And then at intermission we sort of nodded to each other and met up and talked. And the whole time, I just kept remembering what you and Allie had said."

Megan remembered what Allie had said. But she was clueless on any advice she'd given out. She certainly wasn't in the position to give relationship advice, that was for sure.

"What I said?"

"Yeah. In the bakery that day. You said people change."

"And so you think Sean has changed?" As far as Megan could tell, Sean appeared to be the same nice guy he'd been in high school. But if Janey had thought he'd changed somehow and that led the two of them together, more power to the both of them.

So she was surprised when Janey said, "Actually, no. I suddenly realized that all along it wasn't Sean who had to change."

"It wasn't?"

"No, it was me. I needed to change."

"Well, don't change too much." Megan laughed. "I've grown accustomed to all your quirks and weirdnesses over the years."

But even as she said that, she could feel a twinge of envy

resurfacing. There was a calm about Janey that she'd never witnessed before.

Janey laughed. "Oh, I don't mean that. Not things with you and me. I mean with guys. I realized I needed to stop being in competition with them. Needed to stop making up stories about them to myself about who they are and what they're like before I even got to know them. And, Megan, oh my gosh!" Her cheeks flushed red against her creamy white skin again. "It's been so great. Sean and I have hung out every night this week. I can't believe how well we get along. I'd been carrying around a grudge since high school for no reason at all. It was so stupid." She waved a hand to the past. "And you know after we talked about it, we realized Stacy Littleton was the one who got us pitted against each other at the senior prom."

Megan remembered Stacy well. A girl who could have five guys liking her at one time but was never happy unless she was stirring up trouble for someone else.

"You didn't mention Red to Sean, did you?"

"I had to, Megan. I wanted to start clean. Be honest, like Allie suggested."

"What did he say?"

She laughed. "He knew it was me all along."

"But he'd asked me about the mysterious redhead."

"Figuring you wouldn't rat me out anyway."

Megan bit her lip. "He doesn't think I'm awful for not telling him?"

"No, just thinks you were being a friend. And he thinks I look good as a redhead, too." She giggled then looked around, sobered, and shrugged. "I didn't see Mac's truck out front. Is he coming?"

"He said he'd be late." She started to tell Janey the reason why but then stopped herself. Mac's business was his and his alone. If he wanted anyone to know his whereabouts or about changes in his life, that information should rightfully come from him.

"Oh! I have copies of the photo I took when Sammy won. I made five-by-sevens for you actually." She removed an envelope from her purse. "I thought you guys would like it. It'll run in tomorrow's Sunday paper, recapping the event and talking about next year's plans. Which was good I had a photo of the co-chairs anyway. I brought one along for Mac if you can help me remember to give it to him when he gets here."

"No problem, I can do that." Megan laid the envelope on the foyer table. "We'll put them here so we don't forget. Thanks, Janey. That was so sweet of you to make copies." She put her arm around her friend. "Guess we should join the party, huh? And go visit with that new beau of yours?" she said, not even bothering to open the envelope and glance at the photos of the three of them.

She couldn't at the moment. Not if she hoped to keep smiling.

Huge as it was, O'Hare's overcrowded airport terminal felt small and stuffy to Mac. Especially the designated section where he sat squeezed between two weary-looking travelers. He'd been sitting that way for over an hour waiting, which shouldn't have bugged him as much as it did.

After all, the quick trip out to California had been extremely worthwhile, and after meeting with the Miners' people the night before, he was heading back to Loveland, verbally assured he'd be playing ball next season for a stellar team and making more money than ever before.

But the day had been filled with delays. His initial flight held up because of a mechanical malfunction, and then further delays because of heavy thunderstorms in the Midwest.

For a while it didn't look like he'd make the connecting flight in Chicago, but after all the setbacks, he'd gotten there in the nick of time. With the hour time difference, he could make the tail end of Sammy's birthday party as planned.

That is, if his connecting flight got off the ground in the next fifteen minutes. Otherwise. . .

He hated to think about it.

Hated to think he'd made a promise to Sammy and had little to no control to make that promise come true.

Tired of not seeing any movement out the steam-filled windows and too agitated to sit still any longer, he got up and stretched his legs then picked up his carry-on and made his way over to the attendant at the boarding desk.

"Look, is there any reason we're not boarding yet? Isn't the flight scheduled to leave in the next fifteen minutes?" He knew he sounded huffy, but he couldn't help himself.

"Sir, I'm going to be making an announcement in just a moment."

"And then we'll be boarding?"

She looked at him but wouldn't give him an answer confirming or denying that.

"Trust me, miss, you can fill me in now. I won't tell anyone, I promise. It's just I have to get to a party."

"A party?"

"For a little boy. He's seven today." He glanced at his watch. "And I can still make his party if the flight leaves pronto."

Her face softened at the mention of a seven-year-old. "Well, I'm sorry to tell you, I'm about ready to announce that all the flights are being canceled."

"Canceled?"

She nodded. "Heavy mist. Poor visibility."

"Canceled temporarily or for the rest of the day?"

She shrugged. "We don't have any control over the weather, sir."

"I know, but. . ." Telling her how he had to get to the party again was a waste of time, he knew, and only made him sound ridiculous. "Of course you don't," he said instead. "Thanks for your help."

Lifting his cell phone from his shirt pocket, he went to sit down again. He plunked his bag on the floor and this time sat in a chair that faced away from the menacing weather. If nothing else, he could at least call Megan and ask to speak to Sammy and wish him a happy birthday.

He could. . .if only weeks ago he hadn't deleted Megan's cell number from his phone. He'd deleted her mom's cell number along with it, figuring it'd be too easy to reach out to her in a moment of weakness.

Tired and perplexed, he hung his head in his hands. Nothing seemed to be working out for them. Not a single thing. Every time he turned around there was something else keeping him from Megan, and Sammy, too, for that matter. First Megan and her out-of-the-blue dismissal of their relationship. Then the trade offer. And now a simple flight.

It must not be in God's plan, he decided. It must not be. And he'd simply have to get used to it. Even if he didn't want to.

"Aww. . ." he groaned into his hands and stayed like that for a while, a million thoughts jumbled in his mind.

Finally, he lifted his head and started to lean back in the chair and close his eyes. He may as well nap. It wasn't as if he was going anywhere. But before he could lean back, his eyes lit on a woman and a little boy. They were holding hands, walking down the aisle between the gates.

The two reminded him so much of Megan and Sammy that it made his heart ache. Reminding him of how much he'd wanted to be a part of their lives. Reminding him of how he'd changed for the better to the depths of himself, and Megan's heart still remained elusive to him.

But what was he supposed to do about it? Beg her?

Frustrated, he tried to tear his eyes away from the mother and son. Until a baseball hat fell from the boy's pocket and the pair kept walking, not noticing.

Jumping up from his seat, Mac went to pick up the hat. Over the pockets of travelers, he called out to the mother. "Excuse me. Miss? Ma'am?"

Somehow the woman heard him and turned. She eyed him curiously.

"Your son." He strode toward them, the cap in his hand. The little boy immediately moved closer to his mother, hugging her leg. "He dropped his baseball hat."

"Oh, thank you!" Gratitude shone in her eyes as she reached for it. "He would've been so upset if he'd lost his hat," she told Mac. "Wouldn't you?" She looked down at her son who replied with a nod.

"Yeah? Is he a big White Sox fan?" Mac asked her, since her son appeared to be somewhat shy. "Did one of the players autograph it for him or something?"

The woman smiled. "Oh no. Nothing like that." She gave a slight shrug. "It's special because his daddy bought it for him."

Mac stood and watched the two of them for a moment, but they blended into the crowd and disappeared so quickly he wondered if he'd really seen the mother and son at all.

But it didn't matter. He'd seen what he needed to. Suddenly, he knew what he had to do.

He'd never given up in a baseball game. He'd always tried his hardest, to the bitter end. How could he give up on Megan when he loved her more than anything he had ever loved in his life? And Sammy—the boy was too much a part of him now.

Unfortunately, his pride had kept him from questioning Megan much that night she said they didn't have to see each other anymore. Even though it didn't seem like something Megan would do—to lead a guy on—his pride kept him from talking to her all the days that followed.

He'd been so hurt, he hadn't considered anything that was going on in her mind. Only in his own. He kept telling himself not to worry, to get over it. That he could have his pick of any woman.

But the truth was the only woman he really wanted lived in Loveland, Ohio, with her son.

And no, he wouldn't beg her to listen to him. He wouldn't beg her to tell him what all was going on in her head.

Unless, of course, he had to.

"Okay, God," he whispered under his breath. "I get it. I do. Thank You, Lord, for making me see. Thank You."

He glimpsed at his watch, set to eastern standard time. "Home" time. The party would be ending soon, and there wasn't a chance under the heavens that he'd get there for that of course. But Loveland was less than five and a half hours from Chicago. And if he didn't waste a minute more, he might be able to still get there before Sammy's birthday was completely over.

Picking up his carry-on, he made his way over to the boarding station again, realizing that despite all the good news from Miners' staff the night before, he really hadn't felt like smiling all that much. Until just now.

"Hey, one more question."

The attendant held up her hand to stop him. "Sir, I just told you there's nothing I can—"

He cut her off. "Trust me, I heard you. And I apologize if I was even slightly rude before. But now I need to know, where's the nearest rental car agency?"

Chapter 23

D on't need to put jammies on," Sammy mildly protested hours after his birthday guests had gone home.

In contrast to his slight crankiness, the Happy Face balloon still bobbed and smiled widely at Megan as she pushed his wheelchair down the hallway.

"Honey, it's that time of night." She paused in the doorway of his bedroom and flicked on the wall switch. A ceramic lamp with a catcher's mitt base illuminated from his nightstand. "Time for bed."

"Buh Mac still coming. Don't want to be in jammies when Mac come."

Sammy was still wearing the bowling glove Rachel had given him and the cotton sweater vest Mrs. Biddle had knit for him while she'd been recuperating. He also had the photo Janey had taken on All-Stars Sports Day laying in his lap and would've been clutching the new bowling ball her parents had given him if she hadn't urged him to leave it in the family room with the rest of his gifts so they'd all be in one place in the morning.

Megan couldn't blame him for wanting to hold on to his special day awhile longer. But holding on to the notion that Mac was still coming wasn't as easy to deal with. It pressed on her heart.

"Sammy, Mac had to fly clear across the country, and sometimes people get tired or delayed. There were a lot of storms everywhere today. You saw it raining here off and on." She pulled back the covers on his bed, not wanting to make excuses for Mac. But not wanting her son to feel dejected either. The part about the weather was absolutely true. Even though it could also be true that at the last minute Mac had decided not to come after all. Not that she could blame him. She'd given him every opportunity to excuse himself from their lives. Left the door wide open and practically pushed him out of it, giving him full permission to exit. To be gone from them forever.

"Did he call and say he not coming?" Sammy asked, his question more logical than anything she'd been thinking.

"Well, no, he didn't. But—"

"Then he coming. He told me he always be here," her son announced. "He be here," Sammy said emphatically. "Tha why I can't go to bed. Can't put on jammies. Say prayers later."

"Okay." She gave in. Against her better judgment. After all, how disappointed was he going to be when he woke up in the morning and found out Mac hadn't shown up?

But she was far too tired to think about all that now. It had been a big day for both of them. She'd simply deal with tomorrow, tomorrow. "Then how about you keep your clothes on, we take off your shoes, and then you can lie down and rest for a bit?"

"Rest till Mac get here." Sammy nodded agreeably with the new plan and didn't balk at all while she took off his shoes, picked him up, and laid him on top of his bed.

"Do you want the sheet over you?"

He yawned wide then nodded.

"And let's put this picture on your dresser first then, so it doesn't get wrinkled, okay?"

"Uh-huh." He nodded again, his eyes already drooping. "No wrinkle."

She removed the photo from his hands and placed it on the dresser before covering him with the sheet. Tucking him in, she leaned over and kissed his forehead.

"It was a good birthday. And you're a great birthday boy."

"Good birt-day." He yawned once more.

"I love you, my big seven-year-old."

A slight smile tugged at the corner of his mouth, though his eyelids dipped even more. "Love you, Maw-mee. If I. . .sleep. . .you wake. . .when Mac here?"

She stood up straight, wondering for a moment how she could answer him. But then she didn't have to say anything. Didn't have to make him a potentially empty promise. She could tell from his even breathing that he'd already fallen asleep.

Turning off the light switch, she paused in the doorway for a moment watching him. But the sight of him sleeping filled her with so much pleasure, she decided the birthday mess could wait.

A nightlight in the corner cast a dim glow as she settled into the rocking chair across the room from his bed. She hadn't sat in the cushioned rocker for a while. But through all the years, its familiar feel had always been the same, a comfortable place in the black of night where she'd rocked an infant Sammy to sleep. Or soothed him when he could still fit in her arms on nights a fever or a bad dream kept him from sleeping.

But how he was growing up now! She studied the length of him stretched over the bed, marveling at the boy he was on the outside. And on the inside as well. Intrinsically, his faith in people, and good, and God never wavered.

Oh, if only she'd had that kind of faith when she'd first met Mac. That kind of childlike faith that didn't only believe—but trusted earnestly. Then she wouldn't have second-guessed herself or him.

If only she had changed like Mac had—and even Janey. They'd both stopped letting their pasts dictate their futures. But she hadn't. She'd let all her fears of failing at love again overshadow the love she had for Mac. And she'd let all the lies she'd built up in her mind, all the what-ifs, dilute the blessing of Mac's love for her. She'd allowed it all to override the gift of happiness that God wanted to give her.

By focusing on the negative, she'd barely given credence to the positive. In every way, she'd looked at Mac's celebrity as if it were a frightening thing. But lying right on top of Sammy's dresser was proof of something bigger and grander than that. Something more than she'd ever imagined. A photo of her and Sammy and Mac that because of his celebrity might get noticed in the newspaper—and ultimately might change lives and give promise to so many others.

How could I have been so blind? She looked out the window. *How?* She searched the rain-dreary darkness. Finding nothing there, she turned back to the soft glow of the room, cradling her head in her hands.

"Oh dear Father in heaven, I don't want to be like this or live like this anymore. I don't." Her mind cried out like never before. Not even after she'd talked to her mom had she really understood and succumbed to His will. But now was different. Now it was all she wanted to do. With every part of her. "I don't want to try to be in control. I want to surrender. To You, dear Lord." Tears flowed from her eyes. Her heart wrenched with sorrow and repentance. "Please forgive me for my doubts, for not trusting. From this day forward, please know I trust You to lead me. I'm asking You, please, to guide me. I trust that when I close my eyes at night, You won't slumber or sleep and You will watch over my Sammy always. I trust that wherever You lead, I don't need to fear, because You will be right there with me. And I thank You for that, heavenly Father. I thank You for Your mercy and love and forgiveness always. I pray this in Jesus' name. Amen."

She wished she'd realized her mistakes sooner. She wished she'd seen them before now, when Mac was already gone from her life.

But she couldn't control the past any more than she could control the future. Only God was in charge of that. It was all in His hands. She knew that now. She trusted that. And for once in her life it wasn't an unsettling or a frightening thought. It was a comforting one.

Closing her eyes, she laid her head back on the chair cushion and rocked gently, a feeling of thankfulness washing over her as well as a calming peace she'd never known and had only heard about before.

At the time he'd been standing in O'Hare's overcrowded terminal, it had seemed like a good idea to drive from Chicago back home to Loveland. And actually, the weather hadn't been all that threatening on the road. The five plus hours had passed by rather quickly.

Yeah. . .it seemed like the right thing to do. To drive back for Sammy's birthday. Even though Sammy would most likely be asleep, it would prove to Megan that he was a man of his word. More than that, it was a chance to take hold of a situation he'd been too prideful to face before.

But once he pulled the compact rental car into Megan's driveway, his boldness disappeared, like it was stranded out on the highway somewhere. He sat with the engine idling, staring at the digital clock on the dash. It was 11:39 p.m. 11:40. 11:41.

All the hours he'd spent driving, he'd concocted a variety of scenarios. All about what he'd say to Megan. What Megan would say to him. In every one of those scenarios, he'd imagined her changing her mind, saying yes to him and declaring her undying love. He'd never entertained the thought she could say no to the idea of them trying one more time.

At least not until now.

Which caused him to pause. Scratch at the day-old stubble on his chin. And struggle with the choices he had.

He could pull out of the driveway and consider himself lucky he'd gotten home safely.

He could sit and watch the rain run down the windshield all night long.

Or he could do something more constructive than both of those. He decided on his last choice.

Turning off the ignition, he bowed his head and began to pray. He asked for the right words to say. Words from his heart, that Megan would listen to and hear. Words that he meant, ones she could trust. He prayed for God's blessing over the two of them, and then he slid out of the car.

Trickles of rain pelted him all the way up Megan's walk. Standing at her front door, realizing it was midnight and assuming once more Sammy was asleep, he decided to knock instead of ringing the doorbell and taking the chance of waking him.

Once. Twice. Three times. He knocked over and over again, hoping she'd hear. Or maybe she had. Maybe she'd looked out the window and saw it was him and didn't want to come to the door.

It didn't matter. He'd driven a long way, and he'd stand outside in the rain all night if he had to. Ironic as it was, he felt proud of the fact that he'd managed to put his ego away. All in the name of love.

Startled out of sleep, Megan sat up in the rocking chair and blinked. She'd heard something, but what?

There it was again. A knock at the front door. What time was it? She glanced at Sammy's clock radio. . .11:47?

Heart pounding, she got to her feet, stealthily tiptoed out of Sammy's bedroom and padded cautiously down the hallway.

Standing at the edge of her entryway, she didn't know whether to be frightened or worried. She just hoped the knocking would stop. That whoever it was, would go away.

But it kept up. And then, she heard a voice. *His voice.*

And for more reasons than she could even name—hope, excitement, the possibility of disappointment—her heart began to pound all over again.

"Mac?" Rushing to the sidelight windows that flanked the front door, she peered out at his rain-soaked face. Immediately she unlocked the door and let him in.

"Mac, are you okay? Is everything all right?" It wasn't just that his clothes dripped with rainwater that alarmed her. It was the way he stood hunched over, like a man who'd been through something. Though she noticed his eyes glowed as if he might be nearing the other side of whatever that "something" was.

A hundred questions ran through her mind, but so many thoughts did, too. Like how she wished she could reach out and touch his rain-soaked hair. Or wipe the raindrops from his cheek. Afraid she might do just that, she only said instead, "Let me get you a towel."

Starting to walk toward the bathroom, he caught her arm. "Megan, wait. Please." He held on to her. Tightly.

"Mac, why are you here?" She stood facing him. "Sammy's asleep and—it's nice of you to come. But—"

"I know. It's late. I'm sorry." He nodded an apology. "All the flights were canceled. So I got a rental car."

"You drove? From Chicago?"

"I knew I'd be too late for Sammy's party. But I said I'd be here. And. . .I'm here."

He was at that. All six feet of him, filling her entryway the way his love had filled—still filled—her heart. And she wasn't sure what she was going to say. Or how she was going to say it. But this time she wasn't going to let a chance to talk to him pass again.

"Mac, I need to tell you—" she started to say.

But he pressed a finger to her lips.

"Don't. Please don't tell me to go. At least not yet, okay? I have to say something first. Something I realized at the airport today. I saw this mom and her son, and well. . ." He paused, as if to gather his thoughts. Maybe even his nerve?

"You know, when I played ball, for years I thought the measure of who I was as a man was only reflected in my stats. The same statistics that flashed up on the screen every time I pitched or came up to the plate. And the bad thing about that is those statistics can send you on a roller-coaster ride. Lots of ups and downs. With everyone watching. And it's not a good ride, trust me. It can make you crazy. Make you do crazy things." He hung his head before he spoke again.

"But Megan." He looked up, searching her eyes. "These past months, especially the months since I've been with you, let me know that's not true. Now I know the measure of a man is based on his faith. His family. The people he loves. And I love you and Sammy, Megan, I do. And I don't know what went wrong between us. If I did too much. Or not enough. I'm not too proud to say I'm not perfect. I make mistakes. And I made a big mistake that night that I let you walk out of my life without even trying to stop you. But with all that said, I realize it's late, but can we talk now? So I can know for sure there's not still something between—"

It was her turn to stop him. She pressed her finger to his lips, halting him. She had to. She couldn't let him go on, looking in such agony, explaining himself. Especially when it should be the other way around, explaining herself to him.

"Something between us? Oh Mac, there was something great between us!"

His heart lifted with hope. He stared at her looking confused, and rightfully so.

"But then," she continued, "I put other things in our way. All that stuff I said about not seeing each other? I told myself it was best because I loved you too much. I told myself that it was only right to give you the freedom to let your career take you wherever you wanted to go. Not to make you compromise. But that was just a cover-up for all my fears. Fears from my past relationship. Fears of the future.

"I'm so sorry, Mac. I am." She bit her lip, searching her heart for more ways to explain. "I was afraid things wouldn't work out between us before I'd even given them a chance to. I wanted to duck out before Sammy could get hurt. Before I could. And well, I went completely overboard trying to control everything."

"You *can* be quite a mother hen sometimes." A smile tweaked at the side of his mouth. At his lips. "A cute mother hen, but still. . ."

"I don't want to be like that anymore. God brought you into my life, and I want to love you and be with you and accept all that comes along with loving you, MacNeill Hattaway. Whatever that is. I want to try. If you could only give me one more chance, Mac. Please?"

"You? One more chance?" He curled his hand over hers and drew her into his chest, wet shirt and all. She didn't care, it felt good and right and even warm cuddled in his arms. How had she ever dared to let him out of her life for one minute? What a fool she'd been!

"It'll be a tough job," he teased, pressing her close. "But I'm thinking I'm just the man for it." He looked down at her. "When do I start?"

"How about now?" She inched up on tiptoes, gazing at him, not closing her eyes until he bent his head to kiss her. And at the first instant she felt his lips on hers, tears filled her eyes. Tears of thankfulness. Of joy. And of course, of love.

Oh, what would she have done all her life, never knowing the feel of his arms. . .his lips again?

His kiss was slow, thoughtful at first, sending shivers through every part of her. A kiss her once-lost soul could melt into. But little by little, the intensity grew. His demanding lips caressed hers, recapturing all the love they'd almost lost between them. And then, softer again as if realizing the preciousness of that love. Only stopping long enough for him to say, "I've missed you, Megan."

She'd missed him, too. So much. And she could've easily stood there kissing him until the sun came up if it hadn't been for Sammy's voice calling from down the hallway.

"Mac. That you?"

Their kiss ended, but Mac still held her tight. She glanced up at him and smiled. "Seems you have another major fan besides me."

"What can I say? I'm a very lucky guy."

Holding Mac's hand, Megan led him down the hall. As soon as they reached Sammy's room though, she let go. Sammy had his arms raised as far up as he could manage, waiting to hug Mac around his neck.

"You come on my birt-day," her son told Mac once he released Mac from his loving grip.

Mac sat down on the bed beside him. Megan followed his line of vision as he glanced at Sammy's clock. "Yes, I'm late. But it's still your birthday, isn't it? 11:58. Happy birthday, buddy." The two went all out with their secret handshake which was becoming less of a secret nowadays, Megan mused.

"I knew you come." Sammy grinned, looking wide awake as if he'd never been asleep at all.

"Yeah? How'd you know that, bud?"

" 'Cause you said so," Sammy said matter-of-factly.

Mac's eyes shone when he looked from Sammy up to her. She thought he looked like he'd just been given the world and everything in it.

"It's true," she told him. "He never doubted you. Never." Emotion caught in her throat.

And I never will either. I promise, God, I do. Not when You've given me what I'd never dared to hope for—a man I can love and a man I can trust with my heart. . . And as she glanced at Sammy she added, and with my son—my life.

Chapter 24

D id you know that Ohio's state motto is, 'With God, all things are possible'?"

Mac's eyes left the road only long enough to glance at Megan in the passenger seat of his truck. The mid-morning sun came through the windshield, lighting her face, warming the cabin. Pretty woman. Nice end-of-the-summer weather. He'd remember this day always.

"I do know that, yes." Taking a tube of something from her purse, she dabbed glossy stuff over her lips. "Breakfast was really good, Mac. I love First Watch, don't you? Even if we did have to drive all the way to Montgomery, it was worth it."

"Uh-huh. It's great. Great pancakes," he answered, pausing for a moment, acting like he was studying the trees alongside the road when what he was actually doing was biding his time before feeding her more local trivia. "Oh, and do you know what they say about Ohio? They say, 'Ohio is at the heart of it all.'"

"Really? That's nice. I guess they mean the heart of the Midwest?"

It was an effort to act nonchalant, and to ignore the nervous twitch in his left eye. In his most professorial voice, he answered, "Yes. Yes, they do."

"Interesting." She nodded, even though she didn't appear that interested at all. "Sammy loves the First Watch blueberry pancakes." She reverted to the topic of breakfast again. "But I'm sure he's not minding having breakfast at Allie's after his sleepover with Justin and Carrie."

"I doubt it," Mac agreed. Lucky for him after he'd talked to Allie, she'd made all the arrangements for Sammy to stay there, no problem. She'd contacted Megan, acting as if it was all her idea. "I bet he's having fun with them."

"I'm sure he is."

She turned to look out the window, and Mac waited a moment before he cleared his throat and continued. "And by the way, Loveland, coincidentally, is called 'the sweetheart of Ohio.' Have you heard that before?"

Megan turned her gaze from staring out the window and stared at him. "Actually, I'm pretty sure I have." She tilted her head, looking at him in a curious way. "Wow, Mac." She smiled. Teetered on a giggle actually. "I had no idea you were so 'up' on your slogans."

Well, at least now he had her attention. He may as well lay it on before she changed the subject again. Turning his sights back on the road, he rambled on. "Yeah, good old Loveland is an amazing town, for sure. A great community with great schools fingering into three counties. Lots of shops, restaurants, activities. Even has a castle, of all things," he said referring to the locally well-known Loveland Castle. "And plenty of history," he added, as his farm came into view. He flicked on the right blinker. "You do know how Loveland got its name, don't you?"

"Yes, Mac. Yes, I do."

But though she'd just said she knew the history, he mowed right on just the way he'd planned.

"How Colonel Paxton came from Pennsylvania and first settled the area in 1795? But how later on, the name Paxton got replaced by Loveland because James Loveland was the area's first postmaster and an early shopkeeper, and the mailbag always got dropped off at Loveland's. You've heard that story?"

"As I just said, yes, I have," she answered. He tried not to notice the strain in her voice. "Now let me ask you a question." She glanced over at him.

"Shoot."

"Why all the talk about Loveland? I'm surprised you're not giving me fun facts about California. And Sacramento."

"You mean you're not fond of our little burg?"

"Well, of course I am. I've lived here all my life, silly."

A bit relieved at her answer, he pulled the truck onto the gravel drive and slowly made his way up to the house. Knowing the imminent moment grew closer, his stomach rocked slightly.

"I'm glad you wanted to see what I've done to the house. The renovations have taken forever."

"I'm happy you wanted to show them to me, Mac," she replied, but there was a question in her gaze. Which he could understand. He hadn't exactly been acting like his cool, calm self all morning. "I was never quite clear what all you were having done to the place."

"That's why we're here," he said. "So you can see."

Well, one of the reasons. He cut the engine and tried not to think about the other thing he hoped to accomplish as well. Instead, he hopped out of the truck and went around to the other side to help her out. She was already slipping down from the high seat and getting her bearings in her wedged shoes. She had on the same yellow dress he'd remembered her wearing the first time she'd visited the farm, but with a jean jacket over it. Though sunny, there was a slightly cool morning breeze reminding that summer would soon be departing for another year.

"Right this way, ma'am." He splayed out his hands, directing Megan to the new wide walkway that led to the back of the house. He couldn't have been more pleased when she readily noticed the change, oohing and aahing her approval.

"And a wheelchair ramp leading up to the back door?" Her eyes grew wide. "Mac, how wonderful."

"Yes, but that's not all." Trying not to wince at his own game-show host tone, he led her inside. For the next twenty minutes or more, he showed her all of the improvements that had been made, including widened hallways, lowered sinks to wheelchair level and so on—everything that had been done to make the house more wheelchair accessible.

"I can't believe all the changes. It's awesome," she complimented him. "It's a shame though, isn't it? After all this money and work, and now you'll be selling the place once you start playing in Sacramento, won't you?"

They hadn't gotten around to talking about the logistics of their relationship yet. They'd just agreed they wanted to be in each others' lives and somehow they'd make that work. But the more he had thought about it. . .

"I mean, a person has to go where life leads," she added matter-of-factly. "And California, here you come!" Her eyes shone and he knew without a doubt she was behind him all the way. "Sammy's going to love when we come to visit. He can watch you pitch. And after the games, we can take him to Disneyland. And Sea World in San Diego. He'll love it, don't you think?"

"Yeah, I. . ." He ruffled his fingers through his hair. And scratched at his chin.

"Mac, are you okay? You've been acting all jittery ever since we got here."

"Must've had too much coffee at breakfast."

"You only had orange juice."

"Oh yeah. Right."

He did wish he could calm down. His palms were sweating badly. Even worse than the night he first kissed her.

He sucked in a deep breath. "Can you come here a minute?" Taking her hand, he led her from the living room into the kitchen, over by the window. "See over there?" He pointed. "To the left of the baseball diamond? Where there's an open space in front of that grove of trees?"

Megan squinted. "Yeah. There's a lot of land. It's a very pretty setting."

"A nice place for a house, don't you think?"

"Well, sure. If a person wanted to build another home on this property. But it's hard to imagine a person would need another house. Especially when you've made this house so nice and cozy."

None of this was going anywhere. Not his chatter about Ohio and Loveland. Or talk of building a new house. She wasn't taking any of his hints. He had to spit it out, plain and simple.

"Okay, I can do this. I can do this," he murmured under his breath. But obviously not quietly enough.

"Do what?"

"Do you mind sitting down? In the chair there?" He pointed to the kitchen chair.

"Are you sure *you* don't need to sit down, Mac? You look kind of pale all of a sudden."

"No, I'm fine." Which wasn't true at all. He was sweating worse than ever. Like he was on the mound, bases loaded, *and* he was about to pitch to the best hitter in the league.

But he had to man up. He wanted to man up. For sure, Megan was the one. The only woman he ever wanted. He'd known it since the beginning.

"Megan, I know we've been saying we're in for the long haul. But I—I want to make it official. I don't want you to go off and do something silly, like try to kick me out of your life again."

Megan laughed out loud. He smiled at the sound. "Are you going to be bringing that up to me for the rest of my life?" she asked.

"Uh, I hope so. Yeah. I hope forever."

It was the perfect cue. Dipping his hand into the pocket of his jeans, he retrieved a small jewelry box, and then dropped to one knee in front of her.

"Oh Mac!" Her eyes brightened with surprise.

He opened the box, feeling good that he'd spent the time to shop around to find the perfect ring at an antique store in Hyde

Park. "Megan." He gazed up at her sweet face. "Will you do me the honor of marrying me?"

"Mac! Yes. Of course yes!" she said, no hesitation in her voice.

Relieved and thrilled, he started to take the ring from the box and place it on her finger, but then he stopped.

There were just a few more questions he needed to ask.

"And, Megan, will you build a house with me over in the field—that field I showed you?"

"A house for us in the field?"

"And also not mind if I never play pro ball again?"

She shot up out of the chair. He came up off the floor to face her. She plunged her hands onto her hips. He snapped the ring box shut.

What now?

Her flushed expression had gone from ecstatic to concerned to totally confused and even slightly angry in all but a few seconds. "Never play ball again? Mac, what are you talking about?"

"Well, except for with Sammy. I'll always play whatever he wants with him. And with our own kids, if we have them. And with special-needs kids, too," he tried to explain. "Megan, you just said a person has to go where life leads them. And I prayed about it, and this is where I've been led. I want to build a new house for us—for you and Sammy and me in the field where I showed you. And I'd like to make Uncle Jake's house and property a place where special-needs kids can come all year long for sports. Not just one day a year."

He thought she'd melt into him at that. But she didn't. He tried to pull her close, but she stood her ground, holding up her hands to halt him.

"Mac, we've been over this before. You don't have to do that for me. You don't have to pick between what you love. Or quit something you love. Sammy and I will be there, wherever you go. I've already told you that. I'll love you no matter what you do, I will," she promised. "My home is with you, Mac." She corrected herself. "Sammy and I, our home is with you."

He'd been in the limelight for many years of his life. But it never could compare to all the wonder and blessings he'd witnessed by following God's light. Like the blessing of Megan, whose presence in his life dazzled him each and every day.

"Then if it's okay with you. . ." He took the ring from the box and gently lifted her hand into his. "I say we stay right where we are, here in Loveland. Our home sweet home."

Chapter 25

Thanks for dropping me off." Megan leaned against Mac's truck and peeked inside, talking to him and Sammy over the running engine. "You two guys stay out of trouble, you hear?"

"Trouble? What trouble can we get into?" Mac grinned in his signature way. All irresistible man with a hint of mischievous boy blended in. "We're only going to the hardware store to buy a border fence for the bulbs you're planting. Right, Sammy?"

"Right," her son affirmed from the rear bench seat. "Me and Mac be good, Maw-mee. No worry."

"Oh!" Mac leaned across the seat, as close to the passenger window as he could. "Tell your mom to tell your dad that we're a go for watching the OSU game tonight."

"Okay, will do."

"Oh—and there's something else." He crooked his finger. She inched her head into the cab again, closer to his. "I love you," he said.

She smiled. "I love you, too." Their lips brushed in a gentle, knowing kiss. "And I love you, Samster." She blew a kiss to her son.

The first part of their mission accomplished—dropping her off—Mac and Sammy pulled away, leaving her standing on the sidewalk in downtown Loveland. The same part of the walk where her feet had stepped hundreds of times before. Right in front of We Do! Wedding Planners.

Only this time felt different. Because it was. Quite different. She'd never had an appointment with one of the wedding planners inside. And today she did. With her mom.

"Hi, Mom." The door chimed with sweet familiarity as she stepped inside. Even though it was only her mother she was meeting with, the fact that she was meeting with her mother "the wedding planner" caused her stomach to twitter a bit.

"I hope you found a parking space. Lots going on downtown today with the beautiful weather. Plus, people are getting ready for the Bikes, Bands, and Bites festivities next weekend."

"It wasn't a problem. Mac and Sammy dropped me off."

"Oh, that's nice. What are those two up to?" Her mom smiled, her eyes gleaming the way they always did at the mention of her grandson and son-in-law-to-be.

"They're on a mission to buy a border fence for me. I bought some tulip and daffodil bulbs, hoping to get them into the ground in the next week or so."

"You're growing a green thumb?"

"We'll see. I didn't feel like I ever had time before to even think about a garden." But now with Mac jumping at every chance to spend some "guy time" with Sammy, she did. She realized she must have the same disease her mom did because the thought of the two of them made her smile, too. "Mac's made so many wonderful changes inside his Uncle Jake's house, I thought I'd pretty-up the flowerbeds outside."

"Spring flowers are so exquisite!" her mom exclaimed, gathering up wedding albums from the reception desk. "Plant them in the autumn then forget about them. Then after a long, dreary winter, they pop up out of the ground and delight you in the spring. Which is a good thing because who knows how much time you'll have to garden next year—what with building a house. Getting ready for a summer wedding. Working and—"

"Starting All-Stars Sports Ranch."

"Whew, it's a lot. But I know you two will manage." She pointed over to the pair of love seats. "I guess we should get started with this preliminary appointment before your guys get back. Oh, and your dad and I were wondering, are you coming over tonight to watch the game?"

Megan nodded. "Oh yes. Mac said to let you know we will definitely be there."

"Great!" her mom said as they sank into the pink cushions alongside each other. "Well. . .I thought first we'll browse through these books, showing you some of the other weddings Pam and I have planned, just to get an idea of what you think you might like. And then—then we'll. . ." her mom's voice faltered. She dipped her head, put her hand to her mouth.

"What? Mom, are you okay?"

"I'm sorry." Her mom lifted her head, tears glistening in her eyes. "I'm sorry," she repeated. "I told myself I wasn't going to do this. Wasn't going to get all emotional. But, I can't help it. I've never planned such a special wedding before. A wedding for my girl. My daughter. Oh Meg." She sniffed. "I'm so happy you and Mac have each other! I'm so glad you found your happily-ever-after."

Her mom's tears almost made her own flow. But she kept swallowing them back, even as she plucked a tissue from the box next to the china tea setting on the table and handed it to her mom. Rubbing her mom's shoulder till she got a hold of herself, Megan glanced around We Do! Wedding Planners and realized for the first time ever she actually felt comfortable being there.

After all the years of rolling her eyes at her mom's romantic notions of love. . .after all the years of not believing in love's possibility for her life, she noticed that the candy heart pink loveseats seemed to be just the right color. And all the tulle and satin, all the lace and pink bows, weren't overbearing at all. They were just perfect. And precious. As precious as loving someone with all of your heart could be.

"Mom. . ." she said wistfully. "When did you know?"

"Hmm?" Her mom dabbed at her eyes.

"About Mac and me? When did you know, do you remember?"

"Oh, that's easy." She clutched the tissue in her hand and sighed as if content. "It was the day of the Amazing Race. Your dad and I had finished the race and we were walking over to Nisbet Park to rest, and I noticed the two of you along the bike path. Mac was pushing Sammy's wheelchair and you were walking alongside him. And you both looked so—" Her voice cracked a bit. "Happy. Very happy and so—"

"Together?" she asked, to quote her mom.

"Definitely together." Her mom nodded. "Connected."

"Wow, so you saw that in us months ago?" Megan shook her head. "You would've never forgiven me if I would've completely blown it with him, would you?" She smiled. "Actually, come to think of it, I wouldn't have ever forgiven myself."

"Oh Meggie." Her mom chuckled. "The thing is, what I love thinking about most, is that God knew you two would be together. Even before you were ever born."

"You're right. He did, didn't He?"

All those times when she'd plucked daisy petals as a young girl, dreaming of love and marriage. . .all the lonely nights as a young woman when she never dreamed there'd be anyone for her, He'd already had her happiness in place. He knew exactly the daddy He had in mind for Sammy. Exactly the man He'd created for her.

MacNeill Hattaway, former baseball star. Mac, her catch of a lifetime.

Cathy Liggett lives in southwest Ohio with her husband of over thirty years and two grown children. Her passion for all things involved in writing started at a very young age and still inspires her today. She is the author of both fiction and non-fiction.

Check out these other great
Destination Romances from
Barbour Publishing

A Wedding Transpires on
Mackinac Island
978-1-61626-535-9

A Bride's Dilemma in
Friendship, Tennessee
978-1-61626-571-7

A Wedding Song in
Lexington, Kentucky
978-1-61626-573-1

A Bride's Opens Up Shop in
El Dorado, California
978-1-61626-583-0